Blood of the Fallen
The Children of Cain

I0629430

My Little Island in the Ether Publishing
    PO Box 419
    Lewistown, MT 59457

Also by David R Bishop & J Scott Cordero
No Good Deed
Blood of the Father

David & Scott thank Mark Babbey, Janet Cordero, Denise Dunn, and Don Wilson for their feedback and support.

David dedicates this novel to Gary.

Scott dedicates this novel to his loving bride.

Blood of the Fallen

The Children of Cain

Book 2

David R Bishop

&

J Scott Cordero

Prologue

Northern Siberia, May 6, 1945

Twelve had been seated at this table, she thought as she looked around the chamber. Twelve children. She let her eyes drift around the large table made of stone and inlaid with gems, counting each "brother" and "sister" as she did.

"Seven," she whispered.

Four were dead. One by his own hand. Three by the hand of the first child. He was now bound and imprisoned.

The first child was why they were all gathered here in the mountain fortress their father had built as their meeting place. Her eyes fell upon the largest and most ornate chair at the table. It was the chair their father had always sat in. It was vacant now and had been for more decades than she cared to remember. The pang in her heart as she gazed at that empty chair was the only human emotion she could still feel after all these centuries.

Even after their father had removed himself from their presence, the children still came together once every fifty years for what humans might call a family gathering. They would share what they were doing in their part of the world to keep resources flourishing, discuss issues they were experiencing with their stocks, and debate which new investments would yield the best returns. They would also meet whenever a crisis occurred. They had learned over many centuries that despite their best efforts and most attentive care, resources were fragile at best and self-destructive at worst.

The past six years had not completely decimated their resources, but millions had been lost. Millions, before they had decided to step in and remove the first child's power and influence. And now they needed to decide what to do.

The great door made of acacia wood screamed its protest as it was shoved open. A tall man in an impeccably tailored double-breasted wool suit strode into the room. His wingtip shoes were polished to a high shine. His fedora was pulled low, covering his face. Unlike the others gathered around the table, the man looked out of place. He looked like he belonged to 1940s Western high society. The only flaws in his ensemble were his hair, which hung in a long, silky, dark braid down his back, and the katana he carried in his hand as naturally as if it were a part of him.

"Hello, Ronin," she addressed the newcomer.

He removed his fedora, revealing a man of Japanese descent. "Forgive my tardiness." Ronin bowed to her and the others in the room.

The others offered solemn nods of forgiveness.

Setting the katana down on the table in front of his chair, Ronin bowed to it with more respect and reverence than he had for his brothers and sister.

She waited until Ronin had seated himself and filled his crystal goblet before finally speaking. "Welcome, remaining children of the father."

The room fell silent.

"We have much to discuss—"

"We have only one thing to discuss," a voice cut across her.

She gritted her teeth to keep calm. She had expected this. "What is it, Abisare?"

Abisare stood. Looked around the room. "The first child should die for his crimes."

"His name is—"

"I will not hear his name spoken," Abisare shouted as he swatted a hand at the name she was about to speak as if it were a venomous insect. "I don't think any of us should ever have to suffer to hear his name again."

"And what would you have us call him then, Abisare?" she asked.

"The first child and nothing more," Abisare responded curtly.

The other Ancients around the table muttered and nodded their approval.

She had to admit she did not enjoy hearing his name in her ears, let alone the foul taste of his name on her tongue. She nodded with the others.

"Very well," she said, "His name shall be stricken from this chamber and our mouths. He will only be called the first child."

Each Ancient picked up a goblet, raised it high in toast, and then took one sip.

Abisare was the first to set his goblet down, still on his feet. "And now we should discuss his method of execution."

At this declaration, however, the other Ancients stiffened, looking uncomfortably at each other or staring awkwardly at the table beneath their chins.

"The first child is bound and imprisoned." Delilah felt her weariness drape over her like a blanket. Abisare had that effect on people, even the Ancients. "He is no longer the pressing matter."

"If we do not destroy him now," Abisare pressed, "then we are setting ourselves up for failure."

She held up a hand.

Abisare did not speak. Neither did he sit down. "We must destroy him," he mumbled.

The twelfth child spoke now. "We have stopped him from destroying any more resources. We have done what we can, all that our father has allowed. And now we must abide by those rules."

"He didn't abide by the rules, Roman," Abisare spat. "And now, millions are lost, including three of our own. That should be enough reason to destroy him."

"But that's exactly why we cannot destroy him," Roman replied calmly, his eyes staring fixedly at the older Ancient. "The first rule has to apply, even to the one who violated that rule." He added, "It's what father would have wanted."

Abisare snorted. "Father isn't here to tell us what he wants or doesn't want. He hasn't been for three hundred years." He looked around the room. "When's the last time any of you even felt his presence? One hundred years? *Two hundred?*"

Again, the vampires stiffened with discomfort. Abisare now lay on the table the one card each Ancient had silently wondered about but would never dare speak out loud. "I wonder if he is even still alive."

Now Roman was on his feet, fangs bared, eyes burning the same color of bronze in a furnace. He hissed.

Abisare hissed as well, fangs bared.

"When you two are finished behaving like bull elk in Rut," she said softly, but it still thundered in their ears, "we will continue our discussion of resources."

"My apologies, *Mother*," Abisare said in a derisive tone.

The other vampires, even the ones on Abisare's side, knew he had now crossed the line.

Delilah fixed Abisare with a stare so icy that he shivered. "I think you forget your place, *little* brother."

Abisare opened his mouth, but Delilah held up a hand. "Do not forget that since the first child is no longer at this table, I am the eldest." She held Abisare's gaze until the younger vampire dropped his eyes.

"I am..." Abisare cleared his throat. "I apologize for my rudeness and disrespect."

Delilah nodded.

Abisare sat down.

"Roman," Delilah addressed the twelfth child, "what news do you have for us from Germany?" She raised her glass. "I would like to acknowledge what you have accomplished in Europe to bring this...mess to an end."

The other vampires, even Abisare, raised their glasses high, then sipped.

Roman stood and nodded, accepting their acknowledgment. "Hitler is now dead. Germany will unconditionally surrender in two days. America will then focus its efforts on the surrender of Japan."

"What do you think America will do?" Delilah asked.

Roman looked levelly around the room. "America is very close to successfully detonating an atomic bomb. Once that happens, pressure will mount to use that weapon on the Japanese, and I must admit I don't know if I disagree."

Delilah turned to Ronin. "That would destroy many of your herd and contaminate the remaining stock for decades."

Ronin's face was expressionless as he nodded with cold sobriety.

Roman continued. "But compared to the resources already lost, it is a small loss that we can recoup."

Ronin smiled wryly. "The long-term return on investment is worth the loss, in other words."

Roman nodded.

The other Ancients murmured amongst themselves.

Roman continued, "The loss of resources is regrettable, but the loss will be greater if the Americans do not—"

Abisare interrupted Roman, not wanting to pass on the opportunity to cut two brothers in one sentence. "It's not like that island is your only resource." His voice sliced with accusation as he turned to Ronin. "You haven't just invested all your time cultivating this one culture like some banzai tree. You have—"

"Forgive me," Ronin cut across Abisare, and though his voice was calm and quiet, the room reverberated with his fury, "but these are

5

more than just my *resources*. These are my *people*. I am one of them."
He looked around the room, the fury now blazing in his eyes. "Why shouldn't my stock subjugate the world? They have contributed more than all the other civilizations combined." He looked at Roman. "That return on investment you're talking about is centuries old, and the world has benefited from that investment."

Ronin's gaze fell upon the katana sitting before him on the table.

Abisare opened his mouth to continue, but Delilah held up a hand. "*Silence,*" she hissed.

Abisare's eyes bulged as the cords of his neck stood out, straining like a man choking on a chicken bone. He tried to move his hands, his head, anything, but his body was no longer his to control.

And suddenly his body was his again. He collapsed into his seat.

Delilah turned to Ronin, who stood oblivious to what had just transpired between her and Abisare. "Ronin." She paused. "I'm sorry."

Ronin's gaze moved from the sword to Delilah. "So am I." He swept up his katana and exited the room before another word could be spoken.

The room sat blanketed in awkward silence until, finally, the Ancient who'd been sitting across from Ronin leaned forward. "So...uh...do you remember...umm...before the Industrial Revolution...just how good the blood tasted?" He looked around the room, waiting to be silenced or remonstrated. But the others in the room seemed not to hear, or even realize, that other Ancients were in the room. He continued. "I think...we need to take steps to...um...clean up the environment."

A few of the Ancients looked at him, puzzled looks on their faces.

"Take better care of themselves," he offered.

Delilah's stare was incredulous.

The Ancient smiled, gaining confidence, encouraged by the silence. "In fact," he cleared his throat, "I have some ideas on how we can help our resources recover to those pre-industrial days." He licked his lips and then laid out his plans.

1

Miami, Florida, Present Day

Roman stood just inside the tree line across from the once-grand Miami compound, now nothing but a heap of charred wood, blackened cement, ashes, and pandemonium. Smoke shimmered from hotspots like smudgy apparitions, trying but failing to take form. The thick salty air was perfumed with the acrid tang of melted wiring and other detritus that make up a home. And something else. Something ancient. Something only Roman could smell.

Across the scarred landscape, humans scurried over the smoldering remains like so many insects over a picnic meal. Each wore a jacket or jumpsuit emblazoned with the tribe to which he or she belonged. FDLE. DEA. FBI. OCSO. CSI. OPD. OFD.

Humans really do enjoy their brands, Roman thought, bemused. How appropriate.

He'd watched, unnoticed, since the first investigators had arrived on the scene, chain-smoking cigarettes, guzzling coffee, and swapping Cain Dvanaesti stories as they waited for clearance to enter and begin their work. Cain was loved, admired, and even revered. All of them wanted to find out what happened. They wanted to know who, or what, to blame.

No one saw Roman as he stood, taking in the scene before him. He was just another tree on this side of the road. And no one would notice him when he began to move, which he did now.

Roman stepped from the tree line and crossed to the compound. He moved without hurry, without a care in the world. He knew he would go unnoticed. He had a gift for going unnoticed. A dark gift he'd been honing for centuries. He wasn't invisible, but a blind spot.

8

When someone looked at him, their eyes would look past him or slide to the right or left of him.

As he moved, he felt her strong and steady pull as if he had a rope tied around his waist, drawing him. Roman imagined he looked like a slow-motion photography effect directors used, except in reverse. The world and all the insects around him moved in super-slow motion as he moved at his unconcerned, unhurried pace.

His unhurried pace took him past the line of reporters who spoke in urgent yet somber tones about the impending tropical storm and how investigators were quickly scrambling to secure as much evidence as possible. Roman could hear the adrenaline pump through their blood as surely as he could feel their barely suppressed excitement at the thought of six o'clock ratings and, more importantly, personal network exposure.

As if on cue, a cool wind gusted. The barometric pressure dropped. Every cop, investigator, reporter, and onlooker turned toward the water as if they'd just heard their name called.

Roman kept walking, allowing that invisible rope to pull him. As the humans continued to look toward the water, Roman stopped. Looking down, he nodded his approval at the place she'd chosen to secret herself until he came for her. She knew he would.

He closed his eyes as he breathed in the myriad of putrid odors surrounding him, and, focusing until one aroma permeated his nostrils, his lungs, his being.

"Isabella."

Roman began to dig.

2

Venice, Italy

Wasim could hear his wife, Aliya, yelling his name from the back of the store as he began to count the register. Pretending her cry was just the vacuum cleaner, a pretense he'd become expert at after twenty-two years of marriage, he started with the five-euro bills.

"Wasim." There was a slight uptick of irritation in her tone.

Wasim's tongue slipped out between his lips as he concentrated on the count and not the vacuum cleaner. *Eleven. Twelve. Thirteen.* His tongue drifted to the right, aiding Wasim in his multiplication. *Thirteen times five equals...sixty-five.* His tongue moved to the center of his mouth, tip pointing towards the ceiling with triumph.

"Wasim," the vacuum cleaner bawled.

His tongue slipped back behind his teeth as he set the five-euro notes back into the register and selected the ten-euro bills. His tongue made another appearance to help Wassim count and multiply. *Ninety.* He set them down and picked up the twenty-euro notes. The tip of his tongue signaled its pleasure at the thicker-than-usual stack as it pointed toward the ceiling. There had to be at least two hundred eighty euros in that compartment of the till alone. Yesterday had been a very good day.

Good day? It had been a *great day*. It had been a day to be written in gold letters, as his adopted countrymen liked to say.

He scolded himself for leaving so much money in the till overnight, but he reminded himself that Aliya had been browbeating (she would say reminding) him that they would be late if he didn't close the shop early.

"A silver wedding anniversary only happens once in a marriage," she'd chided, referring to their friends, Aldo and Lucia.

"Wasim." The vacuum cleaner was now somewhere between a yawp and a caterwaul.

Wasim's tongue shot back behind his teeth like a frightened rabbit into the safety of its den. He lifted his gaze from the till and sighed.

Wasim and Aliya had moved to Venice from Pakistan and purchased the Alimentari (small grocer) three years ago. At first, the idea seemed exciting, even romantic. Just the two of them. Arriving together. Working together. Stocking. Cleaning. Exchanging smiles as they helped customers. Perhaps a little making out in the back room in the middle of the day when the store was empty. Then, after a long but satisfying day, they would close the store, turn off the lights, and head back to their residence hand in hand. Happy. Satisfied. Eventually, they'd make enough money and get a place in the countryside. Hire help to run the store.

Reality couldn't be any farther from the dream. They still lived in the apartment above the grocery. There were no glancing smiles or make-out sessions in the backroom. Aliya ran a tight ship, and Wasim was grateful for that. Every minute of the day should be accounted for. When there were no customers, that was the time to clean, inventory, order, and repair. After closing for the day, they trudged up the stairs to their apartment, ate dinner, and then completed the professional chores that hadn't been finished before starting on the personal chores. At Eleven, they collapsed into bed and slept the sleep of the hardworking middle class the world over. Yet, when they reconciled the books at the end of the month, they found themselves in the same financial position as the hardworking middle class the world over. There was no money for a home in the country. It was only recently that there was money for an employee.

Still, their life had been better here in Italy than it had ever been in that small village in Pakistan.

"WASIM!" The vacuum cleaner was now a shrill siren.

"Coming, my love," Wasim responded as he closed the till, forgetting the count.

"What have you been doing?" Aliya barked as he entered the backroom. Her hand gestured for him to stop talking before he opened his mouth. "That lazy boy you hired didn't take the trash out again last night when he closed. And I bet he closed early. I told you, you should fire him."

Wasim stared at his wife and wondered what had happened to the young woman he'd married twenty-two years ago. Where was the woman who left Pakistan with him for this dream of a better life fifteen years ago? What had happened to the woman who, despite not being able to have children, was quick to laugh, quick to smile? Who saw every small blessing as larger than any big disappointment? He wanted to ask her, but instead, he exhaled a steadying breath and said, "I will speak with him." He picked up the bags of trash. "I will take it out. It's no problem."

"It *is* a problem, Wasim," Aliya spat back. "If you *pay* someone to do a job, then they should *do* that job. If not, then *you* should *fire* them. The problem is that you are too nice to people."

"I will take care of it. It won't happen again," Wasim answered.

Aliya put more frustration, disbelief, and discontent with Wasim into the roll of her eyes than any words could've conveyed.

Wasim rolled his eyes back, but only after making sure his back was to her as he made his way to the back door.

The alley behind the store was dark. It was still early, and the sun hadn't risen enough to provide sufficient light. Glancing up at the broken light over the door that Aliya had told him several times to replace, he vowed to change it today. Like the light, he'd forgotten to tell his new and only employee that part of his job was taking the trash out every night.

Wasim made his way to the bins but stopped when he heard a crunching sound from under his foot. He looked down to see what appeared to be a rat. Cursing in his adopted language, he set the bags down and squatted to get a closer look. It was a rat. He squinted. The rat was desiccated.

Wasim's brow wrinkled with confusion. How long had this been here? He'd seen his share of living and dead rats and found dead rats in the alley before, stiff with rigor mortis. But never remembered seeing one that looked fresh yet dehydrated. How long did it take for a rat to dry up? Did rats dry up? Wouldn't other animals, or maybe insects, eat it before that happened? One thing he was sure about. He'd better get this rat cleaned up before Aliya sees it. He grabbed the bags, stood up, stepped, and stopped.

Pale morning light now filled the alley, revealing more dead rats strewn across the ground in front of the collection station. Wasim's tongue slipped out between his lips as he counted more than a dozen. All dead. All desiccated. And something else, Wasim noticed now as the sunlight grew stronger. Their fur was darker around their necks, as if it were stained by something. In pure astonishment, he knelt, picked up one of the rats by its tail with his bare hand, and raised it close to his face for a closer look.

Wasim swore in his native language. The neck had been ripped or torn open. He could see the bite marks on the ragged edges of flesh, reminding him of the zombie movies and television shows so popular recently. Wasim now saw in his mind's eye some half-crazed human tearing into the rat's neck.

His stomach roiled as a wave of nausea washed over him, knocking him over onto his butt. Dropping the carcass, he saw the same tear on the necks of the other rats. The same tooth indentations. His mind's eye showed him a clearer picture of a human picking up the rat, eyes filling with lust as if seeing a roasted chicken leg, mouth salivating from the first bite into the meat.

His head swam. His tongue retreated down his throat. He heard the click of his teeth as his mouth clamped shut. He did not want to vomit. He wanted to get up, to run, to get inside the safety of the Alimentari.

He was on his feet, running for the back door, trash bags forgotten. Once inside, he leaned back against the door, feeling his heart pounding against his breastbone. His forehead and armpits were slick with sweat. He could feel the adrenaline surging through his bloodstream.

"Have you been in the alley all this time?"

Wasim held up a hand to silence Aliya.

"Don't you hold your hand up to me—"

"Shut up," Wasim roared at his wife. "Just shut up. And get me the phone." He took a breath, held it, then exhaled. His voice was thin when he spoke. "I need to call animal control".

3

Illuminati Compound,
Baton Rouge, Louisiana

The room was a ten-foot square concrete box. The man currently residing in it knew. He'd walked it enough times.

He focused on the room. He used this as a defense mechanism to keep her out of his mind. She was all he could think about since waking up. He knew the number of paces from corner to corner. Two paces from where he stood to the hospital bed on which he'd slept seven nights. *Well, seven sleep cycles, anyway.* Three paces from the bed to the stainless-steel, lidless, prison-style commode he used to relieve himself after each sleep cycle. It was four and a half paces from the toilet to the vault door, which, except for a narrow slot at its bottom through which trays of food and fresh scrubs were passed, never opened. He knew it was three and a half paces from the door *to* the preformed concrete table and seating area where he ate. Two and a half paces from the table to the stainless-steel sink inset into the wall with a motion-activated faucet.

A toothbrush rested in a Styrofoam cup set on the escutcheon. Soap and toothpaste dispensers hung on the wall beside the mirror. A glass mirror, the man had noticed. Not a polished sheet of stainless steel, which might have finished the maximum-security cell ambiance. One towel and one washcloth for sponge bathing hung from small built-in hooks in the sink.

Except for the vents in the concrete ceiling keeping fresh, conditioned air circulating, this room, which he'd been in for he had no idea how long, had no windows, no cracks, and no crevices. He'd looked. Artificial light filled the room from canisters recessed into the ceiling. The light snapped on regularly in what he assumed was morning and snapped off in the evening. He thought the room must be underground.

He had no evidence to support this hypothesis except that if he inhaled deeply, he smelled cool, damp earth. At least, that's how it started. After seven days of breathing in this room, he'd learned all he had to do was focus on the odors in the air. He'd come to understand that everything, living or inanimate, had an odor, and he'd learned to differentiate. He'd learned to smell only the soap, the toothpaste, or the damp earth. He'd learned that at specific regular intervals, the odors of cologne, deodorant, sweat, and the body odor the cologne and deodorant were trying to mask were present. They were faint, like they were wafting in on the conditioned air, but he knew they weren't. He couldn't explain it. These fragrances weren't *on* the air. They were *in* the air.

The same was happening with his auditory system. He could hear the footsteps of whoever brought the food tray to the door. He didn't think he should be able to. The vault door had to be at least three inches thick and sealed airtight. And not just the step but the weight of the step. He heard the rustle of clothing as the individual knelt to place the tray on the floor. There were times when he thought he heard voices burbling. Like the odors, the voices weren't on the air, but they were a part of it somehow.

He'd been lying on the bed, but now the man got up and began to pace. And to think.

Seven days of breathing in the air, of the lights switching on and off, eating, pacing the room, and counting his steps. *Where is she?*

The man thought of that first time waking in the room. He was lying on the bed, dressed in pale blue hospital scrubs, like the ones he wore today. He had no idea how long he'd been in the room before waking, nor where the room was on Earth. He assumed he'd awakened in the morning only because a tray came through the door slot a moment after he had sat up and taken inventory of his surroundings that first time. The tray held a hot cup of coffee, orange juice, very wet scrambled eggs, undercooked bacon, slightly burnt toast, and a cup of fresh mixed fruit. The man thought whoever had cooked this had no experience preparing this type of...could you call this breakfast?...but gave it the good ol' Joe College try for the first time this morning. The cups, plates, and utensils were all plastic.

He hadn't been hungry but decided to eat anyway. Despite how it looked, the food smelled delicious, except for the burnt toast, and he felt his stomach grumble its happiness. Looking at the toast, he remembered a time when he would have scraped the blackened pieces of bread away, slathered it with butter and jam, and eaten it without hesitation. Now, the aroma of burnt bread weighed so heavily in his nostrils that he felt he'd scooped the dead embers of a campfire and shoved them up his nose. He didn't even want to imagine what it would taste like. It almost made him shiver.

The eggs were surprisingly good despite the wetness. Just the right amounts of salt, pepper, and...what was that third spice? It was on the tip of his tongue. That little pun had put the first grin on his face in he didn't know how long.

Paprika.

The man stopped chewing, the grin slipping from his face. How had he known that? He wasn't sure. He only knew he was right. He also knew that for all his life, he'd always been able to differentiate the ingredients in food, savory or sickening. But with this meal, he could isolate the flavors, drawing each out and spotlighting it. Placing another forkful into his mouth, he chewed: Equal amounts of salt and pepper and just a dash of paprika.

He'd never been a fan of crispy bacon, so he was relieved to see the bacon meat pink, the fat glistening. He loved the texture between his forefinger and thumb and relished it on his tongue. Good thing this bacon was cooked today, he thought as he chewed.

It would have turned by suppertime. He wondered what sensitive digestive system might still feel those effects later this morning.

The coffee was served black, with a sugar bowl and a small creamer. The man spooned in sugar and poured creamer until the coffee was the color of mocha, just the way he liked it. He sipped and grimaced. The coffee- a dark roast- had sat just a little too long at the bottom of the pot. To call the creamer a chemical concoction was generous. This was definitely a low-end product bought in bulk to make it even cheaper.

But the fruit? *Aaahhh*. That was the pièce de résistance of the meal. The honeydew was a pleasant, soft green with just the slightest firmness as he bit into it, releasing a sweet, floral flavor. Likewise, the cantaloupe, grapes, and pineapple were equally vibrant in sight and taste. The man remembered the first time he'd tried strawberries with champagne, how the champagne cleansed the palate and dried the tongue, preparing it for the explosion of sweetness and tartness of the strawberries. This was like that, only better, even after the tepid coffee.

Perhaps the cook was preparing breakfast for a large group of people, like someone putting out a hot breakfast at a hotel, he thought to himself as he took one last sip of coffee and wiped his lips with the napkin. Maybe the wetness of the eggs was just a fluke. He'd eaten everything except the burnt toast, which he frowned at, and though his stomach felt full, he'd found he wasn't satisfied. It'd been that way with every meal since that day.

The man had eaten breakfast and lunch and now paced around the room. He rubbed his chin and frowned. When he'd looked at himself in the mirror that first day, he thought someone had shaved him while he was unconscious, but seven days later, his face was still as smooth as it had been after a fresh shave. He remembered how much she loved to touch his face when it was freshly shaven. And though he sponge-bathed regularly, he felt that if he stopped, he would not begin to stink.

He walked over to the mirror, inspecting his chin and cheeks closely. Rubbing his hand over his chin and neck, he focused on his chin, trying to peer into the pores as if he could see the follicles ready to emerge—

There was a smudge on the mirror. No, not on the surface. *In* the glass. Or maybe it was on the back of the mirror. A scratch or defect in the coating on the back of the glass causing the blemish. Except he'd noticed the smudge move. And then there was the faint odor of cologne. Deodorant. Sweat. And another scent. He couldn't place that one. But like the cologne, deodorant, and sweat, it was close. He inhaled again. Very close. Like on the other side of the looking glass, close. He leaned closer to the mirror, concentrating on looking through his reflection, through the smudge.

Now that other odor, which bore the acrid tang of vomit and the putrid stench of raw human waste, grew stronger. It burned his nostrils. At once, he knew what that odor was. He didn't know how he knew, but he knew as sure as he knew the size of the room and the number of times he'd walked it. He was smelling fear. And it was close.

Leaning even closer so that his nose should have been touching its reflection, he felt he was looking through a windowpane at the forms now taking shape like shadows clothed in fog. He concentrated harder.

The forms snapped into complete focus. Five people crowded around what the man realized had to be a two-way mirror. The faces of the two youngest people, one man and one woman, were gaping in horror. Another man with gray hair cropped close to his scalp and wearing black military fatigues stared at him unfazed. A tall man in a suit stood beside him. He was younger than the fatigued man but older than the younger man and woman who had now taken a step back. His eyes were wide with surprise only.

Front and center of the crowd was an older man with a nearly bald scalp. His eyes twinkled, and he smiled as the man looked directly into his eyes. The man nodded. "Good afternoon. My name is Caiaphas."

The man straightened up and found he could still see the people in the other room as if the mirror had been removed. He cleared his throat. "I am Cain Dvanaesti."

4

Athens, Greece

"**W**hat is so important that you had to come to Greece to speak with me in person about it, Abisare?" Delilah questioned, not looking up from the document she was reading. She had not stood when Abisare entered but had remained seated at her desk.

Abisare remained silent.

Delilah glanced up to see the agitation clenching Abisare's jaw, furrowing his brow, and his hands balling into fists. The abyss set on fire radiated from his eye sockets.

This wasn't a new state for Abisare; Delilah knew all too well. But usually, her brother didn't need an invitation to verbalize his upset, much less wait for one.

Delilah closed the folder, signaling her willingness to give her brother her undivided attention. "All right, Brother. What is it?"

Abisare's glance cut to Eleni, Delilah's assistant, still standing at the door.

Delilah sighed, pushing back from her desk, letting her hand graze the olive wood. The surface was smooth, and the design was elegant. It was not a grotesque, massive slab of wood and metal whose true function was to dominate a room, stroke its owner's ego, and intimidate guests. No, this desk captivated the room with its flawless beauty and strength.

Just like me.

"Thank you, Eleni. That will be all," Delilah said.

Eleni nodded at Delilah, letting a disapproving frown tug at her lips as her gaze flicked to Abisare.

Delilah stifled a smile as she motioned to the seating area across the room. Her staff's dislike of Abisare was well known to her. Equally unknown to Abisare. Their disparagement of the Ancient stemmed from his high degree of self-importance, which was only matched by his low opinion of everyone else. Standing, Delilah walked to a small credenza, also of olive wood, that held crystal decanters filled with various colored liquids.

"Would you care for a drink?" Delilah asked, selecting the one holding a pale golden-yellow liquid. The decanter was one of two sitting on a small warming pad inlaid into the top of the credenza. The second was filled with dark red fluid.

She poured an ounce and a half into a Neat Glass. Holding the glass by the stem, Delilah swirled the glass close to her mouth, closed her eyes, and drew a slow, deliberate inhalation through her nose. Her face relaxed into a sublime expression.

Hemolytic Anemia. Also known as Rh Null. *The Golden Blood.* Delilah's lips curled in anticipation of the rarest blood type in the world. It was a moment to be savored. Relished. Anticipation was truly the second-best moment in life.

After a moment, she turned, facing a discomfited Abisare, and shrugged. "Well, regardless. I'm going to have one. Something tells me I'm going to need it," Delilah said as she took a small but satisfying sip.

Abisare regained his usual disgruntled demeanor. "What are we going to do about Roman?" He demanded, not waiting for Delilah to take a seat.

Delilah ignored his rudeness as she sat across from him. Sipping, she stared at Abisare as if she were the one who had asked a question and was waiting for a response.

"Well?" Abisare asked in an agitated voice.

"Well, What?" Delilah responded.

"Roman," Abisare thundered. "Something has to be done about him." His voice was now shaking with frustration and anger.

Delilah ignored Abisare's raised voice. "I know you've never been fond of your younger brother," Delilah replied, her voice soft with condescension.

Now, Abisare chose to ignore Delilah's tone. "He is out of control. All of his...experiments and projects. He's never once asked permission, let alone kept the rest of us informed. And now one of his *schemes* is growing beyond his control," Abisare stated.

"If you're referring to the Illuminati, then, Brother, you are being hypocritical," Delilah responded. "You, yourself, have used them as a tool before. We all have. They have proven to be a powerful asset."

Abisare wouldn't be deterred. "What about the abomination he created?" Abisare hissed. "His son. You can't tell me that it doesn't bother you."

"And what exactly would bother me?" Delilah asked.

"His audacity to name *it* after our father," Abisare spat. "He should have been punished for that alone."

"Yes, at first. I did take some offense at it. But after speaking with Roman, it was a sign of respect, nothing else," Delilah placated. She sipped and smiled. "Very human of him. Very...sentimental."

Abisare scoffed with disgust.

Delilah's patience didn't wane. "It's humorous, Brother, that you should take such offense at Roman's schemes, permission or not. What would the family think of your adoption agency?" Delilah asked, smirking.

"Or your distillery," Abisare retorted, pointing at his sister's glass. "How many humans in the entire world are Rh Null?"

"Less than fifty." The answer put a smile on Delilah's face as if she were tasting something delicious. "This one," she flicked the rim of the glass, making it ring, "lives more lavishly than Musa." She knew the reference to Mansa Musa would tousle Abisare's emotions, stroking his pride while rankling his narcissism. But she couldn't help herself. Men were so easy to manipulate. Even her brothers. To further inflame him, she added, "At *my* expense."

Delilah hid her grin behind another sip as she watched Abisare's nostrils flare with satisfaction while his lips pursed from disapproval.

"I still feel something should be done," Abisare spouted, regaining his composure.

He won't be dissuaded or distracted for long, she thought. I'll give him credit for that. But. He needs to be reminded of his place, which is not at the head of the table.

Delilah locked eyes with Abisare. "*Your* feelings do not govern *our* family." Delilah's tone suggested that her brother was not an equal or even a subordinate but an aberrant child.

The arrow had not missed its target. The fire was back in Abisare's eyes. His teeth ground so hard that Delilah wondered if they wouldn't crack inside his jaw, which was rippling like a snake across hot sand.

"You will regret this, Sister," Abisare said as he rose. "We all will." He started for the door.

"Brother," Delilah pleaded.

Abisare ignored her.

"Abisare." Delilah's tone stopped him as if he'd walked into a wall.

"I do heed your counsel, Brother," Delilah said in a gentler tone. She gazed at the last swallow. "We're becoming as flippant as the young ones. We all must be careful. Calculated. Roman included." She swirled the glass, looking through the liquid in contemplation. "The young ones. Perhaps it's time for a culling." She swallowed the last of the golden blood. "I will take a closer look at Roman's activities. And in the meantime, perhaps you could find a way not to be so confrontational with him." Delilah said, looking for confirmation from Abisare. "Yes?"

"Yes, Sister," Abisare said as he turned and exited the office.

5

Venice, Italy

"**Alessia**," Nico kept calling out, like a four-year-old wailing for his mother.

"I'll be right there," Alessia responded over her shoulder as she finished writing down the blood pressure and temperature of the patient she was with. She smiled at the older woman.

"Your blood pressure is a little high." No wonder, she thought, as the smell of stale wine wafted off the woman and the remnants of her last meal stained her dress. The food served at the neighborhood soup kitchen was so high in salt. "I want you to sit here for a few minutes," she said as she pressed a bottle of water into the woman's hand, "and drink this."

"Alessia!"

Alessia sighed and then gave the woman a weary smile. "I'll be back in a moment." Patting the woman's shoulder, she rose and headed to Nico.

Alessia Mantalto had been on her feet for more than sixteen hours: a twelve-hour shift at the SS Giovanni e Paolo hospital Emergency Room, and now more than four hours at the clinic. She loved being an E.R. nurse, even after ten years, and usually left her shift exhausted but invigorated, especially when heading to the clinic. But now that she was in her thirties, she'd noticed her stamina waning after fourteen hours. Only a heart and a natural gift for the caretaking of others sustained her. That and the espresso she drank on her way to Nico.

Her heart and gift were discovered when her mother was diagnosed with Stage III breast cancer when she was thirteen years old. While Italy's universal healthcare system helped defray many of her medical bills, it didn't cover all. And the family still had to eat. Her father worked three jobs to cover the costs of treatments, medications, and household bills. That left Alessia at home as her mother's primary caregiver. As her mother deteriorated, Alessia blamed herself for her mother's worsening condition. She couldn't help but think that if she only knew more, she wouldn't have lost her just three years later. It wasn't the truth, however.

After her mother's passing, Alessia decided she wanted to know more and dedicated all her time and energy to her studies, hoping she could receive a scholarship to nursing school. She made that wish a reality by attending Sapienza University of Rome on a full academic scholarship. She fell in love with emergency medicine during her rotations and felt fully satisfied when she married that with clinical care of the indigent.

Three days a week, Alessia volunteered at a homeless shelter, treating the people who came there. Nico was a regular. What's worse than a man who's homeless, one of the longtime workers had asked Alessia when she first started volunteering at the shelter. A man who's a homeless hypochondriac, the worker answered Alessia's puzzled look. What's worse than a man who's a homeless hypochondriac, she asked Alessia next. Nico, she quipped.

She met Nico during her first evening of volunteering. She fell in love with the old man. Not only was he a hypochondriac, but he was also paranoid. Alessia wondered if he was an undiagnosed schizophrenic as well. Add to that his flair for the dramatic and love of storytelling about his life when he was younger, and he was quite an entertaining, albeit harmless, character.

After that first meeting, he always seemed to know when she would be at the shelter. He showed up with some new self-diagnosed ailment: from Aneurysms to Yellow Fever. During the COVID pandemic, he appeared with a new case of the infection every week.

The staff joked they should submit him to the Guinness Book of World Records or at least to the Director of Istituto Superiore di Sanità for medical study. Everyone knew why he was really there.

"ALESSIA!"

As she crossed the room to where Nico was sitting, she could tell that something was wrong. More wrong than usual, even for Nico.

"How are we feeling today, Nico?" Alessia asked, smiling.

Nico either didn't hear Alessia's question or chose to ignore it. "He...he's real. I'm not crazy. I saw him. It. I don't know," Nico muttered.

"Who's real, Nico? What are you talking about?" Alessia questioned, feeling alarmed at the sight of Nico. The wild look in his eyes. His whole body vibrated.

"I know what I saw," Nico bawled as if Alessia had suggested that perhaps he'd been dreaming or mistaken a shadow for something else. A sneer crept across his face, revealing crooked brown teeth. "The others laughed at me, too, when I told them." He swallowed hard like he was struggling to get a pill down his throat dry. "But I know what I saw," Nico replied.

Swallowing down her anxiety, Alessia placed a hand on Nico's shoulder. "Tell me what you thought you saw," Alessia soothed.

Nico shrugged Alessia's hand off as he turned to face her. "I don't *think*," Nico roared. "I *know*."

"Okay." Alessia held both hands up in surrender. "I'm sorry. Please. Tell me what you saw," Alessia asked again.

Nico chuffed, turning away from Alessia. "You don't believe me either. You think I'm just a crazy old man," Nico answered. "Just a poor homeless hypochondriac. I know what they say about me here."

Alessia risked another hand on Nico's shoulder. "Nico, it's me. Of course, I believe you." She put as much reassurance as she could muster into her voice. "Tell me what you saw, and we'll figure this out together." Alessia hoped her comfort would calm and focus the old man.

It seemed to. Nico exhaled a shuddering breath as he sagged back in the chair. He stared at the floor. "Rats," he whispered. "He-...it feeds on them," Nico spoke in a hushed tone, now trying to gain control of himself. "We've all been seeing them. The rats, I mean. Hundreds. Maybe thousands. More than usual, anyway. Like something was...calling them. Then killing them."

"Calling...the rats?" Alessia questioned.

Nico nodded.

"Then killing them," Alessia repeated.

"Feeding on them," Nico muttered, his body trembling as his eyes stared beyond the floor at something only he could see. Some vision rekindled that wild look in his eye. Whatever it was, it terrified him.

Alessia swiped a blanket off the table beside her and draped it over Nico's shoulders, hoping its weight and warmth would quell his agitation. "You saw someone eating a rat?"

Nico's head shook back and forth. "Not eating. Drinking. He drinks their blood. It's always the same. There's nothing left but skin and bone." Nico replied in a frantic tone. "He looks like a man. But he's not a man, he's a monster, a demon." Nico continued to ramble, his breathing ragged and uneven. "I...I saw his face. His eyes were black. And his teeth. More like a...a dog or something. I don't know. His hands looked like they had claws instead of fingers. It was a demon. I'm telling you a demon," Nico said, growing more fevered.

Alessia wanted to distract him. Placing her fingers on the inside of Nico's wrist, she said, "Okay, Nico. I believe you. Let me check your vitals."

"Don't patronize me," Nico shouted, jerking his wrist out of her hands. He stood from the chair and tossed the blanket to the ground. "I don't have a fever. I'm not hallucinating. I'm not having a panic attack or mental breakdown." He shook his head in disgust. "I told you, you wouldn't believe me," Nico said as he marched towards the front door.

"Nico, wait, please. I'm sorry. I didn't..." Alessia stopped and sighed as the door closed behind Nico.

6

Illuminati Compound,
Baton Rouge, LA

Marcus loomed before Caiaphas's desk, waiting for the older man to respond. He felt like the proverbial broken record objecting to his Master's obstinate view that he must put himself in harm's way. But Marcus was feeling just as bullheaded in voicing his dissent.

Caiaphas only stared up into his executive officer's face, jaw set, eyes blazing. He remembered a silly little rhyme his mother repeated whenever she needed a moment. Closing her eyes and balling her fists, she would suck in a deep breath, hold it, and then repeat the words until she ran out of air.

One, two, a bucket full of poo. Three, four, throw it at the door. Five, six, whatever sticks. Seven, eight, it's just idle prate. Nine, ten, to fill the bucket again.

He wasn't sure what had reminded him of the old verse. But Caiaphas repeated it to himself under his breath like a mantra as Marcus said, "I will continue to register my misgivings at your decision to enter into the mons- man's room until you change your mind."

The fact that Marcus had almost said monster was not lost on Caiaphas. He recited the words again as he wished for more than the first time today, and perhaps the fifty thousandth time since appointing the man to the position of Marcus, that the younger man could learn to trust the older man's instincts. He would need to trust others' instincts in addition to his own when he assumed the role of Caiaphas. He would also need a small portion of recklessness to follow those instincts. He'd had that when Caiaphas had appointed

31

him to Marcus. Well, maybe a bit too large an allocation of recklessness. He'd told Marcus to rein in the recklessness. Balance it with common sense and intuition. Marcus had done more than rein in the recklessness. He'd locked it in a cage with common sense and intuition, regarding all instincts like an enemy.

"There's no reason for you to enter...*his* room," Marcus tried again. "When we have the intercom system in the observation room." He brightened. "He can see through the mirror, so it's not like you would be a voice in the walls. The two of you can see and hear each other. It would almost be like you were in the same room." He added quickly, "Without sacrificing your safety."

"Would it relieve your misgivings if I said I'd asked Augustine to escort me into Cain's room?"

Marcus did look relieved. The lines on his face lessened, and his stature straightened as if a heavy pack had been removed from his shoulders. "You did?"

"No." Caiaphas stood and turned to take a book from the shelf behind him. He could hear Marcus's growl of frustration. Caiaphas couldn't help but smile.

The smile quickly faded, however, when Marcus muttered, "Foolish old man."

Caiaphas spun on his heel.

Marcus stepped back from Caiaphas's gaze as if his superior had taken a swing. Immediately, his shoulders slumped, and his head dropped as if he were searching the ground for something. "My apologies," he said in a small voice.

Caiaphas turned away from Marcus, sucked in a deep breath, held it for a count of ten, and then repeated his mother's rhyme in his head until he was out of air. Finally, the rage ebbed away.

In his role as Caiaphas, training Marcus to assume his position upon his death or inability to perform his duties, it was not unlike a father teaching his son how to be a man and a father. The bond between Caiaphas and Marcus was not the same as that of brothers in arms. The bond was more familial.

He had to admit to himself, and here he would've smiled if the moment was not so grave, that he had felt the same way when he had been Marcus. He had looked at his superior, his Caiaphas, as not only his superior but as his father. He had revered and respected the man when he first stepped into the position of Marcus, but as time passed, he had been like a petulant teenager, second-guessing every decision Caiaphas made. He knew better. After all, he was younger and certainly more brilliant. That more than made up for his lack of seasoning and sophistication. Caiaphas was stuck in his old habits, unwilling or unable to adapt to the times. As time went on, however, as the time neared for him to assume the position of Caiaphas, he found he revered his Caiaphas as a middle-aged man might revere his aging father. The roles had changed. He second-guessed not out of petulance but out of genuine love and concern.

Marcus, he realized, was at that place. Marcus had instincts. He had common sense and the right portion of recklessness to be Caiaphas, but not where his Caiaphas was concerned. Where it concerned his Caiaphas, Marcus was the fiercely loving and protective middle-aged son of an aging father.

And now he smiled. Marcus was ready. None too soon, Caiaphas thought to himself. Caiaphas walked around the desk and placed a hand on Marcus's shoulder.

Marcus looked up to see Caiaphas smiling kindly at him and noticed the smile reached his eyes. He felt his shame slipping off his shoulders like a wet jacket.

"Thank you, Marcus," Caiaphas said, hoping Marcus heard the appreciation. "Your concerns are noted and not without merit. However, this is one of those moments in our history that is unprecedented and, to use a phrase from this current generation, a game-changer. Cain Dvanaesti is not human. Nor is he a vampire. He is something else, something...perhaps something greater. He could prove to be our greatest ally or our worst enemy. How we act in this moment could help decide which he will become.

"That's why this meeting must be face-to-face and not through a two-way mirror. As with all great alliances throughout history, a man must look another in the eye. He must talk, listen, and find common ground, hopefully more than political. He must be able to reach out his hand in friendship, or at least in comradeship, and have that gesture returned. To grasp that hand and feel his hand grasped. Alliances are best when all involved feel they are not only on common ground but have equal footing on that ground."

Marcus thought over the words Caiaphas had just spoken and finally nodded. "You are right, of course, as always."

"No," Caiaphas said, smiling, "not always." He shrugged. "Most of the time, but not always. And you should continue to voice your opinions and concerns." He gripped Marcus's shoulder warmly, "but not so rudely, hmm?"

Marcus smiled and nodded again. "Thank you for your patience."

"Just remember to exercise that same patience when you appoint and train your Marcus," Caiaphas said, sounding more like a father than a commander.

Marcus nodded. "With your permission, I will not go with you but watch from the observation room."

With one hand on the panic button, Caiaphas thought. But Marcus was right. It would be prudent to protect him. What Caiaphas wasn't sure of was which man needed safeguarding more at the moment.

Caiaphas nodded his permission and watched Marcus exit the office.

7

Roman Dvanaesti's Estate, Italy

Roman Dvanaesti sat in the straight-back wooden chair, still as a statue. His eyes, never blinking, were intent upon the creature lying in the bed across from him. He watched a blackened flake of skin, the size of a compact disc, fall from its shoulder to the floor, revealing fresh, violent red skin. It was like watching burning flesh in reverse.

Inhaling, Roman caught a scent only another Ancient would: Life.

Eight weeks ago, the form in the bed had been a piece of charred and grizzled meat carved in some grotesque Salvador Dali-esque artistic vision of a human. There'd been no way to identify what type of human, man or woman, it was, let alone who it was. But like one of Roman's favorite sculptors, Michelangelo, whom he'd commissioned to carve from marble a larger-than-life piece entitled *The Rebirth of Pontius Pilate*, he could see the beauty beneath. He also knew that while fire might consume, it could not destroy. So he'd ordered continual blood transfusions.

At first, the blood leached from the black meat like water through a sieve, soaking the sheets and settling into the mattress. Its rancid stench offended the noses of the nurses who said nothing, but Roman knew what they were thinking: *Hopeless,* and *what a waste,* and *better off dead.* Those who entertained that last reflection found themselves donating to the cause and thinking that last thought of themselves.

After two weeks, no fluids seeped from the grizzled form. The blood transfusions continued as the edges slowly turned to a greasy gristle, resembling a well-done steak kissed passionately by the fire.

And today, the last charred flakes of skin fell away. Now, the nurses could see what Roman had always seen.

Isabella

Roman remembered the day he'd dug Isabella's charred body from the ground. Cain Dvanaesti's Miami mansion lay in smoldering ruins, and though it was August, cool gusts blew across the estate from an impending tropical storm. The blackened ashes of home, books, papers, and personal belongings rose upon the wind and danced to a macabre tune only these dead things could hear. Investigators and other law enforcement personnel scrambled frantically to secure the estate grounds and as much evidence as possible before the storm hit Southern Florida. At the same time, every local, state, and national news affiliate recorded the proceedings for posterity and their six o'clock news ratings.

Unfazed and untouched by all this tumult, Roman walked through the grounds to where Isabella had buried herself. He knew exactly what had happened to her and what she had done. He knew her pain, her torment, how once she'd buried herself, she had forced herself to sleep, the closest thing to death a vampire as old as Isabella could inflict on herself. She knew he would come for her. Take her back to his villa in Italy. She knew he would restore her. This was part of the symbiosis between the maker and the made. This symbiosis was strongest between the father and his twelve children. It was almost as strong between the twelve and the children they made, and weakened with each generation.

Roman moved through the grounds of his "son's" estate without hurry to where Isabella was, unearthed her, and carried her away, all without any investigator, reporter, news crew, or gawker noticing or catching him on tape.

"She no longer requires your attention," Roman said to the nurse who entered the room.

Esmeralda jumped at being addressed. Roman had not moved since taking his seat to watch over Isabella eight weeks before, and she had forgotten he was there. He was just another piece of furniture in the room to be ignored as she took care of her charge.

Her startlement was quickly overcome by resentment at being told her job. She didn't care who Roman Dvanaesti was. That wasn't true. She cared very much. She'd only been a vampire for twenty-eight years, and Roman Dvanaesti was an Ancient. He was one of the original twelve. She had great respect and admiration for him. It's why she sought the position on his staff. She'd been a nurse before she was reborn, and she was one now. She took that very seriously.

Before her rebirth, Esmeralda hadn't cared if the patient was indigent or a dignitary. She provided the same level of care to each. She didn't care who the patient's family was, either. She didn't allow anyone to stand in her way of taking care of her patients. And besides, as she looked over Isabella and brushed a few flakes off to reveal an angry red chin, the woman looked the best she had in the past two weeks. Esmeralda had been astonished at Isabella's healing. A younger vampire would not be halfway in her recovery for another six to eight months. But still, she could see the woman was not out of trouble.

Esmeralda opened her mouth to tell Roman when she was distracted by an odor. She looked at the woman reclining in a chair to the left of Isabella's bed. This woman was a pasty white. Noticing that the line from her arm to Isabella's was no longer dark red but empty, Esmeralda placed her index finger on the woman's wrist. Nothing.

"Yes, sir," was all she said as she released the dead woman's wrist. "I'll have her removed and another donor brought in." She exited the room, not making eye contact with Roman. She chose to forget the other three donors reclining around Isabella's bed, blood-filled tubing running from each one to Isabella.

8

Washington National Cathedral,
Washington, D.C.

JOIN US AS WE HONOR
  The Life of
  Sandra Day O'Connor

Remember a woman who
was an inspiration to millions.
DEC 18 / 9:30 AM
Washington National Cathedral

Harold Darby watched his tears stain the invitation. Just two weeks prior, he had received the news that his friend and mentor had passed. He remembered sitting in his office, ignoring the phone ringing. The buzz from his cell phone. Even the knock at the door from his assistant, who had grown concerned about his ignoring calls.

"Mr. Darby? Sir? Are you okay?" Carol asked.

Darby didn't respond.

"Harold?" Jacquelyn said, touching his hand.

Harold looked up to see Sandra-no...Jacquelyn, standing next to him with his assistant standing in front of the desk, biting her bottom lip, her eyes darting between Darby and Jacquelyn like she was watching two opponents square off in a bar. Her whole body trembled, and Darby realized she'd never seen him like this. It had unsettled her. He always knew what to do, so she always knew what to do.

Jacquelyn must have realized it as well.

"Carol, why don't you get Mr. Darby a glass of water?" Jacquelyn said. Her tone was soft but prompting.

Darby had never realized before now just how much Jacquelyn looked *and sounded* like a young Sandra Day O'Connor. He inhaled the fragrance of *Wild Fern*. She even smelled like Sandra.

"Sure. Water. I'll go get some water," Carol said as she rushed out of the office.

Jacquelyn sat down on the edge of the desk next to Harold, still holding his hand. Her other hand reached out, touching the picture of Sandra Day O'Connor that Harold Darby had on his desk. "She was a remarkable woman," Jacquelyn said.

Darby noticed the familiar way that Sandra-...Jacquelyn brushed the cheek and jawline of the image. The smile on Jacquelyn's face was tender, and her eyes were filled with longing. It was, Darby thought, as if the young woman beside him could remember posing for this picture, which had to have been taken well before she was born.

"You two were close," Jacquelyn continued.

"Yes." Darby's voice quavered. "She was...is...will always be...very dear to me." His voice choked on a sob.

"Did that ever bother her husband?"

This question made Darby chuckle in surprise. "Bill?" His headshake was dismissive. "No, Bill knew I was in love with the law. I was harmless. I would never be more than an ardent friend and admirer of Sandy. I never wished I were Bill or tried to seduce her away from him. As a husband, Bill was the best man for the job."

"Mrs. O'Connor is why I became a lawyer," Jacquelyn said.

Darby was not surprised. Many women had confided in him about Sandra's inspiration. And not just attorneys. Women had been inspired to forge paths in other male-dominated fields because of her.

"Sandy was a remarkable woman," Darby said as the tears flowed freely down his cheeks.

"She's always been a hero to me," Jacquelyn said. "As much of an inspiration as an aspiration. A true advocate of the law." She looked down, almost embarrassed. "Perhaps, one day, the same will be said of me."

Darby knew what Jacquelyn was saying. She hoped one day young women would look to her as she had looked to Sandy. "I have no doubt you will. You are a remarkable woman as well, Miss Dvanaesti," Darby said.

"Jacquelyn, please." Jacquelyn patted his hand with consoling affection.

Darby couldn't believe how much it felt like Sandra's touch. That same movement of three pats and a squeeze of the top of his hand as he told her how his beloved Golden Retriever, Justicia, had passed when he was a boy. He'd never owned another dog. Or when he lamented to her his view of the declining love of the law among the graduates applying for jobs at his firm.

"You take all the time you need. I'll let Carol know you're not taking any calls," Jacquelyn said as she stood and walked toward the door.

"Thank you, Jacquelyn."

"I'll give you some time, Mr. Darby," Jacquelyn said.

"Harold," Darby interjected. "Thank you."

"You're welcome, Harold," Jacquelyn said.

"Jacquelyn?"

She stopped and turned back to Darby.

"Would you like to accompany me to the service?"

Darby watched Jacquelyn's face light with that broad gap-toothed smile that radiated up into Sandy's hazel eyes.

"I would love to. Thank you, Harold." Then she left the office, closing the door behind her.

That was two weeks ago. Now, Jacquelyn sat beside him in the Washington National Cathedral, her hand in his. He'd been holding it together until Jay O'Connor, Sandra's son, spoke of his parents' love of dancing, even learning to disco dance. Darby remembered that after their children, Sandy and Bill loved to dance. His mind's eye took him back to the O'Connor house for a Saturday lunch back in Nineteen eighty when *More Than a Woman* came on the Hi-Fi. Bill and Sandra immediately stood up from the table and, as if no one was there, started dancing. John Travolta would've genuflected in reverence had he been there. He hadn't. But Darby had. When they finished, he was on his feet, applauding. The couple had forgotten he'd been there.

It was this memory that finally broke Darby. The tears began to fall as strong and as heavy as a Spring shower. He felt a feminine arm wrap around him, and a hand patted his shoulder three times and then squeezed. Darby placed his hand over the squeezing hand. "I miss you, Sandy."

A voice whispered into his ear. "I miss you, too, Harold. But like Lady Law, I'll always be right here."

Darby felt Sandy's hand on his chest over his heart. It was like swallowing nitroglycerin. He felt strength and vitality he hadn't felt since his days as a student at Harvard Law. He gasped. And then wept all the more.

9

Venice, Italy

Detectives Antonio Frederico and Marco Scalia stared wide-eyed and gape-mouthed at their boss, Chief Inspector Alberto Donatello. Their incredulity couldn't have been greater than if he'd ordered them to exchange their badges for dust brooms.

"Dead rats?" Frederico felt the urge to light a cigarette and take a long drag, but settled for rubbing the Chantix patch on his forearm like a talisman and popping two pieces of Nicorette into his mouth. Gnashing down hard and fast on the gum, he felt a wave of lightheadedness. It wasn't as strong or as satisfying as a hit of nicotine from a cigarette. But with the patch and a quick prayer to St. Michael, the patron saint of law enforcement, perhaps he should be praying to St. Jude, the patron saint of lost causes, for this assignment, he wondered; he kept himself from cursing out his supervisor.

Donatello stared back at him, unblinking.

Scalia looked between his partner and Donatello. "You want us to investigate dead rats?"

Donatello swore under his breath. "Are the two of you detectives or parrots?" He stood up, placed his fists on the desk, and leaned over the two men. "Rats. Dead. Rats. Lots of them. More every day."

"And you want us to find out who's responsible because the city wants to give them some kind of...commendation?" Scalia asked.

Donatello ignored the question. "We have what might be an epidemic of dead rats and a growing hysteria among our citizens. People are thinking it's a disease like the Bubonic plague. And others think it might be a cult sacrificing the rats." He picked up a stack of

43

photos and tossed them to Scalia. "We've had more than two dozen businesses in the last month alone calling to report finding dead rats in and around their establishments."

Scalia caught the pictures and started thumbing through them, his incredulity giving way to his instinct. He was a detective and a good one. *Sub lege libertas.* Freedom under the law. That wasn't just the motto of Italian Law Enforcement. It was his. Anything, even public hysteria over dead rats, which threatened the freedom of its citizens, warranted investigation. Warranted justice. That, and Scalia loved a mystery, no matter how weird.

Frederico resisted the urge to pop another Nicorette into his mouth and instead opened his mouth to protest, but Donatello held up a hand. Frederico closed his mouth and stood up.

Scalia continued to thumb through the pictures.

Donatello and Frederico locked eyes, and at that moment, he understood why he would be spending his foreseeable future investigating rats.

Frederico also loved a mystery and believed in *Freedom under the law* even more than he did in *Hail Mary, full of grace.* It's what made him a good detective, he thought. Good? He was the best. He and Scalia. So, this assignment was more than a slap in the face. More than an insult. Worse than a request to trade their badges in for dust brooms. This was personal.

Frederico wanted to step up to Donatello, get in his face. Donatello was a big man. Over six feet tall and pushing three hundred pounds. The extra hundred pounds made him appear doughy. Frederico was also just over six feet but weighed in at a healthy one hundred ninety-eight. And he was twenty-five years younger. Donatello had spent more years behind a desk now than Frederico had been a cop. He would win and leave Donatello's office in handcuffs.

Instead, he slapped Scalia on the shoulder and motioned for him to follow. Then he turned on his heel and exited the Inspector's office.

Frederico threw himself down into his chair, fuming.

Scalia plopped down in his chair across Frederico, still looking at the photos. "These rats look like they've been...dehydrated. You know, like all their blood's been removed from their bodies. Not like they've been eaten at all. They're intact."

But Frederico wasn't listening. "This is all *your* fault, you know," He spat with accusatory venom at his partner.

Scalia looked up from the pictures, his eyebrows halfway up his forehead. "*My* fault?"

Frederico nodded his head with such passion that his neck muscles creaked.

Scalia tossed the photos down on his desk. "How do you figure?"

"The Christmas Party? At the Inspector's house?"

"Yeah?" Scalia put his elbows on his desk and interlaced his fingers. "What about it?"

"You kissed his sister." Frederico's tone was thick with blame.

"I didn't know she was his sister," Scalia said, hearing the defensiveness and cursing himself for it. He was an adult, not some teenager caught making out with a girl in the school janitor's closet. And she may be the Inspector's sister, but she's also an adult. It was nobody's business but theirs.

"Of course, you didn't, you stupid little Don Juan," Frederico's voice boomed. "Your motto is to kiss first and ask her name later."

Now it was Scalia who wanted to step up on Frederico. Scalia was a couple of inches shorter and twenty pounds lighter, but he'd scored second place at the Italian National Brazilian Jiu-Jitsu Championship a couple of years ago. He was more than evenly matched, and he knew that Frederico knew that too. And just because Frederico was scolding him like he was a teenager caught making out with a girl in the school janitor's closet didn't mean he had to behave like said teenager. Besides, Frederico wasn't just his partner. With what they'd been through together on the job, he was closer than a brother.

Scalia held up placating hands. "It was Christmas. We just both happened to be under the mistletoe." Then, to lighten the mood, he added, "You know the old saying, when in Rome?"

"We're not in Rome. We're in Venice, you twit," Frederico hissed.

"So you think we're investigating dead rats because I hooked up with the Inspector's sister?"

At this, two detectives who shared the desk across from Frederico and Scalia burst out laughing.

Frederico turned to look at the other two detectives.

"It's because you *didn't* hook up with his sister," one said through his laughter.

"Huh?" was all Scalia could think of saying.

The other detective cleared his throat. "Donatello's sister came to spend a little time with him after being jilted at the altar. *A second time.* It was only supposed to be a couple of weeks, but that was four months ago."

"So Donatello's been trying to hook her up with every single guy in the department," the other detective said through his laughter.

Frederico looked hard at his partner. "You've got to make this right."

"Me?" Scalia stared at his partner as if he'd just suggested that maybe the two of them should trade their badges in for dust brooms.

"We are this close to a promotion." Frederico held up his thumb and forefinger, showing an inch of space between them. He then slammed that hand down on the table. "And I am not going to spend it investigating dead rats."

10

Venice, Italy

The man's head cocked to the right like a German Shepherd's when hearing a new and strange sound. It had been high-pitched. Loud. Sudden. Piercing. Very different from the sound his current food uttered, like the one held in his hand, when he drank from it. Different but...strangely the same. Terror. Pain. A desire to survive. The intensity and pitch stopped abruptly, but the man could still hear it. It came in jagged fits and starts.

Removing his fangs from the now desiccated rat, the man dropped it, forgotten, letting it clatter among a dozen other withered rodents. He licked his lips, cleaning them of the remnants of blood, and swallowing as he closed his eyes, focusing on other sounds he could now hear. Grunting. Hard breathing. Struggling.

The man concentrated on the sounds. Memories fluttered at the back of his mind. The high-pitched sound...scream. It was called a scream. It had been uttered by a...by a...

Woman.

The man's head cocked to the left and back to the right. The *woman's* now muffled *screams* were coming from...

Head turning in the correct direction, the man's body pivoted and began walking. He was still several...blocks. That was the word. He was still several blocks away. The shuffling, scuffling, and grunting were clearer, confirming he was heading in the right direction.

The man didn't know he was a man. Or had once been. Didn't know he'd once lived among other men in a city over four thousand miles away from where he was right now. He wasn't aware he'd worn clothes, eaten in restaurants, and slept in a bed. He'd owned a home and a car, had friends and lovers. A career. A bank account. He didn't know or remember any of those things. He didn't even dream about them. But then again, he didn't sleep either. He just was. The only thing he knew was hunger. Voracious, all-consuming hunger from the moment he'd awakened.

That was his memory. Waking in the sewers of Venice, though he didn't know he was in Venice, nor was he aware he was in the sewers. He didn't know his food was rats. Nor did he recognize that the stench that assaulted his nostrils and burned his lungs was human waste. He only knew he'd learned how to sate his hunger. Among the feces and urine, soap, hair, and vomit that filled the tunnels was food. It skittered and chittered all around him but left him alone. The food seemed to understand he was a predator.

Those primal suspicions of him were soon confirmed when a morsel tarried near him. It kept a wary eye on his form as it inched closer to what it considered some morsel of food too tempting to leave untouched. He waited until the animal began nibbling. His arm moved faster than the animal could have imagined. It felt the predator's hand clasp around its body. Felt fangs pierce its flesh.

The man heard the food squeal, a single, piercing note echoing through the sewer. It quickened his heart. Adrenalin coursed. He opened his mouth, feeling fangs spring from his gums. It was acutely painful and euphoric. His mouth flooded with saliva. The squealing food tried to shake loose, but the man's grip was vise-like as he lifted it to his mouth and sank his fangs into it.

Warm fluid gushed over his teeth and tongue and down his throat. His gut wriggled with delight. His head swam. Strength surged through his body. His eyesight, olfaction, and hearing sharpened. Not only did he see food, but now he saw the individual food items. He watched them creep away from him. Tracked them. He snatched another one. Sank fangs into it. He felt the heady giddiness from his increasing strength. The individual food items fled in different directions, but he was too fast for them. Within a few moments, he'd consumed twelve of them.

Soon, his food learned to keep a distance from him. The man had to hunt them, following them through the tunnels. His relentless stalking was only matched by their terror of him, driving them into daylight and the world above.

The constant torrent of sounds flooding his ears and brain simultaneously had driven him mad. He'd retreated into the comfort of the sewers of Venice. They were dark and quiet and still offered food. As he continued feeding, he learned how to wait and lure prey close to him. He learned to separate the images he saw. Recognize them. He differentiated odors and scents. And he mastered drowning out noises and focusing on others. He grasped that when the space above the tunnels was dark, the cacophony lessened.

Feeding not only strengthened and sharpened his senses but also quieted his mind. He became less crazed by hunger. His mind understood there were times to hunt, stalk, or wait. The man was always hungry. But now other cognitive skills were kindled: experimentation and curiosity.

His curiosity drew him on, his nostrils filling with the scent of fear. He'd never smelled it so strongly, not even when the sewers were filled with food. There were other odors as well. The man's mind separated them into pleasant but useless and unpleasant but also useless. But one aroma...that one stopped him like he'd run into a wall. He singled that one out, forgetting the others, and concentrated on it as he filled his lungs. It sang to him. His head spun. His fingers, toes, and scalp tingled with it. Someone watching his eyes close as his face slackened would have thought him a junkie taking his first hit of cocaine after months of sobriety. The aroma was stronger than the scent in the sewers where he fed. Richer. He had to have it.

The man entered the alley where a...woman, he remembered, lay on her back on the ground, struggling. A...male, yes, male, had one meaty hand grasping both of her wrists above her head while the other hand tried to lay across her mouth. The woman's head shook back and forth, allowing her screams to escape. Another male grunted for her to shut up as he lay on top of her while undoing his belt.

The woman bit down on the man's hand.

He cursed as he yanked his hand to his chest.

"HEL—!"

The male slapped her across the face as he cradled his injured hand to his chest. Blood stained his shirt.

The scent of blood reached the man's nostrils. Though the trio was in shadow, the man saw the trickle oozing. He moved.

The woman felt the jerk as something hit the man holding her wrists, and then they were free. She looked up. The male was gone. She could hear struggling in the darkness behind her and a suckling noise. Then silence.

"What the—?"

From the darkness, the man turned and watched the other male rise to his feet, looking for his friend, while pulling his belt from the loops. Although invisible to the male, wrapping his belt around his hand, he could see the male standing above the woman, quickly covering her body as if bright noonday sunlight flooded the alley.

This was new. Nothing like this had ever happened while feeding in the sewers. All of his senses heightened. He'd never felt stronger.

"All right, punk. Show yourself."

The man understood the words. He understood what he'd just interrupted. He understood what he'd just done to one of the rapists. He understood what he was about to do. The male standing before him was about to take his last breath.

The world seemed to slow as he moved towards the male. Picking him up with one hand, he sank his fangs into his throat and began to drink. Euphoria coursed through his body. He drained him in a matter of seconds.

And now, who he had been, where he'd come from, and what had happened to him came crashing into his mind like a thousand plates spilling over his head from an overstuffed cabinet. A wave of nausea washed over him as his vision blurred. He bent over and began to vomit blood violently.

"Gabriel," he breathed when he'd finished. "My name...is Gabriel. Gabriel Hawthorne."

He heard a snuffling behind him and turned to see the woman lying on the ground. Gabriel turned to her, trying to calm her down.

"It's okay—" Gabriel stopped, not recognizing the voice coming from his throat. It didn't even sound human.

The woman scrambled to her feet and ran.

Gabriel watched as the woman exited the alley. Gabriel looked down at the lifeless body of the man he had just killed. He fought back as another wave of nausea washed over him. Gabriel noticed the woman's purse lying on the ground next to the body. He picked up the purse, seeing a name badge clipped to the strap.

"*Alessia Mantalto.*"

11

Washington, D.C.

"Could we please have a short recess, your Honor?" Jacquelyn requested.

Howard Williams turned from the witness to the table where Jacquelyn sat. He approached her with a look of disgust as he snatched the legal pad from her hand that had the witness's name and questions for the cross-examination on it. He'd just addressed the witness by the wrong name. Again.

This was not the first mistake he'd made that day. Earlier, he'd gotten the dates wrong while questioning the defendant's alibi, then further hurt their client by suggesting he'd not been confused but was outright lying. Jacquelyn could tell that, despite the strength of the case they had built, Williams was simultaneously losing the jury and paving the way for a successful conviction for the prosecution.

"That won't be necessary, Your Honor," Williams said over his shoulder as he scowled at Jacquelyn.

Despite the breath mints, Jacquelyn could smell the bourbon on her boss's breath. She took in his three-thousand-dollar suit, two-hundred-dollar tie, and four-hundred-dollar shoes and realized his haircut cost more than the witness's entire suit, tie, and shoes. Yet, the bourbon he'd chosen to imbibe that morning had been of the cheap variety.

Jaquelyn didn't mean a cheap price. She knew there were some quality bourbons under thirty dollars. But Williams hadn't selected one of those. Instead, he'd spent money on a spirit that was a direct reflection of his own. Harsh, yet lacking complexity. Flat.

An idiom came to Jaquelyn's mind: Still waters run deep. In that case, she thought as she met his hard stare with one of her own, Williams was just a mud puddle.

"I think we all could use a break," Judge Michaels replied. "Court will resume in fifteen minutes," he said with a weary clap of his gavel on the bench.

Williams didn't wait for the judge to enter his chambers. "Just what do you think you're doing?" Williams spat at Jacquelyn, punching the desk hard.

Heads in the gallery snapped up to watch the growing spectacle.

Jacquelyn was unfazed by the crowd and even less so by Williams's outburst. "Trying to save this case and salvage your reputation," Jacquelyn replied.

"We only need to put doubt in their minds. If you had been practicing law for more than a week, you would know that," Williams barked as he leaned over Jacquelyn.

"Well, you've definitely put doubt in everyone's minds today." Jacquelyn's voice was calm and even as she stood to meet Williams's glare. "The jury's now wondering just how guilty our client is. The prosecution's wondering what to send you as a thank-you gift. The judge is wondering if he should cite you for contempt because you're slightly inebriated. Or because the rumors that you pay off jurors to win must be true. And everyone's doubting if you've ever legitimately won a case."

A vein at Williams's temple pulsed hard enough to tug at his hairline. His face was now the shade of a red onion. His right hand shook with the urge to slap the mascara right off Jacquelyn's face.

Jacquelyn could hear his teeth grinding. *Good.* She decided to press him. "You're a small man, Howard. I'm not talking about your bank account, and I don't mean your height. You strut around the office and the courtroom, thinking everyone's impressed or intimidated by you and your big swinging—"

"*STOP,*" Williams roared.

"But in reality, it's just..." Jacquelyn held up a pinky and then let it curl.

Williams's hand was up and moving. He wasn't thinking. He wasn't seeing. The rage, fueled in small part by the cheap bourbon coursing through his veins and in large part by his realization of just how badly he'd been screwing up, exploded in an emotional inferno at Jacquelyn's audacity. He only knew just how good the *smack* would feel and sound. It made him giddy.

Jacquelyn knew the *smack* was coming. It's what she'd been hoping for. She'd been planning for it since their introduction. She wanted a way to take him down that he couldn't just bounce back from. Everyone knew he was a self-absorbed prick. It hadn't ended his career. Not even the exposure of his juror tampering would end him. That might get him disbarred, maybe a little time in a white-collar prison. But he'd come out just as cocky and either hit the speaker circuit, become a special legal expert for some media outlet, or wind up hosting a show on whatever incarnation Court TV takes next.

So after a long think, she realized the one thing that would end him. Strike her in the courtroom in front of witnesses. Maybe someone would even be quick and bright enough to pull out their smartphone and film the incident. The video would go viral globally within hours. He'd become a pariah by sundown. Williams would be judged guilty in the court of public opinion and summarily executed. He'd go to prison, and not a white-collar one. He'd be disbarred. Darby, Langley, and Luna would want to distance themselves from him. True, he might get a quiet settlement if he just slipped away. But knowing Williams, he'd make it a public spectacle and thereby make things worse for himself. He wouldn't be able to go anywhere in the world and not be recognized as the brute of a man who assaulted a professional woman.

So she'd waited for the right moment to provoke him. She knew she'd been successful, had planted her feet to take the strike. She just hoped that the smartphones recording and the devices around the world that replayed the assault would show just how good that smack looked and sounded. She was counting on it, expecting it.

What she wasn't expecting, neither was Williams, was Bailiff Orlando Sandoval. Before his duties as a bailiff, he was a highly decorated street cop. Before entering law enforcement, Sandoval was a triple threat at Howard University on the football field, basketball court, and track. He could've become a professional athlete, but his dream was always to be a police officer. Sports were only a way to pay for college. Sports and an academic scholarship. His strength, speed, and agility were only surpassed by his powers of observation.

As soon as Williams had turned back to Jacquelyn and snatched the paper, Sandoval kept an eye on the attorney. His eyes darted away only long enough to see Judge Michaels close his chamber door, then he was back on the two bickering lawyers. His instincts told him tempers were escalating quickly, which always led to bad behavior, so he took several unobtrusive half-steps toward them. As soon as Williams's hand moved, Sandoval shot forward.

Williams felt a vice grip around his wrist.

"Easy there, Counselor," Sandoval said.

Williams glared at the bailiff, who only stared with a dead calm back. Williams understood the look on the bailiff's face.

Give me a reason.

Taking a deep breath, Williams exhaled and relaxed, nodding his acquiescence.

Officer Sandoval let go of Williams's wrist but didn't step off.

Jacquelyn's exhaled frustration was mistaken for relief by the two men. She squelched the desire to berate the bailiff for interfering and instead smiled at him. "Thank you, Officer Sandoval."

Sandoval nodded and didn't move.

"You think you know what everyone's thinking, hotshot?" Williams asked with a devilish grin. "Then why don't you handle it from here?" Williams said as he started to walk away. He stopped at the door and turned back. "And when you blow this case, we'll see what Darby thinks of his new golden child." Williams continued as he walked out of the courtroom.

Jaquelyn watched him go.

Mistaking her gaze, Sandoval placed what he thought was a comforting hand on her shoulder and said, "Don't worry, Miss Dvanaesti. He'll be back after he cools off."

"Not if he's smart," Jacquelyn said, too low for Sandoval to hear. She patted Sandoval's hand as she shot him a thank-you smile. "Well," she said after a sigh. "I guess I'd better get ready." She sat back down and pretended to prepare her questions.

"All rise," Officer Sandoval said.

Jacquelyn jumped to her feet as Judge Michaels entered the courtroom.

Judge Michaels looked around the courtroom for Williams. Noting his absence, he looked to Jacquelyn. "Are we ready?"

Jacquelyn locked eyes with the judge and smiled. "Yes, we are, Your Honor."

12

Secret Vampire Compound,
Somewhere in the World

Kevin tapped the toes of his boots in rhythm with the tune he was humming as he leaned back in his control room chair. Checking his watch, he frowned, realizing he had six more hours in his shift. He also noticed it was the top of the hour. He selected a new tune to hum and kept tapping his toes.

"Hey, it's time," Abraham announced as he shot Kevin a reproving glare.

"What's the rush?" Kevin replied, toes tapping as he glanced at the four thermal images of a chamber. Each image was of a different perspective of the chamber. Each image focused on a shadowy form of something lying on the ground, chained to a pillar. If whatever was lying on the ground moved, at least one camera would capture its movement. But the form never moved. Never spoke or uttered a sound. It could be a pile of rocks or dirty clothes, Kevin thought. "Nothing ever changes. Every hour on the hour, we flood the cell with UV light and then nothing. The whole thing's a waste of time and resources if you ask me," Kevin continued, waving an arm in an expansive gesture to indicate the entire facility.

"No one's asking." Bomani's voice rumbled with menace from behind them.

Both vampires sprang to their feet, spun, and stood at attention. Neither dared to make eye contact with the six-foot-five-inch vampire filling the doorway.

He looks like the love child of Djimon Hounsou and Dwayne Johnson. The thought caused Kevin to bite hard on the inside of his mouth to keep from smiling. Knowing Bomani, that would be the last thing he ever did. He didn't know if it was just Bomani or that he'd been in this god-forsaken fortress too long, but the man had no sense of humor.

"Nothing ever changes because every hour on the hour we flood that cell," Bomani pointed at the screen, "so that whatever or whoever is in there stays there. "It is vital that you follow your orders to the letter."

"Yes, sir," Abraham responded, nudging Keven with his elbow.

"Yes, sir," Kevin repeated with a nod. He was sure he'd seen a slight tremor in his commander's pointing finger.

Ignoring the two men's affirmations, Bomani walked to the console and pressed a button. The image of the chamber disappeared in white light so bright that all three squinted as they watched the monitor. A sixty-second timer above the monitor started counting down automatically. The counter reached zero, and the light cut off. A second later, the thermal images of the chamber filled the screen. The shape was still there. Still unmoving. Silent.

But this time, the silence and lack of change to the form unnerved Kevin. It was more than Bomani's presence and his speech. He had the distinct feeling that whatever lay on that slab was looking through the thermal camera directly into his eyes. And was smiling.

Kevin remembered a quote his high school history teacher had hanging on the wall in his classroom. He thought it was Nietzsche. He didn't remember the whole quote, but the ending had always stayed with him. It seemed especially poignant right now. *And if you gaze long enough into the eyes of the abyss, the abyss will gaze back into you.*

"I still don't see the point," Kevin said, studying the image on the monitor and trying to suppress a shiver. "I have been here for almost six months, and I've never seen any movement from who or what is in that cell." He sneered at Bomani with false bravado. "How do we know if whatever it is is still alive?"

The next thing Kevin knew, he slammed into the wall across the room. Before gravity could pull him to the floor, Bomani had moved across the room and now had him by the throat.

Kevin could feel the older vampire's fingernails, sharp as razors, biting into his skin. His eyes bulged as he realized his superior was about to tear out his throat.

Abraham also realized Bomani's intention. "He's only been one of us for a short time," Abraham stammered. "His lack of understanding and apparent flippancy are my fault, sir. I have failed him in his training. Please give him another chance," Abraham pleaded.

Kevin felt Bomani's nails dig deeper into his throat.

"Please," Abraham pleaded again.

Finally, after what Kevin counted as an eternity, Bomani dropped him.

Kevin landed hard, crumpling into a pile on the floor. He rubbed his throat, which was already healing, soft pink blemishes the only remnant of where Bomani's nails had pierced his skin.. Kevin realized the older vampire had only wanted to get his attention. He had never intended to destroy him. At least, that's what Kevin decided to believe.

Bomani moved to the doorway, then stopped. His head dropped, and his shoulders sagged. He was thinking. Weighing. Finally, he decided, punching the steel wall, leaving a dent the size of a salad plate. He turned back towards the room.

Kevin still lay on the floor. Abraham stood where he'd been.

"We had someone like you back when I was first posted here," Bomani smirked at the thought. "Like you, he thought this job was pointless. A waste of his time. Beneath the *Akhkharu*." His eyes flit upward as if searching the ceiling for the strength to continue.

"We had different protocols back then, and the technology wasn't as advanced. Teams of eleven men went into the chamber to administer the UV light. When it was his team's turn to enter the chamber, he didn't feel the need to follow procedure. What was the point?" He stared off, reliving a memory. When he looked back at them, Kevin and Abraham wished he hadn't. "I lost ten friends that day. In a matter of minutes. Seconds really. Another five men were lost before we finally regained control."

Bomani walked towards the monitor, now showing the thermal images of the chamber. He leaned close to the image, which, Kevin was convinced, showed whatever was there staring back.

"That was almost seventy-eight years ago. And I still don't know who he is." Bomani announced, continuing to stare at the prisoner's image on the monitor. "And I don't want to."

13

Illuminati Compound,
Baton Rouge, Louisiana

Cain Dvanaesti lay on the bed beneath the covers, eyes closed, breathing deep and steady.

Caiaphas wondered how he should wake the sleeping man. Call out his name? Shake him? Gently, of course. He found himself adverse to putting a hand on the form. Caiaphas wasn't afraid of Cain Dvanaesti. Caiaphas had never been fearful of men, or monsters for that matter. And as he aged, the less he feared. But placing a hand on someone lost in slumber seemed a violation to Caiaphas. The waker got what he deserved from the awakened. But Cain Dvanaesti wasn't just a man or just a monster. He was...something else, and waking him might just cost Caiaphas his life. Caiaphas wasn't afraid of death either. Still, meeting his end by waking something seemed frivolous.

"I didn't know if you were real." Cain interrupted the older man's ruminations. "Back in the mirror. I wondered if you were just a dream. I hoped you were just a dream. The alternative was..." Cain's voice trailed off for a moment. "I guess a hallucination wouldn't be too bad. They can always find a medical explanation for hallucinations, right? Auditory hallucinations aren't just voices in your head telling you to do things like hurt yourself or others. So dreams and hallucinations are better than...But then I heard your conversation." His tone was not of a braggart, nor even as a matter of fact, but of surprised revelation, like a child realizing for the first time he was riding his bicycle without a parent holding onto the back of the seat. "Out in the corridor. More of a disagreement, really. I could hear it as if I'd been standing right there with you." He sniffed the air.

Caiaphas appraised the man, the vampire, the being, lying on the bed. He looked and sounded as he had on television. And yet his countenance was different.

"I could even hear a motor hum, soft as a whisper." Cain pointed to the bathroom mirror but didn't look at it. "From there." Cain wasn't sure why he volunteered this information to the old man leaning against the wall.

"What's the last thing you remember?" Caiaphas asked.

Cain opened his eyes. "I was with Claudia. On my jet headed to..." He sighed. "We were in an accident. And then I woke up here." Sniffing the air, he asked, "Where's Claudia?" He breathed in the air again. "I can't smell her. Where is she?"

"You can smell her?" Caiaphas asked, still leaning up against the wall, unable to keep the troubling feeling he was experiencing out of his voice. He clasped his hands in front of him.

Cain felt a slight twinge of irritation. "No. I can't." He sat up. "I can smell cologne and fear from behind the mirror." He looked at Caiaphas. "I can smell," he inhaled, nose wrinkling, "something...unsettling wafting off of you."

Caiaphas's hands immediately dropped to his side as he pushed himself off the wall. His mouth dropped open in surprise, but he quickly recovered himself. It had been a very long time since Caiaphas felt a mustard seed of victory taking root in his chest.

What Cain had said he could see, hear, and smell had not surprised him. As the ultimate apex predator, Caiaphas knew that vampires had heightened senses that other apex predators would envy. What he hadn't expected was how even more heightened Cain's senses seemed to be. Fear. Sweat. Blood. Body odors. That stood to reason. But unease? A slight emotion he'd smelled. Not seen in body language or heard in intonation. Caiaphas quickly calculated just how powerful a weapon Cain would be.

Caiaphas could hardly contain himself. He wanted to raise his hands in victory. He wanted to shout and dance around the room. But that was premature, he reminded himself. Cain was not yet his ally. He needed to tread carefully, not allow the mustard seed to bloom just yet. Walking to the wall opposite Cain, Caiaphas asked, "Do you have any idea how long you've been here?"

Cain shook his head. "I don't even know where *here* is." Cain felt his irritation blossoming as he sniffed the air again. Tossing his legs over the side of the bed, he moved to Caiaphas and spun him around so that the two were facing. "I have answered all of your questions," he said with an edge. "Now answer mine. Where is Claudia? Where am I?"

Caiaphas heard the edge in the younger man's voice, knowing he might well be playing with fire; Might very well be provoking this...whatever he truly was. He seemed very much an ordinary man at the moment. Ordinary, but for some very extraordinary powers. Cain didn't know what he was. Caiaphas could see that. Cain had no idea how easily he could leave this place, and there wasn't a thing they could truly do to stop him. After all, he'd survived the attack on his home and his aircraft, which had plunged into the sea, and had been the only one to survive a crash no human could, or should, have survived. Only days after that crash, his body bore no evidence of it.

Caiaphas let out his breath and found his heart pounding in his chest and his hands coming up in a uselessly defensive gesture. It was only a motor reaction, a fight or flight instinct, but he still cursed himself for doing it. And it was obvious, to him now, at least, that Cain meant him no harm. He was only manifesting his frustration. Cain's life had been altered radically in a very short time. Few humans understood what that radical change felt like.

His mind was intact and his body healthy. But as far as the world knew, he was dead. He was now a man without a country, a home, or a family. He'd lost his wealth, affluence, and political power. Lost his home in Miami and the Governor's mansion in Tallahassee. Lost his confidant in Isabella, his "father" and mentor in Roman, and his lover in Claudia. In short, he'd lost every single tie to identity, his self-worth.

Caiaphas couldn't help but look at the...vampirically enhanced young man and feel pity for him. No, Caiaphas thought, not pity. Pity was a useless emotion. Pity was contained within a person and seldom led to action greater than a shaking of the head and a shrug of the shoulders.

Sympathy would be a more appropriate emotion. Sympathy implies the ability and the desire to enter another's emotional experience. Sympathy was power; the power to act, to intervene in another human being's (vampirically enhanced or not) distress and pain to bring healing. That was a power Caiaphas could embrace and would embrace as he looked at Cain.

Before Cain's healing could start, Caiaphas knew he would have to inflict additional pain. The darkest moment comes right before dawn. It was time to inform Cain of the truth. Now it was time to help Cain find himself and begin forging the ties to turn Cain into an ally, a weapon.

Caiaphas opened his mouth, but didn't get a chance to say anything.

Cain's head had turned, his attention piqued by what he heard behind the mirror.

14

"SIT. BACK. DOWN." Marcus's voice boomed through the room.

Caiaphas's mouth shut with an angry, frustrated snap. He heard his teeth grind as he realized what had just happened. Everything he'd said to Marcus in his office, all of the lessons he'd thought his Second had taken to heart, had been nothing more than wisps of smoke in the younger man's head, blown away by the gentlest of breezes. Or, in this case, the simple movement of a desperate man.

"I SAID SIT DOWN. NOW!"

Caiaphas could hear the panic rising in Marcus's voice. He needed to regain control of the situation. Looking at the bathroom mirror, he held up his hand. He couldn't see Marcus, just his and Cain's reflection, but he knew his successor was standing there, hand on the panic button. "Marcus." His voice was steady, calm. He tried to inflect his next word with as much command as ever. "No."

Cain had heard voices and scuffling behind the mirror, which had distracted him. His head had snapped back to Caiaphas at first, thinking the older man had screamed, but then he'd followed Caiaphas's gaze to the mirror. And there, behind the reflection of Caiaphas and himself, was the shadow of a man. It could've been nothing more than a trick of the brain caused by a blemish in the chemical coating on the back of the glass, but Cain knew differently. He knew the man whose voice he'd just heard was standing behind the mirror.

It's happening again, Cain thought to himself. A mixture of terror and awe constricted his chest, and he struggled for breath.

He took a step towards the mirror and squinted with concentration. The man was no longer a shadow but more like the form of a man standing behind gauze. He took another step forward, pursing his lips, his eyes now no more than slits as he brought the form into sharper focus. His breath caught in his throat, and his forward motion stopped as suddenly as if he'd walked into a wall.

The man, Marcus, that's what Caiaphas had called him, was standing in front of Cain just as clearly as if the mirror had been removed. Cain could see his dark gray suit, the darker gray pin striping on the suit, the individual black diamonds comprising the print on his burgundy tie, and the beads of sweat on his forehead. He could also see Marcus's arm stretched out in front of him, but to the side of the mirror.

"Cain," Caiaphas called, "it's all right."

Cain turned towards the sound of Caiaphas's voice. He'd been so consumed with seeing Marcus through the mirror that he hadn't heard Caiaphas stepping up to him. When he turned, he turned right into Caiaphas, knocking the man backward.

Marcus heard Caiaphas tell Cain it was all right as he stepped towards the monster, then saw Cain turn and strike Caiaphas. That was all the provocation he needed. If he'd been willing to search his heart, he would've known it was more a want than a need. His hand slammed onto the panic button.

Phase Two gas shot from nozzles recessed into the ceiling in a light blue haze.

Cain had reached out and caught Caiaphas. He still had him in his grasp and had opened his mouth to apologize and ask Caiaphas if he was okay when the Phase Two gas settled on his skin and invaded his lungs. He felt like he'd been plunged headfirst into a red ant hill. A million ants swarmed over his exposed skin and eyes, down his throat and into his lungs, biting in unison. His vision blurred as blood-filled tears poured from his reddening eyes and snot gushed from his nose. He opened his mouth to inhale fresh air, but only croaked and sputtered as more ants and their venom clogged his lungs. He jerked and stepped back, throwing an unsuspecting Caiaphas forward and into the corner of the stainless-steel sink. Caiaphas crumpled.

Gas filled the room so thick that the bed, sink, and the forms of Caiaphas and Cain disappeared. Marcus had failed to hit the kill switch. He ran from the observation room, or tried to, struggling with the door. He'd unconsciously locked it when entering. He finally unlocked the door and threw it open.

"Open the door," Marcus screamed at the guard. "Open it."

The guard fumbled with his keys, finally finding the right one, and unlocked the door. Before he could open it, Marcus crashed through it.

Phase two gas washed over Marcus and the guard so thick it was like an ocean wave, invading their lungs like seawater and causing the two men to cough and sputter. A twenty-second spurt of the gas would've been enough to kill a room full of vampires. Marcus had let the gas run until the tanks were dry.

Marcus and the guard waved at the gas, trying to clear it from the room. It crept out of the open door and past the two men at an excruciatingly slow pace, and as it did, forms began to take shape. Marcus could make out the bed, the sink, and Caiaphas lying in a heap on the floor.

"Caiaphas." Marcus leapt forward and scooped up his Master.

Caiaphas was dazed. Blood covered his face, pouring from a large gash on his forehead. "Where's...Cain?" He asked in a whisper.

As if in answer, a grunt came from the mist. The grunt turned into a wheezing growl.

The two men turned toward the sounds and watched as a form emerged from the fog. Caiaphas gasped while an involuntary squeak escaped Marcus's throat as they gazed upon what Marcus would later call a nightmare.

Cain no longer felt the effects of the Phase Two gas. In fact, except for the frog in his throat, he felt as strong and healthy as he ever had. But upon hearing Caiaphas's gasp and Marcus's squeak, he looked down. Ice filled his chest as he drew his hands up to his face. He couldn't call them hands. The skin was a mottled black, dark green, and gray. The fingers were long and spindly, with nails like talons.

The ice dropped through a hole where his stomach had been. Not again, he thought to himself. He turned slowly towards the mirror and stared at his reflection.

"NNNNOOOOOOOO!!!"

Cain's knees buckled. His legs failed him. He dropped as if he'd been shot in the head.

Without thinking, Caiaphas stepped towards the creature crumpled on the floor. He heard Marcus shout in protest as he felt the man's hands grasp him, stopping him from taking another step. Caiaphas's head snapped around.

The look on Caiaphas's face caused Marcus to release his master and step back. It was not anger or even fury. Though he wished with all his breaking heart it would have been. No. The look that had pierced Marcus was one of utter and complete disappointment.

Caiaphas turned and rushed to Cain, dropping down next to him.

Cain's weeping sounded more like a whimpering beast than a human's cry.

Caiaphas knelt next to Cain and placed his hand on him. "Shhh," he soothed as he began to pat him on the back. He continued until the former governor's talons receded, and his skin looked like human flesh again.

15

Tokyo, Japan

Abisare gaped at the giant glass building as the Rolls-Royce Ghost pulled into Ronin's private drive. The structure reeked of money, even for Shirokane, one of the wealthiest neighborhoods in Tokyo. This was Abisare's first visit to Japan, and he was surprised his brother had built such a modern edifice. The entire building appeared to be made of a solid piece of glass, the seams invisible to the naked eye. Naked *human* eye. But Abisare had to admit he hadn't noticed them until one section of the building opened, revealing a sloped drive leading to an underground garage.

He rolled his eyes as he took in the garage's sleek concrete and steel construction. Not one inch of this space reflected Japanese culture or tradition. Abisare smirked as he recalled Ronin boasting how he was one with Japan, bragging that it was the oldest country in the world, blustering endlessly about its beautiful landscapes. The Japanese, his brother swaggered, are one with nature, as evidenced in their music, art, literature, poetry, architecture, and dance. One word came to Abisare's mind as he surveyed what he'd seen of Ronin's house.

Audacity.

Ronin, Abisare thought as he gritted his teeth, built this monstrosity in the middle of Japan's capital for one reason: to flaunt his wealth to his family. And his minions.

No one escaped Abisare's judgment or matched his hypocrisy. He'd flown to Japan on his private Boeing 747, painted a bright yellow with red and green pin-striping. Abisare always insisted on a Rolls-Royce Ghost meeting him on the tarmac, not a hangar. He wore an English-style bespoke suit that traveled well and would've cost him more than sixty thousand dollars if the tailor didn't work exclusively for him. The cufflinks he now adjusted were encrusted with seven-carat blue diamonds.

The Rolls stopped before a tall Japanese man dressed in a black suit with tails, and Abisare exited the vehicle before the chauffeur had his hand off the gearshift.

"Kon'nichiwa," he said, bowing to Abisare. "My master is expecting you." The concrete wall behind him parted, exposing an elevator.

Stepping onto the elevator, Abisare nodded at the still-bowing man as the doors closed. There were no buttons on the inside of the elevator. He tugged again at the blue diamond cufflinks and adjusted his tie as he examined his reflection in the elevator's mirrored walls.

My master is expecting you.

The statement troubled Abisare. Of course, Ronin knew he was coming. Abisare had requested the meeting. But he had the sneaking suspicion that Ronin knew why he was coming. Had Ronin discovered that Abisare had already visited several of their other siblings? Unsatisfied with Delilah's response, he had visited two regarding Roman just days ago. That discussion was swept from his mind as the elevator doors opened.

"What the...?" Abisare gasped, not believing his eyes. Stepping from the elevator, he found himself in a beautiful garden wrapping around a house. Both looked like they belonged in ancient Japan. Walking across the bridge towards the house, he gazed at a Koi Pond snaking its way through the garden. Now he realized the real reason for the mirrored glass surrounding the compound. Standing on the house's front steps, Abisare saw that the entire interior facade surrounding the home and garden was a digital mural of the Japanese countryside. He'd been transported into the past.

"My master will see you now," A soft voice said from behind.

Abisare turned to see a beautiful Japanese woman standing at the front of the house. Vampire, Abisare reminded himself, just like the tall male in the garage. Unlike him, she was wearing traditional Japanese robes. Her jet-black hair was pulled up in a traditional Japanese hairstyle. Her emerald-green eyes flickered from the torch flames illuminating the garden. Blood-red lips glistened on her porcelain skin.

Sliding open the door, she knelt before Abisare as he approached. She gestured toward his feet. Abisare considered ignoring her request and would have if he hadn't wanted Ronin's help. Abisare kicked off his wingtips and slipped on the slippers that the vampire set before him. She rose to her feet and gestured for him to follow.

Abisare followed her down the corridor. Two sliding doors to their right were open, revealing a large room showcasing several suits of Japanese armor. The walls were adorned with various types of swords and spears. She led Abisare to another set of doors on the opposite side of the hall. The doors opened, revealing Ronin sitting at a short table in the middle of the room, drawing Japanese characters on a scroll. Mats and thin pillows surrounded the table.

"Irasshaimase," Ronin greeted Abisare, gesturing to a mat across from him.

"Perhaps I should gift you with some chairs, Brother," Abisare said as he knelt at the table. He immediately regretted his remark as he saw disdain flash on Ronin's face.

Ronin's face relaxed as he placed the brush back into a vial that Abisare thought to be ink, but now knew it wasn't, as the scent of blood wafted across the room.

"Let's move to another room, Brother, to toast your arrival." Ronin sprang to his feet in a blur. The blur seen through Abisare's vampiric eyes would have been invisible to a human.

Abisare forced himself not to roll his eyes or show any sign of judgment. Ronin was showing off. *What are you playing at?* Abisare pondered as he followed Ronin into another room further down the main corridor.

"What brings you to Japan?" Ronin led Abisare to a small round table surrounded by pillows in the middle of the room. "You have never visited my home before now. Although I did attend one of your gatherings," Ronin stated.

"I've never been invited," Abisare rebutted. Could you really not know why I'm here, he thought as he pointed out, "And yes, you did attend *one* of my gatherings. Despite receiving invitations to all of them, Brother."

Ronin's smile was wry. "Once was enough. Let's just say your...proclivities aren't exactly aligned with mine. Besides, how could you ever top Rio de Janeiro?" Ronin asked.

"Ah...Carnival." Abisare couldn't help but grin at the memory. "Now *that* was a party. Rio always offers such a delightful menu. Don't you think?" Abisare's grin broadened into a mischievous smile.

"You would know," Ronin said, sitting on one of the pillows.

Abisare kept quiet this time as he sat across from Ronin, wondering at all his theatrics.

"This is Hayami," Ronin said as the young vampire who had exchanged Abisare's shoes for slippers entered the room.

Hayami offered Abisare a shy smile and nod as she placed a tray holding a small porcelain jar and two cups on the table before kneeling between the Ancients. She said nothing as she filled the two cups from the jar.

Abisare watched, mesmerized. She moved with grace and power; no motion was wasted. He felt like he was watching a prima ballerina. It was impressive.

"Kanpai," Ronin said as he raised his glass towards Abisare, encouraging him to do the same. Ronin touched his glass to Abisare's and quickly shot down the beverage.

Abisare, still distracted by Hayami, did the same.

"Saké," Ronin answered the unasked question, chuckling as Abisare coughed and sputtered. "It's an old family recipe." He gestured for Hayami to pour another for each of them.

"No more for me." Abisare covered his cup with a hand before Hayami could begin to pour. "Like you said. Once is enough," Abisare said, turning his gaze toward Ronin.

The smile fell from Ronin's face as if Abisare had struck him. "To refuse would be considered an insult," Ronin replied, his voice as rigid as his posture.

"I meant no offense, Brother," Abisare said, quickly removing his hand and nodding to Hayami, who refilled his cup without a word. Raising it to Ronin's, he shouted, "Kanpai."

Ronin laughed. "I'm just fooling." Ronin took Abisare's cup, downed the liquid, and handed it to Hayami. "Please prepare something else for our guest," Ronin said in Old Japanese.

Offering Ronin a shy smile and nod, Hayami stood and left the room.

"So what do you want from me, Brother?" Ronin asked after Hayami slid the doors closed behind her.

"Roman," Abisare answered.

"What of Roman?" Ronin asked, unperturbed.

"You were at the Agora. You saw his arrogance and lack of respect. And now this mess with his bastard," Abisare spat.

"You're referring to his son, Cain Dvanaesti?" Ronin asked, still looking puzzled.

"Abomination," Abisare protested.

"I had heard about the attack on his home and that he was missing. Possibly dead." Ronin turned towards the doors as they slid open.

Hayami escorted a young Japanese couple, each wearing a kimono, to the table.

"I don't have time for this nonsense," Abisare said, frustrated by the interruption.

Ronin's eyebrows rose in mock surprise. "First, you don't like my saké, and now you refuse my alternative offering?"

"Brother. This is important," Abisare said in an insistent tone.

Ronin reached out his hand toward the young man.

A wistful smile tugged at the man's lips as he knelt beside Ronin. Rolling back his sleeve, the smile turned triumphant as he shot the woman a furtive glance.

She didn't see the man's glint, though. She was looking with longing at his scar tissue from previous feedings.

Ronin gestured toward the woman, who now stared at Abisare with a look of hope.

Abisare shook his head and waved her away.

Ronin nodded in acquiescence and then sank his fangs into the man's wrist.

The man shuddered a groan of pleasure as he lay his head on Ronin's shoulder.

Watching Ronin feed from the man, Abisare fought to cover his frustration. He watched Ronin stroke the man's hair as he drank, unsure if his frustration was with Ronin's games or himself for turning down the woman. She did look exquisite.

"My question for you," Ronin said after drawing away from the man's wrist, "is why are you so concerned with Roman and his *bastard,* as you call him?"

Hayami knelt and handed Ronin a towel and a small basin of water to wash.

"I would think you'd be happy that his bastard is dead," Ronin said as he lifted the man's head off his shoulder with all the gentleness and care of a lover.

Hayami assisted the man, lifting him to his feet and leading him out of the room along with the now-frustrated woman.

Ronin washed his hands and face, though he hadn't spilled a drop. "I know you and Roman haven't always seen eye to eye on things, but still, this obsession with him is getting a bit old, don't you think?" Ronin watched the anger in Abisare become visible. "Wait, it wasn't you, was it?" Ronin asked with a curious smile as he dried his hands.

"Don't be absurd," Abasaire spat. "It was his...*Illuminati*," Abisare continued in disdain.

"Really?" Ronin allowed his excitement and curiosity to show. "And Delilah? What does she say?"

"She said she would speak to him. But you know as well as I that nothing will be done. She's always shown favoritism toward him. And now Roman is out of control. The Illuminati. His bastard, and who knows what else? All without consulting any of us. But we're left to deal with the consequences when they go wrong," Abisare ranted.

"So, what do you think we should do?" Ronin asked, concern in his voice. He sat back and pondered out loud. "If the Illuminati are truly out of Roman's control, then perhaps it is time one of us steps in," Ronin continued.

"Exactly," Abisare responded with excitement in his voice. Finally, one of his siblings was seeing what he saw. He had an ally.

"Were you thinking of doing away with the Illuminati or just taking over their operations? I know they have at least proven useful for the Cullings," Ronin said. "And what of Roman? What should we do with him?" Ronin asked.

"I'm not sure. Delilah would never allow us to touch him, but with your support, I feel..." Abisare stopped speaking as he saw the devilish grin stretching across Ronin's face, which erupted with laughter. Abisare realized that Ronin had been playing with him. Baiting him.

"Dear Brother. You truly are the definition of hypocrisy. You sit back and cast judgment on Roman for the very thing that you are most known for. How many times have your schemes failed? Countless times, you have undertaken endeavors without seeking counsel or approval from any of us. The only difference between your plans and Roman's is that at least they serve us all as a whole. And you wonder why most of us want nothing to do with you and the extravagant parties you throw. You are selfish, Abisare, and your hubris has always been your Achilles' heel.

"How dare you speak to me that way." Abisare reached across the table to strike Ronin but froze as he felt icy steel touch his neck. He looked up to see Hayami standing over him with a sword.

"Let's not go losing our heads, Brother," Ronin said, motioning for Hayami to stand down.

Hayami stepped back and sheathed her sword with the same grace and beauty she had shown while pouring saké.

"She's exquisite, isn't she?" Ronin asked, rising to his feet. "I think it's time you left, don't you?"

Hayami moved to the door and waited for Abisare to start moving. They followed him down the corridor and out the door to the garden.

"Let's try not to let so much time pass before doing this again, Brother," Ronin said as Abisare crossed the bridge.

"It's like you said, Brother. Once is enough," Abisare said without turning as he walked away.

16

Venice, Italy

Gabriel stood in the shadows of the courtyard across from the emergency room entrance. He examined the identification badge again and compared it to the sign on the building fascia.

SS Giovanni e Paolo Hospital.

It was the third time he'd checked, and the third time he'd confirmed he was observing the right building. Looking at the image of Alessia Montalvo on the identification badge, he compared it to the woman exiting the building. It wasn't her.

His gaze shifted back from the woman to the badge. His eyesight focused without effort from the small image of the face on the card to the face of the woman more than a hundred feet away. He was still amazed by his ability to zoom in on the faces of everyone exiting as if he were looking through a rifle scope. Except his eyesight was better than a scope. There was no momentary blurriness before the object he was looking at came into focus. It was just in focus. No matter where he looked, everything was always in focus. Sight was not the only change Gabriel had noticed about himself since that night in the alley, and not all of the changes were for the better.

How long had it been, he wondered, as he checked the image against the latest woman exiting the building since he'd saved Alessia Montalvo in the alley. Five days? Six? Since that night, the first time he'd feasted on human blood, he hadn't consumed it again. Even though human blood had brought him back into his right mind, as well as heightened his senses, he still found it morally repugnant. He'd gone back to feeding on rats. But human blood was just that – a feast. The difference between human and rat blood was as different as the distinction between five-star dining and fast food. Rats curbed his hunger, but human blood sated him. Made him feel alive. Vibrant. Virile.

At first, Gabriel had no intention of looking for Alessia Montalvo, though he'd kept her purse with him since that night. He'd thought of turning it into a police station, saying he'd found it unattended on a park bench, but hadn't been able to part with it. It had become a talisman, an object symbolizing the moment he'd crawled out of the sewers as a mere beast and regained his humanity.

Was that the right word? Humanity? He now knew who he was or had been. A man named Gabriel Hawthorne. He knew that, however, because he'd killed two men. And how had he killed them? By consuming their blood directly from their bodies until they were dry. That's not something humans did. Humans could be inhumane to one another, but they didn't do that.

The problem was that, after feeding on human blood, he wanted more. He would even say he was desperate for more. The hunger came faster now. Stronger. Feeding on rats was getting less and less effective. He knew it was only a matter of time before the hunger overtook him. Gabriel wanted to avoid killing someone again. He justified what he'd done by telling himself he hadn't been in his right mind. He'd been nothing more than a beast. That, and the two men were sexually assaulting a woman at that moment. They'd probably done it before and would do it again. He'd made the world a better place, or at least, a safer place. That was his nature. Wasn't that what he'd been doing his whole life before...whatever this was? He'd been a police officer and then a political operative. Yes, he'd been a corrupt cop, but he hadn't started that way. Dirt digging had made him a lot of money, but that's not why he did it. He'd wanted to make the world a better place.

Gabriel had never taken heroin, but he'd read addicts describe that first rush and subsequent craving. How, eventually, nothing mattered. They didn't care what they did or who they hurt, just as long as they got that fix. That described his hunger.

He could satisfy his craving by hunting murderers, rapists, and child abusers. For how long, though? Even if there were an endless supply, which there wasn't, how could he ensure those were the only ones he was killing? Catching them in the act of perpetrating a crime was the best way, but that wasn't practical. Would the hunger allow him time to research, investigate, and plan? He didn't think so. Eventually, he'd kill an innocent. The only thing worse than that, he realized, would be when it didn't matter who he killed so long as he fed, when people became nothing more than so many cattle in a field.

The rats were keeping him alive. His moral compass was staving off the worst of the hunger pangs. Deep down, he knew that if he didn't get help soon, his moral compass wouldn't matter. The hunger would consume him.

The hunger doesn't care who it consumes.

Gabriel had Alessia's purse, his totem, in his hands when he'd had this realization. The leather had been worn smoother than silk from the constant caressing by his fingers and thumbs. His eyes fell on the ID badge. Alessia was a nurse who worked at a hospital. He had an idea.

Alessia exited the emergency room doors with a co-worker.

Though the two women were across the courtyard from him, Gabriel could hear their conversation as if he were walking alongside them.

"What a night," Alessia said to her coworker, Mia.

"Tell me about it. I don't know what's worse. When Venezia wins a home game or when they lose." Mia said with a chuckle.

"Especially when it's Verona." Alessia shook her head.

The two women passed within a yard of Gabriel without noticing him as they moved from the courtyard into the main atrium.

Gabriel smelled soap, hand sanitizer, and, ever so faintly, the exquisite aroma of blood. It wafted off the woman like a perfume. He almost convulsed with pleasure. He followed the women as they walked out onto the main plaza in front of the hospital.

"I've got the next couple of days off to recover. I'll see you next week," Alessia said.

"Please tell me you're at least going to go home and sleep before you head to that homeless shelter again," Mia pleaded.

"It's on the way home. And besides, I'll get enough sleep when I'm dead." Alessia responded with a laugh. "How about you? You have plans?" Alessia asked.

"As a matter of fact, I have a date," Mia replied.

"A date? With whom? Alessia asked.

"With a very large...strong...bold...bottle of vino," Mia replied, bursting into laughter. She waved as she turned towards the canal.

"Goodnight," Alessia said again, chuckling and turning toward the shelter. The chuckle died in her throat as she noticed the shadowy patches along her path. She pulled the small can of newly acquired pepper spray from her purse, then almost dropped it as she heard the voice behind her call her name.

"Alessia Mantalto," Gabriel asked.

Alessia turned to see a man stepping from the shadows she'd just passed. She'd never noticed him. A fat lot of good the pepper spray will do me if I walk right past a potential threat.

"I'm sorry. I didn't mean to startle you." Gabriel said, holding up his hands as if the canister Alessia pointed at him was a pistol.

Alessia assumed he must be one of the homeless people from the shelter. His clothing was dirty and weathered, and he looked like he hadn't seen a bar of soap in a long time. As her breathing slowed, however, she realized she didn't smell any body odor emanating from him.

"Was there something I could help you with?" Her hand holding the can of pepper spray dropped. "I'm headed to the shelter now. If you need medical assistance, I can help you out there," Alessia offered.

"I brought you your purse," Gabriel said as he pulled something from inside his coat.

"Where did you find it?" Alessia said, reaching out to take the purse. She rummaged through it, taking stock of what was still there. "I don't believe it. It's all here. How? I mean..." Alessia stopped as she finally looked up, staring hard at the man standing before her. "Have I treated you at the shelter?" Alessia questioned. "Your face. Something about your face seems familiar to me."

"I need your help," Gabriel said.

"Okay. I can treat you at the shelter," Alessia responded, trying to keep her tone soothing. "It isn't far from here."

"No. No shelter," Gabriel replied.

She noticed that some of the grime on his clothing appeared to be dried blood. "Are you injured? If so, we need to get you into the emergency room," Alessia said with growing concern.

"No...I'm not injured...I'm...I..." Gabriel tried to find the words.

"Are you sure we haven't met?" Alessia asked, leaning forward, searching her memory for some clue as to who this man might be and why he seemed so familiar.

"The alley," Gabriel said in a soft tone.

Alessia jolted upright as if someone had dumped a bucket full of cold water over her.

"Please...I'm not going to hurt you. I need your help. Please," Gabriel pleaded as he watched her stumble backward.

Alessia couldn't speak. The fear from that night in the alley had overtaken her. She could now see the face of the monster in the man before her. She struggled to inhale as she turned to run, fumbling with the can of pepper spray. But something broke through the chaos, panic, and fear consuming her.

"Please...please..." Gabriel sobbed.

Alessia turned to see the man down on his knees, slumped over. He was crying. Tears rolled down his face as he wept and pleaded for help.

"Please...help me..."

17

Illuminati Compound,
Baton Rouge, Louisiana

Caiaphas sat silently, not wanting to move or say anything until Cain Dvanaesti was ready. Twenty minutes ago, he'd knocked, and when Cain had not said to 'Come In' or 'Go Away,' Caiaphas had entered the room to find Cain slumped on the bed. Cain wasn't asleep or in some meditative state. If Caiaphas had to describe Cain's body language, it would be grief. He draped a blanket over Cain and sat in the chair across from the bed. Cain would speak when he was ready. Caiaphas could wait. He was good at waiting.

"She's gone, isn't she?" Cain finally spoke without looking up.

The question confirmed Caiaphas's suspicion. Believing the truth sets one free, no matter how badly it might hurt, Caiaphas answered, "Miss Bennett did not survive the plane crash. Another innocent pawn sacrificed on your father's chessboard."

Cain's head shot up so quickly that Caiaphas didn't see the movement. "What do you mean?"

Caiaphas looked at the camera hanging in the corner of the room and nodded before focusing again on Cain. Holding up two fingers, he said, "Your father made two phone calls after telling you to come to him. He ordered the flight plan filed, and then he called the hangar. After that call, a flurry of activity occurred. Your jet is probably the best-maintained aircraft on the planet. Even better than Air Force One. After all, Air Force One only has *human* mechanics."

Cain's eyes narrowed. "What are you saying?"

Caiaphas stood and walked to the door. Opening it, a man in black fatigues handed him a manila folder. Caiaphas turned, walked over to Cain, and offered him the folder.

"You're an intelligent man, Mr. Dvanaesti, but emotions like love and loyalty can sometimes blind us from the truth," Caiaphas said as he watched Cain start to look through the folder of photos and documents.

"Exactly what am I looking at here?" Cain questioned.

"It's a transcript of your pilot and first officer's conversation once your jet entered international airspace." Caiaphas sat back in the chair opposite the bed.

Cain read. Surprise, then anger flushed his face.

FO: Did you get it?

P: Yeah. You?

FO: Yeah. Was it the amount you agreed to?

P: (Sigh)More.

FO: Me too. What do you think that means?

P: I think that means it's happening tonight.

FO: I guess I should've known that when she didn't join us to do any cooking for the trip.

P: (Laugh) No real need, is there? Besides, after I saw the payment, I figured it was only a matter of time. I've been eating like a king.

FO: So have I. Tammy's been so happy. Said it was about time I put meat back on my bones. With the love handles now, she's got something to hang on to when we...

(Laughter from both men)

(Alarm sounds)

(Laughter stops)

FO: I feel bad for her.

P: Tammy?

FO: No. Her.

(Another alarm sounds)

P: Yeah, well. She made her bed. Now she's got to lie in it.

FO: Yeah.

P: Nothing we can do about it now. Even if we wanted to.

(Third alarm sounds)

P: All we can do is take care of our own, which we've done.

FO: It's been a pleasure flying with you.

P: You, too.

(Faint screaming from the cabin)

(Screaming from flight deck)

(Impact)

"No radio declaring a mayday," Caiaphas said when he saw Cain had arrived at the end of the transcript. "No report of a malfunction."

Cain looked from the papers in his hand to Caiaphas.

It took all of Caiaphas's years of training not to flinch. But he did blanch.

Cain's eyes, not just the pupils, were black. His skin undulated as if it were alive, crawling across his cheekbones, forehead, and chin. The skin darkened to a mottled gray and black. When he spoke, his voice sounded more like a dog's growl. "How did you get this?"

"We've been watching you your entire career, Mr. Dvanaesti. That's what we do," Caiaphas explained. "Since the announcement of your birth to the proud parents, Mr. and Mrs. Roman Dvanaesti. And the recent announcement of missing presumed dead, issued by your father first and the media second. Not even the United States Coast Guard has been willing to say you are deceased." Caiaphas paused. "We had a team heading to the Miami airport to intercept you before you arrived at the hangar. They were to abduct you and Miss Bennett. They didn't make it in time."

His words came as a surprise to Cain, Caiaphas realized. He watched as the young man's eyes showed white with hazel irises again, and his skin returned to its normal tint. He gestured at the folder. "Keep reading. You'll find medical records indicating your pilot was diagnosed with pancreatic cancer three months ago and given only six months to live. There's also a report on your first officer. He had quite the gambling addiction and had run up a debt of over a million dollars. Stress reduced his appetite, and he'd lost weight over the last few months. His...creditors were threatening to hurt not only him but his wife.

"You'll also see that Swiss Bank accounts were opened in the names of both men, with their significant other listed as Payable on Death. A week ago, twelve million dollars was deposited into each of those accounts. Knowing of those deposits and then hearing of your father's conversation with the hanger, I dispatched a team to follow by boat while another team followed by jet and recorded that conversation between the pilot and first officer."

Caiaphas fell silent, allowing Cain to process what he'd just heard and what he was reading. Cain was a smart man. Once he processed what he was reading and what he'd heard, it wouldn't take his mind long to work out another realization. Caiaphas was not disappointed.

"You're the ones who attacked my compound," Cain said.

"Correct," Caiaphas replied matter-of-factly.

"So you attacked my mansion. And my father attacked my plane."

Caiaphas did not miss Cain's sarcasm. "Correct," Caiaphas replied in the same tone as before.

"And after failing to assassinate me at my compound, you decide to save my life?" Cain asked, shaking his head back and forth in disbelief.

"Correct, Mr. Dvanaesti. That's exactly what I'm saying," Caiaphas stated.

Cain's hand began to tremble. He could feel the rage building inside him. "And you're telling me all this, why?" Cain spat as he tossed the folder to the floor.

"Because you, of all people, Mr. Dvanaesti, deserve to be illumined," Caiaphas answered. "And I hope you'll want to seek reciprocity from your father."

Now, the rage broke over Cain like floodwaters over a levee. He'd been no more than a pawn on his father's chessboard. Not even a knight or a bishop. He hadn't been sacrificed for some greater good, but because he was no longer useful. What was the adage? One man's trash was another man's treasure. Now that his father no longer had a use for him and, throwing him away, someone else wanted to use him for their gain. The love of his life, Claudia, had lost hers. Who else would lose theirs?

"Get out. Get out," Cain screamed as his eyes began to blur with the tears that were forming in them as he thought of Claudia. His flight crew. Isabella.

"Caiaphas said nothing as he stood and walked towards the cell door. As the door opened, he stopped and turned back. "My deepest condolences, Mr. Dvanaesti. I am truly sorry for your loss. *All* that you've lost." Caiaphas exited the cell.

18

Illuminati Compound,
Baton Rouge, Louisiana

Lucia "Wrench" Cano stood outside Marcus's office, feeling like she was back in high school and had just been summoned to see the principal. She'd spent a lot of time there when she was younger. She may still hold the record for most visits to the principal at her school. Every school she'd attended from elementary through high school, now that she thought about it. It put a smile on her face. She'd never do anything serious enough to get her suspended or expelled, but in her senior year of high school, the bad behavior escalated. She remembered her last call to the principal's office.

Wrench had grown up in the San Fernando Valley. Her father tried everything he could to keep her out of gang life. He owned a garage and had her working on cars at a young age. After school, she finished her homework in the office among posters of scantily clad women posing with auto parts, and summer vacations were spent as a grease monkey. After mass on Sundays, they'd go to the garage again. But this time, to work on a pet project: rebuilding a 1967 Ford Shelby GT500 Eleanor. Once completed, they'd paint it silver and black, just like the one Nicholas Cage drove in *Gone in Sixty Seconds*. Except when she and her dad were finished with that engine, it'd make the one from the movie look and sound like it belonged in a Yugo.

They never had the opportunity to finish the Shelby, though. Her father was test-driving a '97 Honda Accord after an alignment to fix a shimmy. The car belonged to a kid trying to join a gang. The night before he dropped off the car, he'd used it in a drive-by on a rival gang as part of his initiation. Unbeknownst to the kid and her father, the gang had ID'd the car. And when they saw it on the road, they followed. When her father stopped at a red light, they saw their opportunity. Wrench was seventeen.

Her grades started dropping. She arrived late to school, if she showed up at all. She argued with her teachers and even swung a hammer at the shop teacher. Then Wrench reached out to a gang who'd been reaching out to her shortly after her father's murder. When word got back to the principal, who still referred to himself as a Marine ten years after his honorable discharge, he called Wrench to his office, where he introduced her to his squad leader in Iraq and now local Corps recruiter. That introduction set her on a different path. At the end of eight years, as she sat in a bar contemplating whether or not she should re-up, she met Rotty. Her life changed again.

One thing was for certain, Wrench thought to herself as she straightened her coveralls, if it hadn't been for the Marines and Rotty, I'd be in prison or dead right now. She brushed at the dirt on her sleeves but wore the grease and oil stains as proudly as she'd worn the ribbons on her Service "A" uniform.

She wasn't nervous or worried by the summons to Marcus's office, but she was curious. He'd never requested or ordered her presence before. To her knowledge, Marcus had never asked anyone to come to his office. Not even Rotty.

Marcus remained a mystery to her. He'd been with the Illuminati and Caiaphas's Second since before she'd joined. He would succeed Caiaphas as the head of the Illuminati. He parroted every belief Caiaphas expressed. He executed every order without complaint or question, so far as she knew. Yet, unlike Caiaphas, he wasn't approachable. Smiles didn't come easily. When you passed by Caiaphas, he would stop you. Ask after you. Inquire into your thoughts and feelings. Marcus, however, was aloof. When he passed you, he would only offer a curt nod of acknowledgment, if at all.

Well, I'll never know if I just stand out here like a hood ornament. She rapped on the door three times.

"Come in," Marcus called out through the closed door.

Wrench walked in and stood at attention in front of Marcus's desk.

"At Ease." Marcus smiled as he looked up. "Have a seat, Wrench," Marcus said, gesturing to the chairs in front of the desk.

Wrench sat bolt upright as if she were still standing at attention.

"I guess it's true what they say," Marcus said in mild amusement. "You can take the Marine out of the Corps, but not the Corps out of the Marine. Please relax. This isn't a disciplinary meeting."

"Then what is it?" The question was out of her mouth before she realized it, and she hoped it hadn't sounded as harsh to Marcus's ears as it had to hers.

Marcus nodded in a way that led Wrench to believe it had. "Fair enough." He leaned back and considered for a moment. "I'd heard you like to speak your mind. That's part of the reason I wanted to speak with you. But first, I'd like to know how you're doing," Marcus said.

"Sir?" Wrench said with a puzzled look on her face.

"I understand that you and Rotty were close. His loss had to be hard on you." Marcus replied.

Wrench said nothing. Her throat parched as tears pooled in her eyes.

"His loss was great. He was one of our best," Marcus said.

Wrench found her voice. "He was the best," Wrench proclaimed. "Better than any of us." She cursed herself for sounding like a seventeen-year-old fangirl.

Marcus said nothing.

"Rotty is the reason I am Illumined," Wrench explained. "He's one of the reasons I'm alive today. And," she added after a breath, "I think he was right about the vampires." She waited.

Marcus was quiet for a long time. Finally, he said, "That's why I called you here. I'd like to know your thoughts about our current strategy."

"We don't currently have a strategy," Wrench answered. "Not one that I'm aware of. Or anyone else, for that matter. Rotty—..." She broke off.

Marcus nodded for her to continue.

Wrench again fought back tears and felt the ache in her chest caused just by saying Rotty's name. But they were soon replaced by the warmth of anger slowly growing inside as she thought about the question. "The Old Man's got us going on every mission with one hand tied behind our back...I mean...Caiaphas. I'm sorry. I meant no disrespect," Wrench stated. Now, she felt like Rotty's parrot. "He still has us watching and waiting, waiting and watching, but waiting for what? We finally have the tactics and firepower to overcome our enemy, but we're still waiting and watching. It's like the old—...It's like Caiaphas is unable or unwilling to pull the trigger. He's grown comfortable just sitting on his *Illumined* throne doing nothing."

Wrench went quiet, horrified at the torrent of words that had just vomited from her mouth. She was sure she'd gone too far. She expected Marcus to scream. Throw her out of her office.

Instead, Marcus smiled. "The Old Man and I don't always see eye to eye either."

That statement surprised Wrench.

"I can't say this outside of this office," he said, leaning towards Wrench, "but I think Rotty had the right vision of our future." He leaned in closer to her. "And I think you could be that future." Marcus paused for a moment, letting his words sink in. "If you're agreeable, I'd like us to start having weekly conversations. Further discussion about our current SOP, and possibly some changes we might make in the future," Marcus said.

Wrench's lips curled into a smile. "I would be very agreeable."

19

Abisare's Mining Complex,
Congo River Basin,
Republic of Congo

Two men dressed in black fatigues and carrying Kalashnikov rifles walked side by side along a perimeter fence. They walked in darkness, their clothes and skin blending into the night.

"You know," the man on the inside said to his partner as they turned and headed down the long stretch of fence, "I can't think of a better waste of our time."

His partner scanned the jungle. "Oh, come on, Fumbe, quit your whining." He looked down the fence line.

"I'm not whining," Fumbe spat. "I'm just saying I did not sign up for this." He walked automatically, his eyes looking everywhere but seeing nothing. "You can't tell me you honestly like this, Wasswa."

Wasswa looked out towards the jungle again. "We all have our duties."

"This is no duty, it's a chore. It's a waste. A waste of time and talent when we have that

hi-tech geek back in the control room watching fifty different camera monitors at once."

Wasswa rolled his eyes. "If it weren't important, we wouldn't be doing it."

"You *can't* be serious?" Fumbe asked, unbelieving.

The two walked along in silence for a moment before Wasswa said, "I take security very seriously."

Fumbe stepped in front of Wasswa, turning to face him. "Security from *what?*" He made an expansive gesture, taking in the

93

jungle outside the fence and the darkened buildings inside. "Wild boar? Are you fearing an army of Silverbacks? Or perhaps a company of commando pythons."

"There are more than beasts and snakes in the jungle." Wasswa sidestepped Fumbe and resumed walking and searching the elongated shadows.

Fumbe laughed. "Peasants with sticks?" Fumbe fell in step beside his partner. "Is that what you fear?"

Wasswa ignored Fumbe.

"It is," Fumbe chided Wasswa. He laughed.

A sharp report cut through the night.

Wasswa immediately spun to face the jungle, pulling his weapon to a firing position.

Fumbe laughed again. "It was a stick."

"Show yourself," Wasswa shouted out towards the jungle.

"It was only a dumb beast stepping on a stick," Fumbe admonished.

Wasswa called out again. "Show yourself. I will give you to the count of three."

Fumbe laughed, but his laughter faded as a shadow stepped from the jungle into a pool of moonlight. It was a young woman.

Fumbe started laughing again. "You see, Wasswa, just as I told you. A dumb beast stepping on a stick."

"What are you doing?" Wasswa demanded.

The woman stepped towards the guard, her hand moving to her mouth, gesturing as if she were putting food into it. She held her other hand palm up, hoping for money.

"Be gone," Wasswa commanded firmly but gently. "We have nothing for you."

The woman continued to move towards the fence and the guards, repeating the gesture, hand still extended.

"We have nothing for you," Wasswa repeated. "Go back to where you came from."

"The dumb beast is certainly persistent," Fumbe snickered as the young woman made it to the fence and continued her gestures towards the two men. Then he had a thought that split his mouth wide to reveal teeth so white they seemed to glow in the dark. "Perhaps guard duty is not so bad. It can, after all," he stared at the girl with lust, "have its perks."

Wasswa shouldered his weapon and turned to face Fumbe. "No. I forbid you."

Fumbe's eyebrows raised. "You *forbid* me?"

Wasswa's shoulders slumped. "All right. Maybe I can't forbid you. But I can report you."

Fumbe's laughter rang out across the night air. "Report me? Report me to whom? And for what? No one cares what happens to a dumb beast. After all," his smile was tinged with malice, "this is Africa."

The young woman didn't seem to hear or understand their conversation, but continued to gesture for food and money. Then, she noticed how one of them was looking at her like she was a piece of meat on a spit. She shuddered. She'd seen that gleam in men's eyes before, that hungry expression on their faces, and had never known it to end well for her. She stepped back from the fence, putting distance between herself and the guards, and wrapped her cloak around her body like it could shield her from their stares and intentions.

The woman watched Fumbe's smile take on an even more wicked aspect. Shrieking, she turned to run back into the jungle. Instead, she ran into Fumbe, who stood in front of her. Her eyes grew wide, and she screamed again. She turned to the fence and saw only one guard frowning at her.

"I told you to go back the way you came." The man said in resignation.

She turned back to Fumbe, who stood there eyeing her up and down. She tried to put distance between herself and the man but backed into the fence, and found both guards standing before her, blocking the way she'd come.

"Please," she sobbed, "please don't hurt me."

"Hurt you?" Fumbe soothed. "We're not going to hurt you."

"In fact," Wasswa said, stepping closer to the young woman, "you may find you enjoy it."

The young woman looked up at Wasswa and found he, too, now wore that same hungry expression on his face. She backed up to the fence. "Please don't rape me," She begged, falling prostrate before the two men. "Beat me. Kill Me. But please don't rape me."

"Don't flatter yourself," Fumbe said.

She looked up, startled.

Fumbe was smiling, his white teeth gleaming in the moonlight. And then fangs slid gently out of his gums.

She looked at Wasswa, and he had fangs as well. She collapsed.

Wasswa and Fumbe grabbed one of the woman's arms and lifted her to her feet. As they did, they caught sight of a metallic cylinder she was holding. It flashed blue. They looked up at the woman who now smiled.

The woman dropped the canister at their feet.

The two vampires stared in confusion at the cylinder. Wasswa looked from the cylinder at his feet to the woman and opened his mouth to speak—

Whoosh!

The young woman turned, pulling her cloak over her head, and dropped to a knee. She listened as the two vampires began screaming. That would be the UV light blinding them as the silver mist began permeating their bodies, she thought to herself. The screaming turned to gurgling, and she realized the gas was now eating away their tongues and esophageal tissue. She began to hear what sounded like greasy meat frying in a pan and another of boiling water. A stench invaded her nostrils, reminding her of when, as children, she and her brother had found a dead boar swollen with decay. Her brother had poked a hole in the boar, releasing a putrid gas from the belly of the boar, like air from a balloon. The stench had caused them to vomit, and she felt the same wave of nausea come over her now.

She knew it was almost complete. Only one thing remained: the pop as the marrow inside their bones boiled. She knew what would happen, had seen it countless times in training videos, and had told herself she had no desire to see it up close and personal. But...

She couldn't help herself. She had to make sure they were dead. So she dropped her cloak and turned.

Pop!

She was showered with the greasy liquefied remains of Fumbe and Wasswa. It sprayed across her face, into her hair, and through her partly opened lips.

She stood and spat. She rolled her eyes, chastising herself. "Perfect," she said and spat again. Wiping her face on her cloak's cowl, she punched the small device protruding from her ear. "The way is clear," she said as she pulled a pistol from underneath her cloak, loaded with Phase Two rounds.

The high-tech geek was roused from his stupor by multiple proximity alarms screaming from his cameras. He sat up and began punching buttons. The cameras tilted, turned, and zoomed. His mouth dropped as he saw ground troops, perhaps fifty to sixty, moving through the forest and across downed perimeter fences, followed by HUM-Vs with what looked like large flat-screen televisions attached to their roofs. He couldn't help himself and moved closer to the monitors, which suddenly glowed white.

He swore and slapped the complex-wide general alarm.

20

Illuminati Compound, Baton Rouge, Louisiana

Cain Dvanaesti sat up on the bed of his cell. He sensed someone standing on the other side of the door. He heard a buzz and then a voice asked, "May I enter Mr. Dvanaesti?".

Cain recognized the voice of Caiaphas. "You don't need my permission," he answered.

"On the contrary," Caiaphas responded. After our last meeting, I feel it necessary to ask your permission. I want to take every opportunity to make up for past mistakes."

Cain paused before answering. It was easy to let his guard down with Caiaphas. He sounded not only honest but genuine. Cain wanted to believe that this man's request was just a tactic, giving him a false sense of control. But he knew that couldn't be further from the truth. The truth was that he had no control. That was his reality. And what made his reality a nightmare was the realization that maybe he'd never had any. Not even over himself.

Still, Cain couldn't help but like the man who called himself Caiaphas. He was open. Honest. Unafraid. He offered answers, and when he didn't have any, he admitted it. Cain was sure Caiaphas had an agenda. You didn't rise to the top of any organization, especially a worldwide secret organization, without an agenda. And even if he didn't, the organization sure did. It was a secret organization for a reason, after all. Maybe Caiaphas wasn't employing a tactic. Maybe Caiaphas understood better than Cain that he'd never had any control. He'd only been a puppet his entire life. Not even a puppet. A pawn. So maybe Caiaphas wasn't playing games or using tactics but just had good manners. One thing did bother Cain, though.

That can't be your real name.

"Come in, Caiaphas," Cain said.

Caiaphas opened the door and stepped into the room. Walking towards Cain, still seated on the bed, he inquired, "Did you sleep well, Mr. Dvanaesti?"

"Like a baby," Cain answered, patting the mattress while glancing ostentatiously at the camera. "You ought to know." He decided not to leave his snark there. "You know, you guys should start advertising. This place makes the Waldorf Astoria look like San Quentin," Cain added as he waved around the room. At that moment, he decided to push Caiaphas.

Caiaphas looked around the room. "I realize this isn't an ideal situation."

"Ideal situation," Cain repeated as if tasting the phrase on his tongue for the first time.

"I hope we can make the best of it for now."

"We?" Cain asked. "You really are a glass-half-full kind of guy, aren't you?" Cain asked.

Caiaphas took a long breath and exhaled as a smile stretched his face. "And you're a

glass-half-empty guy? No. A whose-glass-is-that-and-what's-in-it kind of guy? Mr. Dvanaesti—"

"Just call me Cain," Cain interrupted. "After all, this is San Quentin, right? Not the Four Seasons. Besides, I always hated being called Mr. Dvanaesti. Governor Dvanaesti was bad enough, but *Mr. Dvanaesti* makes me sound like my fa-..." he sighed. "Just...call me Cain."

"Cain." Caiaphas nodded in acquiescence. "First, I'd like to apologize for what happened at our last meeting."

Cain stared in confusion at Caiaphas for a moment before his gaze drifted left as if he were remembering. "Oh," he exclaimed in mock realization. "You must mean when you mustard-gassed me." He nodded. "Yes, that was...an inconvenience."

Caiaphas ignored Cain's sarcasm. "Those responsible have been dealt with. I assure you that nothing of the sort will happen moving forward. You have my word."

"Dealt with, huh?" Cain considered for a moment. "Did you pull out fingernails with a set of pliers? Or maybe some waterboarding? Or was it the old *ssssslitt?*" Cain dragged his finger across his throat in a cutting gesture.

Caiaphas smiled. "You have quite a dark sense of humor, don't you, Cain? I don't remember reading about it in the papers or seeing it at any of your public appearances." Caiaphas shrugged in a 'who knew?' way. "I do truly hope you will accept my apology for the...mustard-gassing as you call it. I want to help you, if you'll allow it."

"And just how do you think you can help me?" Cain asked, standing to his feet without realizing it, face-to-face with Caiaphas.

Caiaphas didn't blink. "To be honest..." Caiaphas's shrug this time was of the 'no idea' variety. "I don't know. But I promise you," he continued, "I will do everything in my power."

Cain looked into Caiaphas's eyes, which stared unblinking back into his own. He could hear the heartbeat pumping blood through Caiaphas's veins. It was slow and steady. He inhaled no scent of fear. These things, and what he already knew of Caiaphas, made him believe the man. That was good, he thought to himself, because he wanted to believe him. Needed to believe him. He nodded.

"I think it's time we got you out of these accommodations. Someplace less San Quentin and more...Hilton, at least. More comfortable anyway." Caiaphas turned and walked towards the door. "I'll make arrangements for a new room. Once you've had time to settle in, we'll talk more then. You have my word," Caiaphas said as he turned and nodded goodbye to Cain.

21

Athens, Greece

Delilah looked at her phone's screen, waiting for the video call to be answered. This was a call she wished wasn't necessary. But knew that it was. Condolences had to be offered. Ruffled feathers needed smoothing over. Order maintained.

Abisare's face filled the screen. "Greetings, Sister," Abisare said with a devilish grin, revealing ivory-white teeth.

"Greetings, Brother," Delilah responded, sensing the sarcasm in Abisare's voice. "I was just informed of the attack on your compound. I'm truly sorry—"

Abisare interrupted. "What's there for you to be sorry about? After all, there's no way anyone could have known that the Illuminati was acting on its own," he gloated. "Who would've thought Roman would or could lose control of—"

"Enough, Abisare." Now it was Delilah's turn to interrupt. She could feel her anger erupting. "I get your point."

"I don't think you do."

"I know you're upset. You've personally suffered a loss. I promise there will be restitution. Roman will answer for this, and you will be compensated," Delilah answered.

"And the others?" Abisare spat back.

"Others?"

"Hahahahaha!" His laugh was cruel. "You don't know, do you?" Abisare asked.

"Know what?" Delilah said it more like a command than a question.

"My compound was only one of four locations attacked. That we know of." He shrugged. "There may be more. We're still waiting to hear. Several locations have failed to report," Abisare hissed. "You were wrong not to listen to me, but you are right about one thing. Roman will pay. I will see to that. Personally."

"I will allow you to confront Roman regarding this. But only in my presence." Delilah responded.

"Allow me?" Abisare barked, eyes blazing.

"Do not forget your place," Delilah shot back like a viper spitting venom. She waited for a beat before continuing. "You and I will visit Roman together. You will have your pound of flesh, but no more. I will see that Roman pays you back for your losses." Delilah continued.

"That dog needs to be brought to heel," Abisare cursed.

"Enough. He is your brother. He will be punished for his actions, but you will still respect his station," Delilah demanded. "We will speak again in a few days. I need to make the travel arrangements. Until then, you will do nothing. Is that understood?"

Abisare said nothing.

"I will take your silence as a yes," Delilah said as she ended the video call.

Abisare stared at the black screen for a long moment before dashing it on the floor, splintering it into pieces. "Understood."

22

Venice, Italy

"**Alessia**? Nurse? Nurse Mantalto," Nurse Camilo shouted.

Alessia turned her head to her coworker and friend, charge nurse Gia Camilo, standing beside her.

"Are you okay, Alessia?" Gia asked, gesturing to the bag of fluids Alessia was holding. Gia had asked her to come change out the fluids for the patient lying in the bed beside them almost forty minutes ago.

"Yes. I'm sorry," Alessia responded, shooting Gia an embarrassed smile. "I just got a little distracted."

"A little? You were staring off into space like a zombie or something. I kept calling your name. I thought you'd fallen asleep on your feet," Gia said.

"I'm just tired, that's all. Too many doubles," Alessia said, trying to sound convincing.

"Well, then you need to go home and get some rest. Cause you just freaked me out," Gia said, trying to lighten the mood. "I'll take it from here. Go sign out. We have enough staff to cover." Gia said.

"I'll be fine," Alessia demurred.

"Go," Gia ordered, taking the bag of fluids from her and pointing to the door.

Alessia opened her mouth to protest further, but when Gia opened her eyes wider and nodded at the door in her 'don't say another word' gesture, Alessia closed her mouth. Making her way out of the room, she headed towards the employee locker room.

Alessia knew Gia was right. She should go home and get some rest. Sleep until she was done, and then sleep some more. But she was afraid. That's why she'd been pulling so many doubles. It had been only a week since her attack and just a few days since her encounter with the man who had rescued her.

But he isn't a man, is he? Alessia thought to herself. The image of what he did to her two attackers burst into her mind's eye like a glass bottle smacking her in the face. She jerked back physically from the memory.

I need...I need blood.

It was a second assault that made her knees buckle, not just the words, but the desperation, the need in his voice. She reached for the wall to steady herself as she rubbed her forehead.

These memories assaulted her more times in a day than she could count and were especially vibrant whenever she closed her eyes for sleep. She didn't like being alone, only going home long enough during the day to change her clothes and feed her cat. She never stayed long enough to shower. And now she was at her front door. The thought of being alone, even with Luca waiting for her right now, terrified her.

Alessia was greeted by her cat, Luca, as she walked into her flat. "Hello, Luca. Did you miss me, boy?" Alessia asked as she knelt to pick him up. "I missed you, too," Alessia said as Luca nuzzled her neck.

Heading to the kitchen, Alessia poured milk into a saucer for Luca and a glass of wine for herself. Her jaw popped and cracked as she yawned. She knew she needed to try to get some sleep. Setting her wine glass on the bedside table, she lay on the bed, where Luca joined her. She yawned again, feeling her frame settle into the mattress, her muscles melting toward oblivion, yet still afraid to close her eyes. She knew that she would see them. Hear him.

I need...I need blood.

Alessia scooped Luca to her chest. The cat didn't mind, nuzzling even closer to her as his body hummed with contented purring. "I feel like I did a bad thing, Luca," she said as she stroked his ears between her thumb and forefinger. "And I feel so guilty for it."

Luca purred on.

"How so, you ask? Well. I allowed my fear to prevent me from helping someone in need who'd helped me when I was in need. I've spent my entire life helping people. I feel like a hypocrite." She rolled over onto her back. "Like a fraud."

Luca crawled up on her chest and rubbed his face against hers.

She laughed, scratching his head. "You're right, Luca. I'm not a fraud or a hypocrite. I got scared. So it's time to put on my big girl panties and stop being such a baby."

Luca purred long and loud in agreement.

"Okay then," Alessia said as she scooped Luca up and held him at arm's length. "That settles it. Tomorrow, we will try to find the man who helped us."

Luca's purr had a 'put me down now or I'll pee on you' growl.

Alessia laughed again, feeling the wine as she brought Luca to her chest and hugged him tightly. Then she rolled over, snatched up the glass, and drained the remaining wine in one gulp. "Good night, my little man," she said as she reached for the bedside lamp and turned off the light. She was asleep before her head came to rest on the pillow.

Luca continued to purr as he curled up beside his master and watched over her as she slept.

23

Washington, D.C.

Jacquelyn exited the elevator and marched into the parking garage. Her nostrils flared as she approached her car. She tracked the scent that wafted from behind the support pillar in the row where she was parked. She stopped, shaking her head and rolling her eyes.

"What do you want, Howard?" Jacquelyn asked, putting the head shake and eye roll into her tone.

Howard Williams stepped out from behind the pillar with a puzzled look, confused as to how she could know he was there, reeking of cigars, bourbon, and Creed *Viking* cologne. He wore it because it was the most expensive of the colognes that some men's magazine had rated as the manliest. He'd been brooding since his plan to embarrass her in the courtroom had failed. Not only had she won the case, but through the legal grapevine, the board had heard, and more importantly, Darby, that it was one of the most impressive closing arguments the judge had ever heard. The jury was more than impressed. The defendant was more than grateful.

To make things worse, Howard had been called before the board, where he was reprimanded for deserting her and abandoning the client, and Darby then suggested that perhaps he should '*take a break.*' That meant the board put him on a mandatory three-month leave of absence, transferring all of his other cases to the partners and executive partners, and forcing his assistants to call his clients to explain that he would be out of the office. It was beyond humiliating. Who do they think they are? Howard thought to himself. I built this firm.

"What do you want?" Jacquelyn repeated, bringing Howard out of his thoughts.

"I...ah...I." Howard struggled to form a thought. He was taken off guard by her directness. He had planned to surprise her. Intimidate her. Hopefully, scare her a little bit. She was none of those. From the disgusted look on her face, with arms crossed over her chest and body weight resting on one hip, she appeared only irritated.

"I don't have time for this, Howard," Jacquelyn said as she turned towards her car. "I have a plane to catch."

"Don't you dare turn your back on me," Howard barked.

Jacquelyn continued towards her car, ignoring his demand. Reaching for the door handle, she felt him step up behind her. She smiled. It was exactly what she'd hoped for. Jacquelyn spun around and grabbed the arm that was reaching out for her.

Howard screamed in pain as he watched her twist his outstretched arm like it was a piece of pulled taffy.

"You *really* are pathetic," Jacquelyn hissed as she pulled him closer. "Your kind is sad and weak, to begin with, but you take the cake."

Howard was in shock. The pain radiating through his arm made it impossible to understand what she meant. Was she one of those feminists who hated all men, he wondered.

"Not men, you fat, stupid bull," she said with a devilish grin as if she could read his mind. She twisted his body till they were face to face, noses touching, and whispered, "Human."

Howard felt a wave of nausea wash over him as his knees buckled. His legs began to give out beneath him, staring in horror at Jacquelyn as her eyes grew black, and inky-black veins stretched across her face. He never saw her fangs before she wrenched his head back and sank them into his throat. Howard watched the fluorescent lighting above his head dim into darkness.

Jacquelyn surveyed the parking garage. No person or camera had seen what had just happened. Popping the trunk with the key fob in her hand, she dragged Howard to the back of the car. As she tossed his body into the trunk like a piece of luggage, her cell phone rang.

"Did you get the itinerary I sent you?" Stacy, Jacquelyn's legal assistant, asked over the phone.

"Yes, thank you so much for booking the flight for me. You're the best." Jacquelyn replied, her voice not betraying what had just happened.

"Are you headed home to pack?" Stacy questioned. "I know this was last-minute."

"I was, but something came up at the last minute that I need to take care of before I head to the airport," Jacquelyn said, looking down at the clump of meat and bone that used to be Howard Williams.

"I'll treat myself and buy some new outfits while I'm there," Jacquelyn said, whimsy filling her voice as she slammed the trunk closed. "I've always wanted to own a couple of truly Italian-made pantsuits."

"Any excuse to go shopping. That's my motto," Stacy replied. "And you definitely have earned those pantsuits." Jacquelyn heard Stacy lean forward and cup the receiver. "And from what I hear, those pantsuits will come in handy around here."

Jacquelyn chose to ignore the bait. She already knew. "I'll call you when I land. We still need to iron out a few things while I'm away."

"Yes, ma'am. Have a safe flight," Stacy replied.

"Thanks," Jacquelyn said, hanging up the phone.

24

Roman Dvanaesti's Estate, Italy

Roman did not need the head vintner to tell him that two unexpected guests awaited him in the wine cellar. He knew precisely where these "guests" were at all times. It had always been that way with the Twelve. As with their father, they could feel each other's presence at all times, and simply by focusing on a sibling, they knew not only *where* that sibling was but *how* that sibling was.

So, Roman knew Abisare and Delilah were in the wine cellar. He knew why they were here on his estate. Knew that they were angry. In good health, but furious. He knew why they'd chosen the wine cellar. It wasn't for protection from the sun. The Twelve did not suffer that side effect of the thinning bloodlines. Abisare, Roman smirked, would have been attracted to its ambiance for their conversation. And Delilah would like it for its privacy.

A snort escaped Roman.

Delilah.

That was the name her human parents had given her. And that was the name with which she'd gained infamy and immortality. Her exploits with a Hebrew boy named Sampson were well known to anyone who'd read the Bible, attended Sunday School, or a church service. But those exploits had also attracted the attention of their father. She was proud of that name, and when their father offered her a new name, she declined.

She was the oldest and strongest of the Ancients to still sit at the table. She could do things the other Ancients could not. She had a formidable mind, spirit, and, of course, body. The rumors of how she'd seduced Sampson were true, after all. What didn't make it into the rumor mill, much less the pages of the Old Testament, was that she wanted Samson's strength for herself. One night, after getting Samson drunk with wine and lovemaking, Delilah pulled a knife she'd spent the morning sharpening until it could split a human hair and sliced four thin but deep cuts on Samson's back. Cuts, if he noticed, his ego would attribute to scratches made from her nails during her ecstasy. She didn't stop collecting Samson's blood until she had a chalice full of his warm, red life fluid. Then she drank. It hadn't worked, but it had made her very receptive when their father offered his.

Roman stood up from his chair in Isabella's room in one fluid motion that belied the years he appeared to be. Like his siblings, he could appear to be any age he wanted. Unlike Abisare and Delilah, who chose to look exactly the age they were when their father had adopted them, Roman found the appearance of middle age more conducive to his plans. But since returning with Isabella from Miami, he had, as Jacquelyn would've remarked, let himself go.

Unlike their progeny, the Ancients, who were the very first children, did not need to feed nightly. Not even weekly. Or monthly, for that matter. Roman had not fed since Gabriel Hawthorne and saw no reason to feed now. He did check his image in the mirror and decided it would not do. A change of clothes was in order.

He bent down to kiss Isabella's forehead. A patch of burnt flesh sloughed off and stuck to his bottom lip. Roman smiled. The pink flesh now gleaming on her forehead heartened him. She was now almost completely restored. Completely healed.

Roman opened the door, turning to gaze upon Isabella one last time, then stepped through the doorway. Shutting the door behind him, Roman looked like the perfect image of health and vitality for a fifty-five-year-old man.

Fifteen minutes later, Roman descended the stairs into the cellar. He'd been ready in five, but knowing his older brother and sister were there to scold him left him feeling petulant.

Abisare and Delilah were waiting exactly as Roman knew they would. Delilah was sniffing a wine cask, a look of sublime pleasure on her face. Abisare had found a corner where he could stand, arms crossed, back ramrod straight, the overhead lamp slicing his body so that only half his sneer was bathed in light. The other half of his face was cloaked in shadow. Ambiance, Roman thought. And theatrics. Abisare should have been on Broadway.

"Caio," Roman said with a bow, first to Delilah, then to Abisare.

Delilah returned the bow, but Abisare only snorted. Roman and Delilah ignored him.

"What you've done here," Delilah gestured about the space, "is magnificent."

"Grazie." Roman bowed again.

Delilah smiled. "And the vineyards. I think they are more beautiful than those of Philistia."

"You honor me," Roman said. The humility in his voice was genuine.

"That's hardly a compliment as the vineyards of Philistia have been dust for three thousand years," Abisare scoffed.

Delilah glared at Abisare, who glared at Roman, who only nodded acknowledgment. He knew Abisare was only sniping at him without thought of how it affected Delilah.

She looked back at Roman, her features softening. "Isabella?"

"Recovering," Roman answered.

Delilah nodded. "We extend our condolences on the loss of your son."

"Thank you," Roman said. He'd been a vampire too long, and Cain had only been a tool, a pawn on his chessboard. He was too powerful to be called a pawn, more like a bishop or queen. But even a bishop or a queen was subject to the player's wants and needs. Roman cared for him like a human might care for his tools. But he always knew Cain might have to be sacrificed.

Delilah, however, was still able to feel. Maybe because she was the only female child left, or because of her sheer force of will, she had learned how to retain and compartmentalize her human emotions. Abisare however...

"His loss was no loss." Abisare's arms fell to his sides as he stepped forward. "He was an abomination." He pointed a finger at Roman. "And you had the gall to name him after our father."

"Abisare." There was a warning in Delilah's tone, but Abisare was feeling his oats. He held up his index finger toward her.

"How dare you disrespect—"

Roman cut across him. "Sons have honored their fathers by naming their offspring—"

"He wasn't your offspring," Abisare screamed in rage, his eyes glowing red, his hands clenched tightly into fists. "He was livestock. No, that's wrong. He was something worse. He was a genetically modified bull."

"We have no laws against the vampiric enhancement of humans," Roman countered.

"That is not why we are here, Abisare," Delilah interjected.

"We should have come for that reason alone years ago," Abisare spat.

"But it is as Roman said," Delilah sounded like a mother patiently explaining to an angry toddler why he must take a nap, "we have no laws against enhancing a human. And personally," she looked at Roman, "I think it was quite brilliant."

"Thank you," Roman said, bowing his head again towards Delilah.

Abisare took advantage of Roman's downcast eyes and Delilah's gaze. He crossed the room faster than a human eye could follow.

If the head vintner had been there, he would've sworn Abisare had vanished, and Roman had executed some acrobatic feat.

Roman did see Abisare moving, though. Watched as Abisare's hand reared back. Felt the backhanded slap, nose breaking, and cheek slicing open. Roman's feet left the ground as the strike launched him across the room. He hit the wall, carving out holes in the stone where his head and shoulder hit, and crumpled to the floor.

His nose was set, and the slice on his cheek was knitted before he hit the ground.

"There may be no law, but there are still consequences," Abisare said, adjusting the rings on his fingers. "That was also for my complex in the Congo. The Illuminati destroyed it, thanks to their Phase Two weapons."

Roman stood up and dusted off his suit. He'd heard the fabric tearing when he hit the wall. It was a thousand-dollar suit or had been. Now it was rubbish for the trash bin.

Abisare started towards Roman, but Delilah touched Abisare's chest with a finger. He looked like he'd just walked into a stone wall.

"Enough, Abisare," Delilah said with a reproving look.

Abisare's jaw clenched, but he said nothing.

Delilah turned towards Roman and gestured for him to come forward.

Roman stepped up to Abisare and Delilah, his tattered suit the only evidence of his flight across the room.

"Abisare is right, though," Delilah continued. "We have lost many progeny around the world to these new weapons. Weapons you knew about but said nothing."

If Delilah realized just how much he knew about the Illuminati's weapons, she might strike him herself. Roman decided to ignore that topic altogether. "Those progeny were of no value," Roman answered. "They were like spoiled brats whose every whim has been indulged by their wealthy parents. They know nothing of the struggles their parents went through to gain that wealth. They do not conduct themselves with the respect the opportunities afforded to them should garner. They would have been sacrificed in the next culling."

Abisare opened his mouth to speak, but now it was Delilah's turn to hold up an index finger. Abisare's mouth shut with an audible snap.

"Nevertheless," Delilah responded, "we were caught unaware."

"As was I," Roman admitted.

Delilah nodded. "Yet you told no one what happened in Miami."

"It is not your decision to make who is sacrificed or not," Abisare said as he glared at Roman. "He knew of these Phase Two weapons before Miami and decided to let them eliminate these spoiled brats first."

Roman heard the taunt in Abisare's voice, but refused to react. Instead, he looked at Delilah. "I was...distracted."

"Isabella," There was no taunt in Delilah's voice, just a simple statement of fact.

Roman nodded.

Abisare rolled his eyes.

"No, Abisare," Delilah said as if she'd heard his eyes rolling. "You have never known love or compassion. He speaks the truth."

Now, she addressed Roman. "I think it best if you no longer watch over the Illuminati. Not while you're distracted. And you will pay restitution to your siblings for their losses."

"And the next time you and I meet," interjected Abisare, "you will not have these *puttanas* to protect you."

Abisare never saw it coming; even if he'd been looking at her, he still wouldn't have seen it. One moment, he was sneering at Roman, and the next, he was extracting himself from an Abisare-sized hole in the rock wall.

Delilah was already up the stairs and outside before Abisare hit the wall.

"I guess Delilah knows what puttana means." Roman offered a hand. "I won't tell Isabella, or she'll rip out your throat the next time she sees you."

Abisare's jaw rippled as he gritted his teeth, waving Roman away.

Roman looked at the damage behind Abisare. "I'll just deduct the cost to repair the wall from your share of the restitution, shall I?"

Abisare brushed himself off, shot Roman daggers with his gaze, and then staggered to the stairs without saying a word.

Roman shrugged and followed.

25

Illuminati Compound
Baton Rouge, Louisiana

Marcus seethed as he crossed the compound towards Caiaphas's office, replaying the episode in the gym in an endless loop in his mind's eye. Each time he did so, he picked up more nuances in tone and body language of disrespect, judgment, and condescension. The scene was turning redder with each repeat.

"Where are the intel reports for the compound attacks?" Marcus had barked as he'd entered the gym, where Collins, one of the team leaders, bench-pressed while a man stood behind him counting.

The man said nothing as he finished the rep, then set the bar back on the brackets. "Hello, Marcus," Collins said as he sat up. "I'm doing well, thanks for asking. How about you?"

Marcus ignored the sarcastic small talk, the daggers shooting from the eyes of the man standing behind Collins, and the two hundred and fifty pounds of weight on the bar Collins was pressing. "You should've finished those reports hours ago."

"Give us a minute, Chewy," Collins said to the man behind the bench, unfazed by Marcus's tone.

Chewy earned his name not because he looked like a woolly mammoth walking on its hind legs but because he did the best Chewbacca impersonation. It was more than an impression. He could carry on whole conversations with people and be completely understood.

At the moment, Chewy looked less like Chewbacca or a woolly mammoth and more like an oversized hound of the Baskervilles. Marcus imagined this was the look of a man who'd been interrupted

117

in the middle of a make-out session with his girlfriend by a Mormon missionary. He said nothing and didn't move. Still, Marcus had to force himself not to take a half-step backward.

Resigned to the fact that Chewy wasn't going anywhere, Collins nodded to Marcus. "I did. And I submitted them."

"I didn't receive anything."

"I didn't send them to you."

"Who'd you send them to?" Marcus stared hard at Collins, who stared hard right back at him. Marcus wondered why Collins had refused a nickname or call sign. He'd just come up with one for the man: The Wall.

Marcus remembered his mother telling him when he was a boy that sometimes his father was a brick wall during discussions, allowing the other person to speak without interruption. The individual could talk without feeling judged. Sometimes, a person needs a wall with a face to reason out the issue on their own. Marcus didn't think that applied to Collins as they continued staring at each other. Chewy's eyes continued shooting daggers.

And it finally dawned on Marcus. "Caiaphas told you to change S.O.P."

Collins nodded. "All intel on operations outside the compound now goes directly to a short list marked 'Eyes Only.'"

Marcus's jaw clenched, his teeth grinding against each other. "And I'm not on that list."

Collins shook his head. "Specifically not on that list."

A hateful smirk curled Chewy's lips.

Marcus wanted to punch the wall that was Collins and slap the smirk off Chewy's face. Instead, turning on his heel, he made a beeline for Caiaphas's office.

How dare you embarrass me like this. Make me look like a fool before the very people I will soon lead as Caiaphas.

Marcus ignored the nagging little voice in the back of his head reminding him how he might have been doing just that when he organized the alliance and carried out operations without Caiaphas's knowledge or approval. He drowned out that voice and the feeling that he was an errant teenager disobeying his father with the conversation with Collins, focusing on the man's last statement, "Specifically not on that list."

"We'll see about that." Marcus spat as he arrived at the door of Caiaphas's office. Sucking in a deep breath, he pushed the conversation with Collins and the errant teenager to the back of his mind. Sharp, shooting pain replaced them, hammering at his temples.

Get a hold of yourself, Marcus thought as he rubbed his forehead. Now is not the time for tantrums or histrionics. Or migraines. It's time to assert myself. Time to convince the old man it's time for him to step down. Time to—

"Come in," Caiaphas said from behind the door.

Marcus glanced up at the CCTV camera outside the office door before grabbing the handle and entering.

Caiaphas sat at his desk, fingers interlaced, an 'I've been expecting you' expression on his face.

"How long have you known?" Marcus questioned.

Caiaphas only nodded at the chair before him.

"I'm fine standing," Marcus replied.

Caiaphas smiled expectantly at Marcus as if waiting for him to answer a question he'd asked.

Marcus huffed and rolled his eyes as he sat, chastising himself for the errant teenager's response.

"Right after the teams were deployed," Caiaphas answered. "Smart of you to have them go dark on comms until they returned," he added.

"So why not just come to me once you were aware?" Marcus hated the whine he heard in his voice, but he pressed on. "Why let me find out this way? To embarrass me? You had to know it would make me look foolish and undermine my authority."

"I could say the same of you," Caiaphas retorted. "You've set quite the precedent."

Marcus looked at him, confused.

"The rank and file of the Illuminati now understand that if they disagree with their leadership, they can simply ignore them. Orders can and should be disobeyed. They can decide which course of action is best. And they can execute that course. They don't need, nor should they, share intel with leadership. Ignorance is bliss. In short, Caiaphas is now as irrelevant to this organization as a parent to a headstrong teenager." He tipped his head to Marcus. "And that's what you'll be dealing with as you assume the mantle of Caiaphas."

His reply cut straight through Marcus. He'd been so consumed with his agenda and ego that he'd never considered Caiaphas's position, let alone his feelings. He'd known that Caiaphas would be angry, even disappointed with him, but he hadn't thought about the position he was putting him in. Or the position he would be putting himself in.

"I'm sorry. I wasn't trying to...I was...just...I mean... I...," Marcus stammered.

Caiaphas held up a hand, silencing Marcus. "I forgive you."

Marcus looked at the man he considered more than a mentor, more than a boss, and felt the migraine thrumming inside his skull like a drummer in the distance announcing his coming. He would prefer a railing Caiaphas. A condemning, expletive-driven dressing down by his superior than this calm, factual, and forgiving old man. But that's why he was Caiaphas. And, as usual, he was right. Soon, Marcus would be sitting behind this desk. And how much of his own leadership had he undercut?

Caiaphas interrupted Marcus's ruminating. "The damage is done. The trust has been broken. It will have to be re-earned. For now, all of your duties remain the same. The only exception is that anything concerning operations outside the compound will go through me. Is that clear?"

Marcus understood the conversation was over. "Yes, Sir," Marcus replied as he stood and walked towards the door.

"Marcus," Caiaphas called out.

Marcus turned and looked at his mentor.

"I still trust you with my life. That hasn't and won't ever change."

Marcus nodded and exited the office, forcing the tears forming in his eyes to subside as the drummer announced he was here and would remain for a very long time.

26

Venice, Italy

Alessia gripped the pepper spray inside the clutch hanging from her shoulder. She hated the fact that she still couldn't control her fear. Last night, with Luca by her side, it was easy to be brave. It was easy to think she'd go looking for the man who saved her from rape and possible murder. She'd fallen asleep imagining herself marching down the street, head up and shoulders back. But now that she was on these streets, as the shadows lengthened with approaching dusk, she fought the urge to run, not home with Luca, but to the emergency room with its familiar people and mayhem.

She tried reasoning with herself. She'd walked these streets hundreds of times over the years. It's where she worked. Where she lived. Alessia remembered how, once, a vagrant outside the shelter attempted to snatch her clutch. Even that hadn't scared her. Maybe because she'd fought back, and the vagrant was weak. She'd botched his attempt to steal her purse. She'd felt empowered. Strong.

Despite her success, Gia had given her the pepper spray she now held onto so tightly after that incident. Alessia thought it was silly and absolutely unnecessary, but Gia made her promise to carry it. Now, she was grateful for it. It helped her put one foot in front of the other as she walked down the street, past the bar where she met her fellow nurses for a drink after a shift. Her legs seemed to get heavier with every step as she turned the corner and walked down the street where it all happened.

Alessia looked down into her clutch, ensuring the canister was facing the right direction. Stopping in her tracks as the alleyway her attackers dragged her into came into sight, she stood there for several moments, trying to convince herself to take another step. Stop being such a baby, she thought. There are people everywhere. You're safe. She continued, willing herself forward. It didn't work. Alessia spun to walk in the opposite direction.

"Hello."

Gabriel Hawthorne put both hands up in surrender as he watched Alessia stumble backward and fall.

Before her mind could register what was happening, Alessia found herself standing face to face with the man she had been looking for. On a well-lit street with passersby and no apparent attackers, she noticed it was a handsome face. Filthy. But handsome. She wanted to thank him for keeping her from falling, but instead, she asked, "Have you been following me?"

Gabriel's eyes popped open wide in surprise. He released her as if she'd screamed for him not to touch her. "No. I sss-...saw you."

"You were going to say something else," Alessia said, studying Gabriel's face.

Gabriel shook his head, eyes darting everywhere as he tried hard not to make eye contact.

Alessia continued to study Gabriel. She could see that he was struggling to find the right words. He also seemed more nervous than she was. Scared even. He had looked past her in all directions several times as if he were looking for something. Or someone.

A passerby commented on the condition of Gabriel's appearance loud enough for others to turn their heads and take notice.

"Let's get out of here. We could go to the shelter I work at." Alessia nodded over Gabriel's shoulder. "It's only a few blocks from here. You could get a shower. Some fresh clothes. Possibly something to eat. I bet there's some panelle or focaccia still in the fridge."

"Food isn't what I'm hungry for." The words were out of Gabriel's mouth before he realized it, and a look of terror flashed across his face as another passerby commented on the sexual overtone.

Alessia knew he meant blood, but she wasn't about to correct the passerby. Instead, she grabbed Gabriel by the arm and spun him toward the shelter. "What was your name again?" She asked as she marched him away.

"Gabriel. My name's Gabriel Hawthorne."

"Mr. Hawthorne." Alessia nodded. "You sound American. What brings you to Italy?" She kept her tone light and airy.

Gabriel bit his lip, not sure how to, or even if he should, answer. It was only after drinking human blood that he'd remembered who he was and why he'd come to Italy: To kill Roman Dvanaesti. That's not something you bandy about in public. *I came to Italy from America to kill an Italian citizen because, despite what you think you know about him, he's really a vampire responsible for killing my ex-girlfriend, whom I haven't dated in more than ten years, and who was about to marry someone else.*

No, that didn't sound crazy at all in his head. That sure wouldn't sound crazy to her or anyone who might overhear it on the street. It didn't matter that she or anyone overhearing might not even know who Roman Dvanaesti was, but he didn't know who he could trust. He didn't know if he could trust her, but he had to trust someone. Why not the woman he'd saved? For blood, anyway. That was enough for now, and he didn't think he could drink another rat.

Gabriel said nothing.

Alessia nodded in understanding and changed the subject. "It occurs to me that I've never thanked you for...well. Thank you."

"You're welcome," Gabriel replied.

It felt strange to Gabriel to be walking and talking with this woman. He hadn't spoken with anyone since...he had no idea how long that had been, but since showing up at Roman's estate to kill him. Since Roman had turned him into this...monster. He wasn't ready to call himself a vampire.

Gabriel's vision blurred, thinking about that. He'd once been a man. He'd never be again.

The two fell silent as they walked the last block to the shelter. Once inside, Alessia found some clothing for Gabriel in one of the donation bins while he showered and shaved. Gabriel stayed under the water until it turned cold, feeling hope for the first time in...

He stopped thinking about time. That sapped his newly found hope.

The clothes fit a little loose but were clean, fresh, and comfortable. Gabriel felt like a new...well, he felt a little like his former self. Old didn't seem like the right word. He exited the locker room and found Alessia waiting for him in the hallway.

"Well, you clean up nice," Alessia said, looking him up and down. She meant it. He was handsome, and she felt a tingle in her belly. She hadn't felt attracted to a man in a long time, especially not since...she changed the subject. "I'd like to give you a quick check-up, Mr. Hawthorne."

"Gabriel. Please."

"Okay. Gabriel." Alessia gestured to an exam room.

Gabriel followed her into the room and climbed onto the table as Alessia measured his blood pressure and temperature.

"So, Gabriel. What brought you to Italy?" Alessia asked.

Gabriel was silent for a long time. She'd seen what he'd done to her attackers, heard his pleas for help obtaining blood. Just how far could he go? Just how much could she be expected to accept? She's still here, he thought, fingers on my wrist, counting my heart rate. Gabriel looked into her eyes. There was no fear, only compassion and concern. He took a long breath and said, "Okay."

For the next hour, Gabriel recounted his story, or at least what he could remember, of becoming a vampire.

A vampire. It still sounds crazy when I say it.

But that was his new reality. Vampires existed, and now he was one of them. Alessia listened. At first, Gabriel could see that she was responding just like he'd had when he was first illumined.

After a while, she decided to let science decide what was truth and what was fiction. She was already concerned by the fact that his heart rate and blood pressure came back far below normal levels. She took a sample of Gabriel's blood. The results were astonishing. The physical appearance of the blood was a dark black liquid, almost like thick ink. She introduced several different blood types to the sample. Clotting never occurred. Instead, Gabriel's blood cells acted as Phagocytes, consuming each foreign blood type they came into contact with.

"Back on the street. You started to say something but then you backpedaled and said you saw me. What was it? How did you find me?" Alessia asked.

"Once you were close enough. I could..." he'd gone this far, "smell you. The scent of your blood." Gabriel answered.

Their eyes locked. Alessia felt the butterflies in her stomach.

Gabriel would describe the sensation as more of a gut punch.

The two stared silently at each other for a full minute before Alessia finally said, "Fascinating." She wasn't sure if she was speaking about Gabriel's story. Or Gabriel.

27

Illuminati Compound
Baton Rouge, Louisiana

Cain Dvanaesti reclined on the exam table, dressed in a hospital gown. He'd agreed to this testing not because Caiaphas had asked him but because he was as curious about himself as they were. He didn't know all of his strengths and limitations. He'd gone from the attack on his mansion to the plane crash to a cell in Baton Rouge. He knew he could now hear heartbeats, smell fear, and practically see in the dark. He knew that in moments of extreme duress, he...changed. He shivered at the memory of his black eyes, talons, fangs, and mottled skin color.

"Are you cold? Would you like a blanket?" Caiaphas asked.

"What? No." Cain tried to cover the shiver with a stretch. "I was just..." His voice trailed off. Just what? Just as scared of what I can turn into as you are? Probably more scared. Because, after all, it's happening to me. You see it. I experience it.

Cain let the word 'just' hang there like a dead leaf at the end of a dried-up tree, eventually falling and drifting away.

Caiaphas seemed to know what Cain was thinking and changed the subject. He touched Cain's shoulder and said, "Dr. Hernandez is going to wave a U.V. light bar over your exposed skin. You won't see the light. Well, I don't know. Maybe you will see the light." His tone was soothing, as if he were explaining what was about to happen to a child.

Cain didn't miss the tone and couldn't resist teasing Caiaphas. He screwed his face up like how he imagined a small child would and asked in a timid voice, "Will it hurt?

Caiaphas was oblivious. "That's what we're going to find out."

Dr. Hernandez, not known for playfulness or a comforting bedside manner, rolled up a trolley with what looked like a curling iron attached to a white plastic box. "We're looking to see if U.V. rays produce any discomfort to you and how that discomfort may present."

"Present?" Cain asked.

Dr. Hernandez nodded. "Burning. Stinging. Discoloration of the skin. Do you perhaps start to cook like a piece of meat over an open fire?" She pressed a button on the box, and it started to hum. She picked up the curling iron.

Cain shouted in his best Wicked Witch of the West imitation, "I'm melting, melting."

Dr. Hernandez frowned.

Caiaphas guffawed.

Dr. Hernandez stared at Caiaphas. "May I begin?" She did not try to hide her irritation.

Caiaphas only nodded as he patted Cain's shoulder.

Dr. Hernandez waved the curling iron, which Cain now realized was the light wand, over the back of Cain's hand. She looked from his hand to his face before waving the wand over his arms, legs, feet, and finally across his neck and face. She said nothing as she turned the nobs on the box and repeated the process. Finally, she set down the wand and looked at Cain.

Cain shook his head.

She looked at Caiaphas. "The subject appears to have no physical response to UV exposure." She gestured at the wand. "At least in this form."

"Subject? I'm right here, Doc," Cain said, chuckling.

Dr. Hernandez ignored Cain. "I'd like to draw some blood and run some tests. I'll get the orders ready." She turned and walked away.

"Perhaps she should get an X-ray. See if her funny bone's been removed and shoved up her—"

"Her husband and two children were murdered," Caiaphas interrupted. "By vampires."

Cain stared at Caiaphas in horror.

Caiaphas remained silent for a long moment, looking in the direction Dr. Hernadez had walked. Satisfied she would not return, he started. "She and her family loved the outdoors. Usually, their vacations centered around hiking. Kayaking. And tent camping." He sighed. "They were supposed to leave for a camping trip in Yellowstone. The plan was for them to camp and hike in the backcountry. Her mother was ill, so she told her family to go without her while she cared for the older woman. They did. But when they didn't arrive home at the appointed time, she alerted the park service, who started looking for them. Two days later, she received a call. Her family had been found. Slaughtered. The park rangers said it looked like a bear attack."

"If they thought it was a bear, how do you know it was vampires?" Cain asked.

Caiaphas's chuckle had no humor in it. "We've seen this before. Vampires, the younger ones anyway, have been blaming their butchery on animals for centuries. The more mature ones exhibit self-control. But the younger ones, the bloodlust takes hold, and they tend towards...extreme violence. An easy way to cover up that violence is to blame wild animals. In this case, it was Yellowstone in August, a popular time for hiking and when bears are searching for the sustenance they'll need in preparation for hibernation."

Cain wanted to ask more questions, but his throat had gone dry.

Caiaphas changed the subject. "So, you are impervious to sunlight. Probably because you've been ingesting Roman's blood your entire life. We know that new vampires can't be in sunlight, but the older ones can tolerate it for short periods, and the Ancients, like your father, have no vulnerability to sunlight."

"Don't call him that," Cain answered agitatedly.

Caiaphas only nodded in acquiescence. "The blood tests should give us more information about your gifts," Caiaphas said.

"Gifts," Cain spat. "You mean curse."

"You can label your new talents and abilities however you want, Cain. Talents, gifts, and abilities do not define a man. Nor are they a direct representation of his character. His choices are the true indication of his character. How you use them will determine if they're a blessing or a curse." Caiaphas eyed Cain. "We all make decisions based on what life throws at us. Sometimes, we have time and control. Sometimes those choices are forced upon us by events out of our control."

"And what gifts have I utilized in circumstances beyond my control?"

"Regeneration," Caiaphas explained at the oblivious look on Cain's face. "You survived a plane slamming into the ocean from ten thousand feet."

Cain scoffed.

"Life is precious. Especially to those of us who have so little of it left."

"How long?" Cain asked, reaching out to keep Caiaphas from leaving.

Caiaphas didn't shrug off Cain's arm but turned and eyed him. "How do you know?"

"I can smell it. Growing inside you. It was faint when we first met, but it grows stronger. Cancer?" Cain asked.

"Yes. It's in my bones now. Caiaphas shrugged. "They're not sure. The doctors. They say months, maybe weeks."

"Do they know?" Cain asked, nodding around the door.

"Just the doctors."

There was a knock at the door, and Dr. Hernandez entered.

"I would prefer to keep it that way for now," Caiaphas whispered.

Cain heard and nodded his agreement.

Dr. Hernandez didn't make eye contact with Cain as she swabbed his arm with alcohol. Knotting a tourniquet around his bicep, she ran a finger over his veins and selected one. She said, "Poke," as she inserted the needle into his vein.

Nothing happened. The needle didn't penetrate his skin, let alone his vein.

She studied the needle tip. Brushed it with her gloved finger. Tried again.

Nothing.

Caiaphas placed a hand on Cain's shoulder. "Let's try something. Close your eyes. Breathe slowly. Think of some relaxing place."

Cain did as Caiaphas suggested.

After a few moments, Caiaphas nodded to Dr. Hernandez, who tried again.

This time, the needle slid easily into the vein. Blood flowed into the specimen tubes.

Caiaphas said, "I think we just found another of your gifts."

28

Roman Dvanaesti's Estate, Italy

The seventh monitor on Roman's wall lit up with the face of Sergei, the youngest of his captains, summoned to this impromptu meeting. In some ways, Sergei reminded Roman of Isabella. Headstrong. Cruel. Efficient. A certain willingness to accomplish objectives outside the rules. And beautiful to look at. What was the modern idiom? Ah, yes, Roman remembered: Eye candy. Sergei had been handpicked by Isabella, the only one she'd recommended.

When he'd first met him, Roman had been sure lust had been the only reason Isabella had brought him to the party, using another idiom, like a sixty-five-year-old beer-bellied millionaire with his twenty-three-year-old Playboy centerfold girlfriend hanging on his arm. Then he noticed Sergei was locking eyes with him, not like a young upstart lion looking to conquer the older king of the pride, but as equals. It was at once irksome and refreshing. Usually, the only vampires who did that were Isabella and Jacquelyn. His siblings were condescending at best, despite his accomplishments. Their offspring always averted their eyes, hoping like an obese child not to be singled out by the physical education teacher. He'd wondered if Sergei were perhaps too young and stupid.

Since that first meeting, Sergei had proven he was neither. He'd been a child of twelve living on the streets of Moscow when Bonaparte's army invaded. He survived poverty, hunger, and the French soldiers before he was a teenager. By the time he was fifteen, he'd moved from crimes of opportunity to petty theft to robbery and finally confidence games. His most lucrative was the false good

Samaritan in which a younger compatriot would knock down a woman, steal her purse, or perhaps a necklace or bracelet, and run off.

Lucky for the distraught woman and her husband, Sergei had happened to see the whole thing and, without request, chased after the miscreant. He was always successful at retrieving the stolen property, but alas, he was just as unsuccessful at capturing the young purse snatcher. He almost always returned, swearing after the urchin who'd bitten him, his bloodstained shirtsleeve bearing witness to the insult. The distraught woman and grateful husband would give what coins they had, and sometimes, if the necklace or bracelet was damaged, the jewelry as well.

Sometimes, Sergei would combine the false good Samaritan with what could only be called the unwilling badger game. He would happen upon a wealthy aristocrat who'd taken up with a mistress. He'd surveil the count or baron for weeks before striking. Upon returning the stolen property to the nobleman and his "wife," Sergei would recognize the man, and more importantly, the woman as not his wife. He received bills, coins, and jewelry in those moments for his silence.

He wasn't always successful, and on several occasions, Sergei had received nothing for his trouble. A couple of times, he had to sacrifice his accomplice to escape law enforcement, and once, he took his cohort's life to save himself. It was after this last occurrence that Sergei decided he needed to leave Moscow. That's when an opportunity presented itself.

Traveling through the shadows of the back alleys, Sergei came across a young man, just a couple of years older than himself, lying in a crumpled heap, barely breathing. By the cut and fabric of his clothing, it was easy to see he was an aristocrat. The man reeked of alcohol, and Sergei wondered if he'd been assaulted and robbed. Checking the young man's pockets, he found more cash than he'd held in his lifetime, and a letter. It was an imperial order of commission. Sergei had taught himself to read and write. The young man was a count and due to report in two days. So, it hadn't been a robbery. He'd just drunk himself to this state. Condolences or a last hurrah? Did it matter?

Sergei reviewed his options. He could take the money and leave the man to his fate. But that also left Sergei to this man's fate. If he lived, the authorities would be looking for a criminal who'd assaulted and robbed a count. If he died, the authorities would be looking for a criminal who'd robbed and murdered a count.

He could take the money and the letter. But that wouldn't work either. Sure, it would slow the process down, but the ends would be the same. His clothing meant aristocratic blood had been assaulted or spilled. This man would be known.

But what if nothing more than a vagabond was found? Then the body would be removed as nothing more than an eyesore and a nuisance and thrown into an unmarked pauper's grave. End of a life. End of a story.

A young count shirking his responsibility to the state and disobeying an imperial order would be too much of an embarrassment to the man's family. The family would want to keep the humiliation as quiet as possible. They might search for him, insist that he would never neglect his family or his duty, but his absence would speak for itself.

The letter stated it would be two days before the young man would be missed. The money gave him the means. The clothing would provide him with camouflage. All he had to do was...

Sergei dropped to a knee, pulled the man's handkerchief from his waistcoat pocket, placed it over the man's mouth and nose, and waited. The man never struggled. He died quietly, peacefully. Sergei thought the man was so inebriated that he would have stopped breathing on his own eventually. But Sergei couldn't risk that. Instead, Sergei exchanged clothing with the dead man. The clothing fit well. They were both of similar size and stature. Pocketing the cash and the letter, Sergei fled Moscow in the style befitting a young count and made his way to Italy.

Roman was a little hazy on the details of how Sergei and Isabella met. The truth was, he really didn't care. Sergei had proven resourceful and unhesitating. The perfect soldier. He followed orders to the letter. The mission was always accomplished to Roman's satisfaction. Yet today, Roman knew, Sergei would be the one to test Roman's patience.

Roman stared at the seven monitors, taking them all in at once. The seven captains stared back at him with silent expectation. Roman preferred to meet in person, but there just wasn't time. These seven vampires were responsible for all of Roman's interests around the world. One was posted on each continent. His orders, which these seven would find unorthodox at the least, had to be coordinated around the globe in seventy-two hours. Any more time and his siblings would question his commitment. So, Roman had called for this remote assembly.

After the visit from Delilah and Abisare, Roman knew it was time. It angered Roman that this meeting was necessary. It wasn't the loss of assets or change that upset him. Roman knew this day would come eventually. Change is inevitable. Assets were like pieces on a chessboard: expendable. What angered him was the lack of respect his siblings had shown him. Not him, per se, but his accomplishments. Though he was the youngest, Roman had done more to help cultivate the herds than several of his siblings combined had.

Now that they were all here, in spirit if not in truth, Roman mused to himself, it was time.

"We are shutting down the Illuminati project," Roman stated as if he were going over line items at a weekly board meeting.

Six of the seven looked visibly shocked. One, however, looked disgusted.

"Shutting down," Sergei exclaimed. "What do you mean, shutting down?"

Roman ignored the outburst. "I want a plan for a coordinated attack on all Illuminati compounds."

"But, sir," Sergei continued to question. "We have been cultivating and policing that project for centuries. And now you want us to burn it to the ground?" Sergei spat the words as if they were battery acid in his mouth.

"I want you to do as I tell you." Roman hissed in Sumerian.

The other six recoiled as if Roman had reached through their monitors and slapped them.

Sergei was undeterred. "But that's just it. We do as you tell us. *You* plan. *We* execute." Sergei sat back. "Now you tell us to plan? What's next?" He smirked. "You're going to execute?"

If Roman were simply a man, he would've perhaps closed his eyes and counted to ten or balled his hands into fists until his nails dug deep into the flesh of his palms. But Roman was a vampire, an Ancient. So instead, he fixed his gaze so that each vampire in the monitor felt he was staring directly at him. "Perhaps execute is exactly what I will do. Maybe my staff is too large. It may be that I don't need a staff at all."

Each vampire knew exactly what that meant. Roman didn't lay off personnel. He didn't downsize. He destroyed. Collectively, they willed Sergei to apologize or, better yet, keep his mouth shut.

Sergei remained silent.

"I expect a briefing," he pointed to where he was standing, "here. In seventy-two hours." Roman killed the feed to all the monitors.

29

Venice, Italy

Detective Antonio Frederico watched as his partner, Marco Scalia, shoved another Gnocco Fritto into his mouth. His stomach roiled as Marco chewed the fried dough. He watched Marco swallow, and felt bile rise in his throat. He popped a Nicorette in his mouth and chewed with fury while he rubbed the Chantix patch on his arm.

"What?" Marco questioned.

"How could you possibly eat? We've spent the day past our ankles in dead rats. We're about to see more, and God knows what else. You're stuffing your face," Antonio replied.

"I'm hungry," Marco said, popping another into his mouth. "You want one?" Marco asked through a mouthful of dough, holding up the bag.

Shaking his head in disgust, Antonio stepped out of the car and popped a second Nicorette into his mouth. "Let's go."

They were met at the door by the restaurant owner, Paola Rossi. "About time you got here. I run a respectable establishment. I can't have my patrons thinking we have..." She looked around to see if anyone would hear what she said next and lowered her voice to just above a whisper, "A rat problem."

Amused, Marco whispered, "A...rat problem?"

Rossi nodded. "And a monster." She still whispered.

"Monster?" Marco blurted out.

Passersby rubbernecked.

Rossi hissed a shush at Marco.

Reaching for his badge, Antonio said, "I'm Detective Frederico, and this is my partner, Detective Scalia."

Rossi put a hand on his. "The last thing I need my patrons to see is police flashing badges." She cast a quick, furtive glance back at the restaurant and then at the two detectives. "This way."

She led them around the side of the building to the garbage bins.

"So, rats, monsters, and cops. Oh my." Marco said in an annoyingly accurate rendition of the lion from *The Wizard of Oz*.

Both Rossi and Antonio ignored Marco.

Marco continued his chant until they approached the scene. What shut him up was the footprint in the middle of one of the rats. "What the...You let your employees walk through the scene?" Marco said.

"Excuse me," Rossi replied with a confused look.

"The footprint." Marco pointed at the ground.

Now Rossie looked scandalized. "That's not one of my workers." She looked around to make sure they were still alone. "That's from the monster," Paola replied.

"It looks human," Antonio said, squatting to look at it.

Rossi's head shook. "That's no human. It's a monster. I saw it. Eating the rats." Her voice trembled as she said this.

"You saw a man *eating* the rats?" Marco's was a mixture of skepticism and nausea.

"I saw *it* eating the rats," Rossi repeated. "That was no man. I mean, it looked like a man. But," she pointed to a broken chain in front of the trash container, "no man could've done that."

Detective Antonio bent down to examine the chain more closely. He could see that one of the chain links had not been cut but pried apart. He rubbed the Chantix patch on his arm as his gaze moved from the broken chain to the bloody footprint and the desiccated rats. Marco's silly little mantra of *rats and monsters and cops, oh my,* didn't seem so idiotic right now. He popped a third Nicorette into his mouth.

Picking up the chain, Antonio pulled it. The links were thick, molded from steel. The chain was heavy. He guessed some muscle-bound gym rat might be able to rip it apart. But last Antonio heard, muscle-bound gym rats weren't scavenging restaurant trash cans for food. And rats weren't the best source of protein.

Antonio looked closer at the rats. They weren't really eaten, were they? There was no tearing of flesh from bone. No bones were pulled from sockets or joints. No. All the rats they'd seen were intact. Whatever had torn the chain apart would've destroyed the rats if it were eating them. Instead, they were...drained, siphoned from two punctures. He ran his tongue over his teeth. Two puncture wounds spaced as if they came from the canines of an adult human. Or something humanoid.

Antonio didn't want to entertain that thought. He was a cop. A detective. He dealt with facts, not fiction. And he'd seen enough of the horrors humans could commit against each other; he didn't need to make anything up. Still, he had a bunch of dead rats, a chain torn apart, and all the food in the bins ignored. One thought, however, he couldn't keep from bouncing around in his brain, and it sent a shiver down his spine. How long before they were called to the scene of a human victim?

"Thank you, Mrs. Rossi." Antonio stood, pulling his phone from his pocket.

"*Ms.* Rossi," she corrected. A coy smile softened her features. Now that the shock was wearing off, she could feel a sense of camaraderie with these Pula, especially this lead detective. He was handsome and wasn't wearing a wedding band. "But you can call me Paola, Detective."

Antonio ignored the invitation. "My partner will take you inside and get your statement and a description of the suspect while I take a few pictures and wait for forensics."

"I am?" Marco asked, surprised at his partner's demeanor. He seemed to think this woman was telling the truth about the "monster" she saw eating the rats. It was obvious to him that she was flighty. Probably loved watching horror flicks or reading Alessandro Manzetti and Stephen King. Probably wanted to write that stuff. Definitely wanted to be involved in an investigation. So she saw some guy breaking into the trash bin, saw the dead rats, and her imagination ran wild.

After seeing the look on Antonio's face, Marco answered his own question. "I am."

"Yes. My partner will take care of you." Antonio said as he smirked.

Rossi nodded, crestfallen, and led Marco into the restaurant through the back entrance.

Antonio called requesting forensics, then walked the scene, taking pictures of everything. He looked over the photos. "So, who are you?" He asked out loud. "And where are you?"

30

Roman Dvanaesti's Estate, Italy

Sergei's six fellow vampires sat behind Roman as Sergei briefed their superior. They had to admit he was doing a magnificent job. He hadn't stumbled over any aspect of the plan, even the new particulars he'd added after the seven of them had finished. Under other circumstances, they'd take issue with what he'd done, but these last-minute details had only made the plan even better. And they liked the fact that those additions were delivered as if they were part of the original plan that the seven of them had agreed upon.

The six were also impressed with how effortlessly Sergei fielded Roman's interruptions. No hesitation. No fumbling over words. No *ums* or *ahhs*. His expression remained placid, as if he knew that Roman would interrupt him at that point and pose the exact question Roman had, as if he'd already formulated his response and was just waiting to deliver it. Each had to acknowledge that Sergei was the right vampire for the job. Each also had to admit that by this time in the briefing, they'd hoped that Roman would've already ripped out Sergei's throat.

In truth, the plan had been Sergei's. He'd offered suggestions which the others accepted. He'd listened to their ideas and tweaked them, making those thoughts preferable. After listening to an idea, he proposed a better one. By the end of the planning session, it was obvious to the other six that Sergei, the youngest of Roman's captains, was their superior. He was smarter, more clever, more attractive, and bolder than his compatriots. What he lacked in vampiric age to his colleagues, he made up for with his audacity. And they hated him for it. They always had.

So, when the operation plan was complete and the question arose of how they'd brief Roman, they saw an opportunity, and the motion was offered that Sergei present the entire offensive. The other six would be there for moral support and to jump in if Sergei faltered. They wanted him to falter, to fail. They hoped Roman would hate the plan. Since he'd returned from Miami with the burnt remains of Isabella, Roman had not been the unshakable, immovable superior they'd always known. He was no longer the epitome of the proverb "Still waters run deep." He was temperamental, quick to display his anger in violent ways. A lot was riding on this plan for Roman, and anything less than flawless might incite him, would probably provoke him against the one who made that mistake. So they hoped Roman hated it. They would have a front row seat when, at the least, Roman put Sergei through the wall, or best, remove his head from his shoulders.

But Roman did not hate the plan. As he'd listened to Sergei and questioned him, analyzed the plan for flaws, Roman concluded he wouldn't have created a better plan. He would've developed the exact same operation. Granted, he would've finished it in one one-hundredth of the time, but that's why he'd wanted them to fashion it; he kept reminding himself as he listened. He was also impressed with Sergei. Not once had he stumbled or looked over Roman's shoulder at his colleagues. He now stood, ramrod straight, eyes focused on Roman's.

"Your plan is a good one, Sergei," Roman finally said, emphasizing the word, *your*. It was an individual effort, not by a committee. "You have done well."

Sergei nodded. No relief or elation brightened his face. His eyes remained on Roman's. He gave no credit to his fellow vampires.

Nor, Roman noticed, did the six behind him dispute that lack of credit. They continued their silence. And why shouldn't they, Roman thought. They hadn't conducted the meeting in turns, each briefing

Roman on a different aspect of the operation. They hadn't jumped in to answer the questions he'd posed or clarify Sergei's answers. They'd been content to be nothing more than statues decorating the room. Roman was not surprised and suspected that this operation plan had been Sergei's, with a touch of Isabella. There were particulars in the plan that bore the scent of her.

Sergei had indeed run the plan by Isabella. The particulars added after the final agreed operation plan were her contributions. He'd presented it to her, not because he feared Roman's temperament and possibly violent rejection, but because he craved Isabella's approval. She was more than his maker; she was his mentor. She was his confidant. She was the sun in his day and his sweet dreams at night. He loved and cherished her, and one day, he hoped she would consent to being called his own.

"You will have assets in place worldwide in seventy-two hours," Roman ordered. A smile slithered across his face, distorting it into the stuff of nightmares. "And twenty-four hours after that, the Illuminati will be no more."

No one else smiled. They remained more still than statues. Only Sergei acknowledged Roman's words with a curt nod of agreement.

Roman stood. "Make it so," he commanded Sergei, ignoring the others as he strode from the room. Pulling a burner phone from the inside pocket of his suit jacket, he couldn't help the heavy sigh that escaped his lips.

Isabella.

She should've been here to witness her protégé in action. She would've been very proud, and probably would've quietly culled the six behind him before he reached the door. If he'd still harbored doubts about her eye candy, Sergei had put those doubts to rest once and for all today. He didn't know what might pass between Isabella and Sergei before she joined him outside the room, and he frankly didn't care, but she would've been right there, pulling the burner phone from her jacket pocket before the door closed, and quickly typing the text he was now sending. But the nurse caring for Isabella felt it best for her not to attend. He decided to acquiesce to her expertise and not rip her throat out, especially since Isabella had agreed with her caregiver.

Satisfied the text had been sent, Roman crushed the burner phone into a small ball and hurled it like an outfielder throwing a baseball into home plate. The ball finally fell to Earth and landed in the Mediterranean Sea. Roman decided he would reward Sergei. The other six? They wouldn't live to see the next culling.

31

Illuminati Compound, Baton Rouge, Louisiana

Marcus hesitated before entering the room where Caiaphas sat sipping his tea. He hated the uncomfortable distance between them since the incident with Cain Dvanaesti, not to mention the recent altercation over his conducting military operations without Caiaphas's knowledge or approval. He was still trying to make sense of what had happened. He didn't feel he'd failed Caiaphas. After all, his sole purpose, after learning from him, was to protect him. What troubled Marcus was the complete disappointment in Caiaphas's expression. That look had pained Marcus more than anything Caiaphas could have said to him. It still made his heart sink into the pit of his stomach like a stone.

Another emotion Marcus was trying to quell was jealousy. He hadn't expected it. He'd never experienced the feeling before, but when Caiaphas had dropped to his knees and comforted a weeping Cain, it had blossomed in his chest, hot and greasy. He'd wanted to kick Cain. Stomp him into the ground. The pang of his failure, still fresh in his soul, stopped him. Froze him still as if he were a statue. He'd stood there, remembering Caiaphas's expression, watching the tableau of Caiaphas soothing Cain, and felt the exquisite stings of ice and fire.

He felt those stings now as he watched Caiaphas. They were distinctly different pricks on his heart, but they produced the same pain. The same regret. And then another thought entered his head, tweaking the pain just a little darker. What if he and Caiaphas couldn't find a way to bridge the gap between them?

"Something on your mind, Marcus?"

Marcus focused on Caiaphas, smiling at him, slipping what looked like a phone nonchalantly into his top desk drawer.

"Or are you merely making sure the doorway doesn't collapse?" Caiaphas asked.

Marcus cleared his throat, pulling his attention from the drawer and back to Caiaphas. "I have an update on Venice." Marcus stepped into the room, feeling like a statue learning to walk. "Our latest report shows-" Marcus stopped as Caiaphas held up his hand.

Caiaphas gestured to the chair next to him. "Sit. Tea?" Caiaphas poured Marcus a cup, not waiting for a response. "We need to clear the air, you and I." He smiled at his pun. "Your intentions were well meant," he added milk to the tea, "though misguided." His tone was soft as he kept his eyes focused on his task. "You are young. Younger than I, anyway." He laid a lemon slice across the top of the tea. "Youth mistakes wrinkles, gray hair, and white stubble on the chin for stupidity. Or worse, ignorance." He used a spoon to dunk the lemon and stir the milk. "I chose you as my Marcus. I chose you to be the next Caiaphas." Satisfied he'd prepared the cup to his protégé's liking, he looked up, locking eyes with Marcus. "You will lead the Illuminati at the most exciting time in its history. Your job is not to protect me but to learn from me. At all times. Learn from my wisdom." He handed Marcus the cup of tea. "And from my lack." He smiled. "Understood?"

Marcus felt the urge to defend himself, perhaps even lash out. Ball his fist, smash it into the table and rail, "It is my job to protect you, you stupid old man. To keep you alive to lead us. To teach me." But he didn't punch the table. He didn't scream at him.

How could he make the older man understand? Caiaphas was like a father to him. More than a father. Grandfather. Mentor. Maybe even a deity. He loved and worshiped the man who'd lectured him while preparing tea. Tea, which he realized when he glanced at it, looked exactly as if he'd prepared it himself. He knew it would taste exactly as he liked it. He knew of Caiaphas's love and reverence for tea and the ceremony in its preparation.

At that moment, he understood. Caiaphas had just built that bridge. The gap was closed. Marcus had been forgiven. He nodded and accepted the cup. Setting the cup down on the table, Marcus sat down. He didn't drink from the cup. Instead, he placed his hands in his lap, so Caiaphas couldn't see him digging his nails into his knees, wiping his palms across his lap.

"Your tea's getting cold."

Marcus's hands stopped swiping over his slacks. He balled them into white-knuckled fists for a count of two before relaxing them, reaching up, picking up the cup, and taking a sip. He was right. "Just like I make it."

Caiaphas smiled at the compliment. "Now then. Tell me about Venice."

The tea was delicious. Marcus took another sip before answering. "Our suspicions were correct. The dead rats are because of a vampire," Marcus stated. "I know we originally wanted to use this as a field study resource, but I think we may want to reconsider that." Marcus could not hide his excitement.

"Well then. You'd best get on with it." Caiaphas said, not missing Marcus's uncharacteristic manner. "You have more news."

Marcus nodded like a six-year-old agreeing to ice cream for dinner. "The vampire responsible is Gabriel Hawthorne." A wide grin spread across Marcus's face, knowing what effect the information would have on his mentor. He was not disappointed.

Caiaphas stopped mid-sip and lowered his cup. Leaning back in his chair, he looked to Marcus like a man who couldn't decide if the information he'd been given was important or extraneous. After a long moment of reflection, Caiaphas locked eyes with Marcus.

"We don't know how it happened," Marcus exclaimed in a rush. "We can only speculate. Whether it was intentional, or he was left for dead, or escaped after being attacked. He showed up on our radar after rescuing a local nurse from a sexual assault. He killed the would-be rapists and then befriended the woman, probably because she's a nurse. We believe she is stealing blood from the hospital and giving it to him. I have a team watching him now."

"It would seem you can put the vampire into the man, but you can't take the man out of the vampire." He added after seeing Marcus's bewildered stare. "Always the gentleman when it comes to helping damsels in distress." Caiaphas's smile was not one of triumph but of opportunity. "I see why you were so eager to share this information with me. Mr. Hawthorne could prove to be a very valuable asset."

"Indeed, sir," Marcus replied before sipping his tea. "Do you want us to pick Mr. Hathorne up?"

Caiaphas picked up his cup. "Keep an eye on Mr. Hawthorne. And his damsel. Look for an opportunity to make contact and prepare for an extraction," Caiaphas stated, smiling as he finished his tea. "And now we must discuss the evacuation of this facility."

Marcus froze, his teacup halfway to his mouth.

A smile curled the right side of Caiaphas's mouth. "You had to know and anticipate there'd be repercussions."

32

Venice, Italy

Marco sat on the bench, sipping his coffee, brooding. He'd come to grips with the fact that it was his fault that they'd been given the assignment, although he would never admit that to his partner, Antonio. The inspector was known for his retaliatory tactics, and he'd been caught kissing the inspector's sister. Marco could admit that the number of rats, drained and not eaten, was curious. Then the restaurateur claimed to have seen a human-like monster drinking from the rats. And now this latest report.

He remembered his joke to the inspector about finding the person responsible so that the individual could receive a commendation from the city. He might make another joke now if his mood weren't so sour. But this was ridiculous, and he couldn't keep it in any longer.

"I can't believe you're actually going to waste our time questioning this woman," Marco barked at Antonio. "What in the world does a woman almost getting raped have to do with our dead rats?"

"I read you the report. Oh, let me guess, you couldn't hear me over your chewing. If you were even listening," Antonio barked back. "She claimed that her attackers were killed by someone or something that drank their blood."

"Are you listening to yourself? It's not bad enough that we got stuck on this wild goose chase with the rats, but now you want to go looking for Dracula?"

Antonio ignored Marco's sarcasm. "I know it's a long shot, but maybe they're related. The alleged assault happened in the same area

149

as the rats and the restaurateur, spotting the man outside her establishment. And right now, it's the only other lead we have."

Alessia left the hospital grounds, carrying a backpack.

"Whatever. Let's just get this over with." Marco pounded down the last of his coffee and stepped towards her.

"Alessia Mantalto?" Antonio questioned.

Alessia stopped, pulling the backpack to her chest as if it might protect her from the two men standing before her.

"I'm Detective Frederico, and this is Detective Scalia," Antonio continued, noticing the gesture. He wondered if it'd been defensive or protective. "Do you mind if we ask a few questions?

"About?" Alessia replied, clutching the bag tighter to her breast and looking between the two detectives.

"About the report you filed." Antonio took the lead.

Despite thinking this was a waste of time, Marco assumed the role of observer, listening and watching Alessia for any signs of deception.

"I'm...I'm not sure what else I could add," Alessia replied, unable to keep the quaver out of her voice.

"There's no need to be nervous, Miss Mantalto. We only want to clear a few things up. It may help us with another case." Antonio followed up.

"Oh no." Alessia's grip loosened on the backpack with the knowledge that these men had attacked other women.

"No, it's not about your attackers. It's about the one you claimed to have killed them," Antonio said.

"Claimed. I don't understand." Alessia hitched the backpack back up in front of her.

"The thing is, Miss Mantalto, neither of the assailants' bodies has been found," Antonio replied. "All attempts to locate your rescuer have been futile."

Alessia's entire body tightened with defensive anger. "Are you calling me a liar, Detective?"

Antonio was relieved to see the body language. He'd struck a nerve, just what he was hoping. He shook his head. "Not at all. The scene is consistent with the activity you described. DNA types your blood and two males there."

"Then why do you use the word 'claimed'?"

"Because until I have a confession or a conviction, it's just alleged. Those are the rules. Please understand me, Miss Mantalto. I do believe you. That's why I'm here." Antonio watched confusion replace defensiveness. "You aren't the first person to report seeing a mon-...man drinking blood."

Both detectives could see the nervous tension growing on her face. Her entire body seemed to vibrate with fight or flight.

"I'm sorry, Detective. I reported the crime and made my statement," Alessia said, the quaver back in her voice. "I prefer not to relive what happened to me. I'm trying my best to put it behind me."

So she's decided to fight, Antonio thought. "I understand, Miss Mantalto, we are just trying to—"

"I don't think you do," Alessia cut him off, squaring her shoulders and lifting her chin. "Not unless you've been grabbed from behind, beaten, and raped, you have no idea what I've been through."

"I thought you reported an *attempted* rape," Marco said. "Saved by a man who drank your attacker's blood."

Antonio cursed Marco in his head. She was finally past any pretense, responding with real emotions and truthful statements. In short, she had started talking.

Alessia shot Marco an icy glare. "Two *alleged* men *attempted* to beat and rape me, but were stopped by a third *alleged* man who might or might not have *assumedly* killed them and then *supposedly* drank-...and then perhaps I fled."

Her shoulders weren't quite as square, and her chin not so high, but Antonio knew they were done getting anything useful from Alessia Montalto. "My apologies." Antonio put as much softness in his voice as he could, hoping she remembered the next time he paid a visit. Alone. Grabbing Marco's arm, Antonio led him away. "Sorry to have bothered you."

Alessia marched away in the opposite direction, glancing over her shoulder several times to ensure the two detectives weren't following as she made her way to her apartment. When she was sure they were not, she ducked into a storefront alcove. She was relieved to see the closed sign hanging on the door.

She pressed her back into the wall, feeling the coolness from the stone seep through her clothing into her skin as she took long, deliberate breaths. As the adrenaline left her system, Alessia giggled from the rush of emotions surging through her. Apprehension about the two detectives ambushing her outside her workplace. Annoyance with herself at her initial reaction to the two detectives. Terror, as she remembered that night. If Gabriel hadn't shown up, she definitely would have been raped and maybe even murdered. Rage at the detective who didn't believe her. Amazement at her audacity in standing up to them. Disgusted with herself for telling the police everything that had happened that night. If she hadn't, the two officers wouldn't have visited her tonight. Relief that the secret in her backpack was still undiscovered. She was still clutching it to her chest.

Dropping down to her haunches, she set the backpack in front of her. Unzipping it, she hefted out the thermal cooler and lifted the lid, inspecting the two bags of blood inside.

33

Mississippi River,
Baton Rouge, Louisiana

Cain watched Caiaphas as he stared out towards the muddy water, unsure whether the older man was lost in thought or basking in the beauty of the moonlight as it danced across the river's surface. Maybe both. It was hypnotic, Cain thought. And tranquil. The wind was warm, and as the boat pushed through the rippling water, it created music and mystique. The moment was tailor-made for nostalgia.

He thought back to just hours before, when he was taken from his cell. At first, he thought he was being taken to see Caiaphas, but his escorts hadn't taken him to an interrogation room or an office. Instead, they exited the building and approached a waiting panel van. The back opened, and an arm gestured for him to enter.

The van didn't have any windows for him to see where they were going, but he knew where he was as soon as the vehicle came to a stop. He didn't have to see it. The stench of fish, living and dead, putrefying clams, decaying leaves, and mud, tangy with iron ore and tannic acid, invaded his nostrils like a cheap perfume that burns the skin where applied and causes the eyes to water. They were near a river. Cain guessed the Mississippi, especially once the back doors opened.

He was ushered from the van to a waiting open-sea barge. Once aboard, he was taken to a cabin where Caiaphas sat, in his customary white shirt, dark tie, dark suit.

He smiled as Cain entered, standing and offering his hand. "Thank you for joining me."

As if I had a choice, Cain thought as he accepted his senior's hand. But Cain had been trained from an early age. Always the politician. Always the diplomat. "Thank you for having me," he said, smiling as he shook the man's hand with the same warm affection he'd had with state legislators.

"My apologies," Caiaphas offered as he gestured to the sofa across from him. "But we need to move to a new compound."

Cain had taken a seat.

Caiaphas sat. "I wanted you to accompany me on this part of the voyage."

"This part?"

"Down the Mississippi."

"Any particular reason?" Cain asked, intrigued.

But Caiaphas wasn't listening. His attention had drifted back out over the water.

Okay, Cain thought. I guess I'll play along for now. So while Caiaphas sat lost in his thoughts, Cain searched his memories for an instance when Roman summoned him for no other reason than spending time with him. There wasn't one. He could remember inserting himself into Roman's affairs with that intention. He could remember lots of those.

Cain snorted with disdain directed at Roman and disgust directed at himself. In the short time he'd known Caiaphas, the man had provided Cain with more examples of what a father should be than Roman had in decades. Roman hadn't sired him, hadn't raised him. He'd left that to Isabella and others. He'd suffered those intrusions into his affairs by Cain for pretense. And when Roman no longer saw a use for the pawn, the tool he'd formed him to be, he'd discarded him.

Caiaphas interrupted Cain's brooding.

"I've always loved the water." Caiaphas's gaze remained somewhere beyond the water. "My mother loved the beach." A sudden smile lit his face. "But my father and I loved any water we could fish on." Caiaphas's eyes left the water and fell on Cain. "Did you fish as a boy?"

Cain shook his head, acknowledging yet another example of Roman's lack. It didn't cause pain, he realized. It was just a fact. Cain could now see with a certain amount of detachment that Roman hadn't wanted a son, but a tool. Everything Roman did as a father was only a sham designed to manipulate Cain.

"Never had much time for things like that," Cain replied. "Every step in my life was designed to further my political path. The only times I went fishing were deep-sea charters, and those were for networking. They weren't for fun or the thrill of the catch."

The corners of Caiaphas's smile sagged with the weight of sympathy he felt for Cain. His heart always panged when he met an individual robbed of the opportunity to have a normal childhood, but Cain's entire life had been stripped away from him. He'd truly been nothing more than a piece on a chessboard, an inanimate object. Yet he thinks of himself as a monster. But even monsters have a reason for what they do. Roman was proof of that.

Caiaphas winced as he struggled to stand, losing his balance.

Cain shot across the cabin to catch Caiaphas, his speed startling them both as he took Caiaphas by the arm.

"I feel like a character in one of those Marvel comics discovering his superpowers," Cain scoffed as he righted the older man. "I don't think I'll ever get used to this."

Caiaphas patted Cain's arm. "I'm just glad you're on our side."

The examples keep coming.

Cain decided to change the subject. "So, where are we headed?"

"You and I?" Caiaphas gestured to a table holding a tea service. "This barge?" Caiaphas sat down and began preparing two cups of tea. He said nothing until he finished. He offered Cain a cup and asked, "Have you ever been to Texas?"

"Does Longhorn Steakhouse count?" Cain grinned.

Caiaphas smiled as he tried to get comfortable in his chair.

"Have you considered trying vampire blood?" Cain asked.

Caiaphas rolled his eyes, but not with exasperation at the question. "We went down that rabbit hole years ago. We'd been working with vampire blood on different cancers long before I became Caiaphas. Unfortunately, there was no way to isolate just the cancer cells. Vampire blood attacks everything living it comes in contact with," Caiaphas explained. "Healthy cells, cancer cells, sickle cells, even cells infected with H.I.V. all end in the same result – Vampire."

"What about my blood? Perhaps it's different," Cain replied.

"We didn't just draw your blood for fun," Caiaphas said with a grin. "And you're right, it's different, like nothing we've ever seen."

"What do you mean?"

"Your blood is unique to you. It has zero interaction with any cell it comes into contact with. It's like oil with water. It neither absorbs nor is absorbed." He sipped his tea. "It's not changed by extreme heat, cold, oxygen, or any other chemical element, for that matter. We know. We tried." Chuckling, he added, "To use your Marvel character analogy, you are a Superman."

"Superman is a D.C. character."

Caiaphas shrugged. He wanted to make a joke, but saw the pain and desperation on Cain's face. He was touched. Cain genuinely cared about his well-being. "It's all right, son." He placed a comforting hand on Cain's forearm. "It really is."

Cain looked away as his vision blurred, wanting to swipe away the sting of saline in his eyes as if it were responsible for Caiaphas's condition. It wasn't fair. None of it. This was a good man. This was a man worth following. A man who'd lived a life worth emulating. A man who would've made an excellent father. He looked at this man and realized he wished he'd been his father instead of the monster he'd had.

Caiaphas understood. He may not have been a father, but he'd been a father figure to enough young men and women in his lifetime to recognize what was going on in Cain. He decided to offer a distraction. "In answer to the question you're bound to ask." He waited for Cain's pain to turn to puzzlement and asked, "So where in Texas are we headed?"

Cain's laughter burst from him with surprise, not humor.

Caiaphas smiled, thinking there was something apropos in his answer, considering all this talk of death and vampires. "Corpus Christi."

34

Illuminati Compound, Baton Rouge, Louisiana

Ezekiel looked across the room at the others standing there, waiting for his orders. He made sure to make eye contact with each man and woman. They were more than just fellow members of the Illuminati. More than just comrades in the cause. They were family. His family. He couldn't have been prouder if they'd been his blood children.

Sparks shot from the server racks that held data the Illuminati had collected for centuries. The data was stored on the cloud and backed up to several locations around the globe. But Ezekiel knew data left images. Any half-decent techie could lift those images and learn everything the Illuminati knew about them. He didn't want the vampires to have any clue, so he'd ordered the self-destruct sequence to be engaged as soon as the compound fell under attack.

The early warning alarms had sounded fifteen minutes ago.

"We all knew this day might come," Ezekiel began, feeling his chest swell with pride. "I'm reminded of what Pericles said when the Spartans invaded Athens. It's as true of us today as it was for the Athenians nearly three thousand years ago." He smiled. "I'll paraphrase. When our forefathers stood against the vampires, they had no such resources as we have now. Indeed, they abandoned even what they had, and then it was by wisdom rather than good fortune, by daring rather than by material power, that they drove back the foreign invasion and fashioned our world to what it is today. What it will be tomorrow," He added. "We must live up to the standard they set. We must resist our enemies in any and every way. And try to leave those who come after us a world that is as great as ever."

The Imminent Threat alert screamed.

"It's been an honor to know all of you," Ezekiel yelled over the high-pitched warning.

"The honor is ours, sir," Carmen replied.

The rest of the gathered soldiers echoed with a combined 'Hua!'

Ezekiel could see it all on their faces. If there'd been time, he would have hugged each one. As it was, a line from his favorite Billy Joel song, *Goodnight Saigon,* played in his mind's ear.

And we would all go down together. We said we would all go down together.

And they would. Today.

Caiaphas, Marcus, and the others had already been moved with arms and equipment to another location. When Ezekiel had taken over special operations after Rotty's death at the governor's mansion, he knew it was only a matter of time before there was reciprocity. It's what he would have done, and the enemy was no different. Staying put was not prudent. But changing locations would not be enough. The vampires knew to expect a fight. They'd be suspicious if they rolled up on the command post they knew housed Caiaphas, the Illuminati's supreme commander, and found the compound desolate.

So he'd convinced Caiaphas to relocate to the new headquarters ahead of schedule. Not one to shrink from the fight or lead from the rear, Ezekiel volunteered to stay behind and continue to operate this compound business as usual. All the soldiers in front of him, Carmen included, volunteered to stay and fight without hesitation or request.

"Not the most flattering thing I've worn," Carmen said with a chuckle as she donned a vest rigged with Phase Two explosives. Ezekiel grinned as he did the same.

"Well, boys and girls. Let's roll out the welcome wagon for these bloodsuckers." Ezekiel announced.

"Hua!" Carmen and the others exclaimed.

35

Venice, Italy

"Keep an eye out. I'm going to check in," Carlos said to the man sitting in the driver's seat of the cargo van. Carlos passed through the privacy curtain to the back of the vehicle. There, he sat at a console with several monitors and other surveillance equipment. Carlos picked up a headset with a microphone and placed the call.

Carlos heard his call picked up after the fifth ring. There was no greeting.

"This is Raven One-Four-Seven-Three," Carlos announced. "Bottom of the fifth."

"Passcode?" A voice requested.

"India-Hotel-Victor-Five-Two-Eight-Nine."

"Hold," The voice replied.

Carlos heard the line ring once, and the call was answered.

"Yes," Marcus said.

"The target has been stationary for forty-eight hours," Carlos reported. "Confirm the secondary target following routine. We don't have eyes and ears inside yet. Should we put a tail on the secondary?" Carlos asked.

"Negative," Marcus answered. "Keep eyes on the target. Prepare for an extraction. I'll let you know once a decision has been made. Any indication our *friends* have noticed you?"

"None."

"Good. Let's hope it stays that way. Report to me immediately of any changes."

"Yes, sir. Raven One-Four-Seven-Three out." Carlos ended the call.

36

Venice, Italy

Antonio approached the door to the Grasso residence. The Grassos had called the station, reporting they had seen a homeless man in the park they passed on their evening constitutional. He was acting strangely, as if he were going through withdrawal. He was arguing with himself or with someone only he saw. But what caught their attention and why they decided to call was that his clothes, face, and hands appeared to be stained with blood.

An officer had gone to the park to investigate that night. When he arrived, the park was empty of patrons. The officer walked the area but found no sign of the bloodstained homeless man. He concluded that because of the couple's age and the time of day, they had probably seen a homeless man, but he wasn't bloodstained. He did, however, issue a Be on the Lookout, just in case. The officer understood that a homeless man, bloodstained or not, muttering to himself in public spaces would not help tourism.

Marco had seen the BOLO and dismissed it, not bothering to tell Antonio. He'd only heard about it after two young officers asked him if the homeless man might be the same one the restaurateur had seen behind her establishment. The policia were just as capable of gossip as the public they protected. Antonio was incredulous when he learned of Marco's discount of the report. Marco was just as dismissive when Antonio confronted him.

"Two geezers out for a walk saw a homeless man and mistook the dirt and grime on him for blood. So what? They didn't see him eating rats or drinking anyone's blood." Marco munched on an apple without concern.

Antonio had argued that although the Grassos said nothing about rats, the park where they'd seen the man was near where dead rats had been discovered. The park was not far from where Alessia Montalto had been assaulted. They reported seeing the man just after twilight. Both Ms. Montalto and Ms. Rossi had reported seeing the man after dark. And wouldn't it have been nice when they were speaking with Ms. Montalto to have brought up the man to see her reaction? Confirm if this might be the same man who rescued her and killed her assailants?

Marco had only rolled his eyes and chewed his apple, reminding Antonio of a mindless cow chewing its cud.

So Antonio decided to interview the Grassos alone, not even telling Marco what he was doing.

"May I help you?" Mr. Grasso asked as he opened the door.

"Signore Grasso. I'm Detective Frederico," Antonio introduced himself, smelling the enticing fragrance of chicken pastina soup as it wafted out the door. "I wanted to ask you and your wife a few questions about the man the two of you saw in the park. Could I come in for just a minute?"

"I already told the other detectives everything I know," Mr. Grasso said with a puzzled look.

"Other detectives?" Antonio asked.

Mr. Grasso nodded. "They came by yesterday."

"What did they look like?"

"Like you."

"Like me?"

Mr. Grasso nodded. "Si. Short hair. Clean-shaven. Suits."

"Did they show you any credentials? Tell you which department they were with?"

Mr. Grasso nodded again. "I don't remember the department. I assume yours."

"How long did they stay?"

"Not long. My wife is ill. They asked their questions and left."

Antonio thought that would explain the chicken pastina soup as his stomach growled. "Did they leave a card?"

Mr. Grasso shook his head. "Should they have?"

"No, but we usually do. In case you think of anything else, you can reach us." So, Antonio thought, two detectives or two people calling themselves detectives interviewed my witnesses yesterday. Why? If they were cops, then what station and department were they with? Why haven't they reached out to him and Marco? Does this mean other areas outside our jurisdiction have the same sightings? The same rat issue? If they're not cops, how would they know about the witnesses? Why would they be pretending to be cops?

Antonio asked, "Could you describe the detectives?"

"I already did. They looked—"

"Like me," Antonio interrupted. "I know. I mean. Could you describe their height and weight? Any distinguishing characteristics?"

Mr. Grasso stared at Antonio, mystified. "Like what?"

Antonio felt his irritation rising at the older gentleman. A week ago, this old man spotted a man in the park just after twilight and volunteered information about his clothing. His demeanor. Can even distinguish between grime and blood. Now he's asked about two strangers he's invited into his home, and it's like he's never seen a crime show on TV.

"Hair color. Eye color," Antonio responded, trying to keep his voice even. "Did one or both of them have a beard? Glasses? Tattoos? Scars?" Antonio couldn't help but wonder if this guy was somehow related to his partner. Or maybe this guy was what Marco would be like at this age? He was professional enough to hope the man would not pick up on his frustration. He didn't want his defenses up. But Antonio had to recognize the man was just that clueless.

Mr. Grasso thought for a moment before shrugging again. "No. Like I said, they looked like you." Looking over his shoulder, he said, "If you don't mind, my wife isn't feeling well, and I'm making her some soup, so if there isn't anything else?"

"Did they at least tell you their names?" Antonio asked. "Can you at least remember their names?"

"I can't remember."

"Could I speak with your wife then, Mr. Grasso? I'll only be a minute," Antonio tried to assure the man. "Maybe she remembers."

Mr. Grasso shook his head so intensely that he looked like a bobblehead toy. "Out of the question. She's ill. "I'm sorry, but I really need to get back to the kitchen," Mr. Grasso said as he closed the door.

Antonio stood seething at the door for a long time. He wanted to knock. Pound on it. He wanted to throttle the man. Question his wife. Find Alessia Montalto's assailants and beat the life out of them. Locate her rescuer and perhaps toss him around the room for good measure. He wanted to drown Marco in Mr. Grasso's chicken pastina soup. But more than any of that, he wanted the truth.

37

Illuminati Compound,
Caja del Rio Plateau, New Mexico

Cain looked up from the book in his hand. It was *War and Peace* by Leo Tolstoy. He'd read it when he was younger. Required reading, but not by any of his schools. His father had insisted he read it in the original Russian. Cain had not been a fan. When he selected the novel this morning, it was not because he wanted to see if perhaps time and life experience had changed his appreciation of the work, but because of its length. With over twelve hundred pages, the average reader will spend thirty-eight hours reading the tome. Cain finished the novel in just under ninety minutes. Read it. Understood it. Comprehended it. And yes, he had a new appreciation of it.

He'd been marveling over the masterpiece when he heard footsteps approaching the door to his new lodgings. The space included a bathroom, bedroom, and separate sitting area with a small library. The quarters looked more like a high-end hotel suite, minus windows and treatments, and less like a jail cell. But Cain knew it was still a cell. He also knew who was approaching his door.

"Come in, Caiaphas," Cain called before the man had raised his knuckles to knock.

Cain had hoped Caiaphas would find his ability to know who was on the other side of the door without any announcement unnerving, or at least annoying. But Caiaphas entered with an astute smile.

You are one wily old man.

Observing Cain seated with *War and Peace* in his lap, Caiaphas said, "I see you're settling in."

Cain looked around the room. "Well. It ain't no Motel Six, but at least it isn't that prefab concrete cell I was in." Cain gestured to the chair next to his. "At least now, I don't *feel* like a monkey in a cage."

Caiaphas ignored Cain's sarcasm. "I wanted to bring you up to speed." Caiaphas sat.

Setting the book on the end table, Cain leaned forward, facing Caiaphas. He studied the man's face, looking for any tics. He listened to his robust, steady heartbeat as he inhaled his scent: a blend of shaving cream, soap, a faint, disturbing tang of nail polish remover, and calm.

If the man were more transparent, he'd be a ghost, Cain thought. But before...whatever this was, his transformation, his illumination of his father and this organization, he'd been a politician. Cain knew that wherever people organized, there were politics. The best at the game, who ascended to leadership, appeared to be the most open while guarding the most secrets. The wizards of Oz, convincing people to ignore the men and women behind the curtain. He'd been no different, and before all this, he now realized, he'd convinced himself to ignore the vampire behind his curtain.

Still, Caiaphas did seem different. Or at least, Cain wanted to believe he was different. He thought maybe needling the older man might help decide if that belief was well-placed. "Like how I was on a boat having a conversation with you and then woke up at the Hilton?" Cain thought back. "Was it in the tea?"

Caiaphas sighed, but not with exasperation or frustration. It was regret. "I apologize for our rudeness, but it seemed the most...prudent decision at that moment. We needed to get out of Baton Rouge as stealthily and unobtrusively as possible. But once we reached Corpus Christi, we needed to move and move quickly."

Cain thought that might be the case. The air smelled and felt different in his nostrils and lungs. Drier. Warmer. It's what woke him. His circadian rhythm and those of the two guards outside his door seemed off. His body had felt...polluted. Like some toxin flowed through his veins. The guards, however, were exhibiting telltale signs. Their heart rates were slightly elevated and increased at the slightest activity. They took turns walking, returning with coffee for each other. The coffee had a wonderful nutty aroma that he was not familiar with. No, that wasn't true. He'd had it once when he'd attended a governors' conference in Albuquerque, New Mexico. What was it called? Oh yes, he remembered: Piñon coffee.

"So you knocked me out and moved me like a piece of furniture. How'd I go? By Mayflower Movers?"

Caiaphas could see what made Cain such a great governor. Such a great leader. Adaptability. Self-awareness. Empathy. Courage. These were just a few characteristics Cain was naturally endowed with before Roman's blood enhanced them. Cain would've made an excellent Caiaphas. That was probably something Roman had never intended or even thought about.

And he was charming and funny. Caiaphas laughed at the joke and then made one of his own. He shook his head and answered, "PODS."

Cain was not expecting Caiaphas to have a sense of humor. He burst out laughing. It felt good to laugh. He couldn't remember the last time he'd laughed. It had to have been before the attack on his mansion in Miami. Before Gabriel Hawthorne had scared the living daylights out of Claudia.

Claudia.

The memory of her jammed the laugh hard in Cain's throat. Hot tears burned his eyes as the pit of his stomach turned to ice.

Caiaphas seemed to understand and offered a distraction by way of an explanation. "We're a clandestine organization, the stuff conspiracy theory novels and films are made of. Fighting an enemy the world believes is a Hollywood nightmare. And you're Cain Dvanaesti, the once and future king of America, who just happens to have recently been on the cover of every newspaper, tabloid, and news program the world over, thanks to your dramatic," Caiaphas made air quotes with his fingers, "death in a plane crash somewhere over the Atlantic after your mansion burned down. It's not like we could just put a pair of coveralls on you and sit you beside a driver as we drove from Corpus Christi, Texas, to Chihuahua, Mexico, to...well. Back into the United States." Caiaphas didn't give Cain a moment to process what he'd said. He continued. "We've been making incredible strides in our weaponry. You had the unfortunate opportunity of experiencing one of our latest breakthroughs."

Cain grimaced at the memory of being gassed in the small prefab concrete cell.

Caiaphas acknowledged the memory with a nod before continuing. "To be honest, we had the unfortunate opportunity of experiencing your potential that day. It was," he didn't try to hide his shiver, "terrifying." He paused a moment in that memory. "These advancements have been, to use the common euphemism, a game-changer. They've allowed us to take the fight to them. And we have. The results have been," he didn't bother to hide his smile, "dynamic."

An interesting choice of words, Cain thought. It suggested the results hadn't just been better than expected, they'd been staggeringly better than anyone could've hoped. And not only that, but they're improving. "The Illuminati has been capitalizing on its success," Cain said.

Caiaphas's nod of agreement was deep. "And that's not gone unnoticed. Consequently, the vampires have been exacting a certain level of reciprocity."

"Certain level?"

"Your father has been...*selective* with his choices of targets."

Cain didn't miss that Caiaphas continued to refer to Roman Dvanaesti as his father. Cain wasn't sure how he felt about that. Had

Roman ever treated him like a son? Roman hadn't contributed to his conception. He hadn't been in love with Cain's mother. She was just an unmarried pregnant woman who crossed Roman Dvanaesti's path at the right time for him, the wrong time for her. She'd just been a pawn, like he'd become.

But let's say he was my biological father, Cain hypothesized. Roman had given his son the equivalent of a performance-enhancing drug from the day Cain was born until the day he tried to murder him. From the day he was born till the day he attempted to murder Cain, Roman had lied, manipulated, controlled, and coerced him. He'd most likely murdered my mother. Definitely murdered my fiancé. Where's Jerry Springer or Dr. Phil? I want to nominate Roman Dvanaesti for Father of the Year.

Instead, Cain asked, "How could Roman be selective?" Then, he had a thought. "Unless he knows all of your locations."

Caiaphas confirmed Cain's thought. "When we first pulled you from the ocean, we brought you to our U.S. headquarters in Baton Rouge. We knew, of course, there would be retaliation. We didn't know when or to what extent. Fortunately, Roman has not been subtle. Also, fortunately, we are aware of your father's knowledge of our locations around the world, and we've taken certain...precautions."

"Precautions?"

"All of our head compounds have an alternate location." Caiaphas gestured expansively, taking in more than Cain's quarters. "We've moved to our alternate in New Mexico. Our compound in Baton Rouge has been destroyed. As a result, we moved vital personnel before the attack," Caiaphas exclaimed.

"Vital personnel. You left people behind before the attack?' Cain said with a puzzled look on his face.

"No one was left behind. They volunteered. They knew if we evacuated the entire compound, then the vampires would realize we knew they were coming," Caiaphas replied.

"I don't understand. How could someone volunteer to wait around to be slaughtered?" Cain said, still confused by the thought.

"We've all had to make sacrifices in this war, Cain. And make no mistake. We are at war," Caiaphas said.

The two men stared hard at each other for a long moment.

Finally, Cain broke the silence. "So why did you save me? Why did you bring me with you? Why didn't you just leave me for Roman to kill or reclaim?"

For the first time since Cain had met the man, Caiaphas looked at a loss. Then, surprise crossed the older man's face. He looked at Cain, somehow older. More frail than even a moment before.

Caiaphas was at a loss. It was the first time in decades that he could remember not having a response. Certainly not since rising to Caiaphas, perhaps even to Marcus, had he not anticipated and planned not only his actions and words, but had multiple backup plans and strategies. Each revealed a version of the truth, but not the whole truth.

But he found, as he spent time with Cain, a desire to be completely and wholly truthful. So when Cain asked, *Why did you save me*, Caiaphas wanted to respond with, *Isn't it obvious? I wanted to take something away from Roman Dvanaesti. I wanted to turn his prized possession against him. I want you to fight with us and end vampires for all time. I want you to assassinate Roman Dvanaesti.*

These were all true, no skewed or edited versions. But no war was ever won with such bluntness. There was always deception. Distraction. A desire to reveal only what was truly needed to know, even among allies. Neither Roosevelt nor Churchill divulged all their secrets to one another while they were allies against Hitler and the Nazis.

So, time for a distraction. Caiaphas rose and gestured toward the door. "Walk with me."

38

Venice, Italy

Alessia quickly stepped inside her apartment, shut the door, and twisted the deadbolt, noticing the trembling in her fingers. She could feel her heart pounding in her chest. Hear her blood thrumming in her ears. Maybe it'd just been the surprise of the two detectives ambushing her outside of the hospital, but her paranoia had been rising since leaving them. She hadn't been able to shake the feeling she was being followed. Being watched. Willing herself to calm down, she turned.

"Aaaggghhh!"

Gabriel sat in the armchair in the corner of the room, watching her, still as a statue. Or a corpse.

"I'm sorry," Gabriel said, standing. "I didn't mean to startle you."

Alessia didn't see Gabriel stand or move toward her. One moment, he was seated; next, he had his hands on her elbows to steady her. She didn't think she would ever get accustomed to his blood-drinking, but she hoped one day she would take for granted the speed at which he moved. Like a professional or Olympic athlete, whose physicality she might marvel at but not freak out about.

Nor did she think she'd get used to his vibrant eyes. They were mesmerizing, causing her heart to skip a beat before racing like a thoroughbred for the finish line in the Kentucky Derby. She forced her gaze to look to the ground, focusing on the dichotomy that was this man. Gabriel was dark and dangerous yet kind and innocent. Like a wolf in sheep's clothing. Or an infant in an adult body. Maybe that last description was the most accurate. He looked like a man. He had a man's voice. But that's where the similarity ended. He didn't understand his strength, the speed of his movement, his insatiable thirst for blood.

"It's not your fault," Alessia finally said, wanting to save his feelings, though not sure why. "I'm just used to living alone, you know. Just me and Luca." She made her way to the kitchen. Placing the backpack on the counter, she opened it and then removed the cooler containing the blood bags. She dropped two bags in the fridge and took the other back into the room where Gabriel was still standing, stopping abruptly as Gabriel's eyes fell on the bag. His nostrils flared. His eyes widened as his pupils constricted with a laser focus on the blood inside. She heard his breath hitch in his throat. No, this reaction was something she would never become accustomed to, and she fought the urge to drop the bag and the glass and bolt for the door.

Gabriel smelled her fear like a bottle of Chanel sprayed in his face. It was almost as intoxicating as the metallic tang of the blood in the pouch in her hand. That pouch looked as good to him as a bottle of cheap hooch must look to a wino, he realized. He'd probably looked like a teenager seeing his first Playboy magazine. Or a meth head gazing at his next score. He'd scared her. He could hear her heart pounding a staccato drum beat from Bose speakers. He needed to distract her. Make her feel at ease.

Pointing at the glass, he jibed, "No thanks. I'll just drink it straight from the bottle."

It did not produce the desired effect.

"I know this has to be hard on you," Gabriel said. He decided to try a different tack. "Why are you helping me?"

"I've dedicated my life to helping others and saving lives. What kind of person would I be if I didn't help someone who had saved mine?" Alessia responded, feeling slightly more relaxed. "I'm not going to lie," she continued as she handed him the blood bag, "trying to wrap my head around this whole vampire thing is really screwing with me. I want to believe this is some kind of virus or infection, some disease that can be treated or cured." She shook her head and set the glass down on the coffee table. "I just don't know. This is all so insane."

Gabriel could hear the frustration and fear in her voice. "You know you have nothing to fear from me, don't you? I would never hurt you."

"It's not you I'm worried about," Alessia replied.

"What is it then?"

Alessia related her run-in with the two detectives, how they'd waylaid her as she left the hospital grounds, and how they seemed more interested in her rescuer than her or her assailants. They seemed to know she was not telling them everything about Gabriel.

"What did you tell them?" Gabriel asked, his investigative instincts kicking into overdrive.

"Nothing. I told them I'd already given a statement and had nothing else to add. I had no desire to relive that night." Alessia felt swelling pride in herself when thinking about it.

"Did they seem satisfied with that response?"

Alessia shrugged. "Not really. But..."

Her voice trailed off as Gabriel heard her heart rate rise. "It's okay. You didn't do anything wrong," Gabriel soothed. He thought of moving to her, embracing her, stroking her hair like he might a child's. But he didn't move. He wasn't sure the gesture would be appreciated.

Moving to the window, she glanced furtively through the blinds to the street below. "My imagination may be getting the best of me, but I felt like I was being followed. After I was sure the detectives weren't behind me, I had a moment when I felt I was alone. And then...all the way home, I felt like someone was keeping pace with me."

"Keeping pace?" Gabriel asked.

Alessia nodded. "Like someone was following me, watching me, but not wanting to stop me. I never saw anyone, but I couldn't shake the feeling. I even took a couple of immediate turns and doubled back to see."

Gabriel smirked.

"What? I watch TV," Alessia said matter-of-factly, placing her fists on her hips like a

petulant child.

A bark of laughter erupted from Gabriel at the sight and sound of the woman before him. He couldn't remember the last time he had laughed.

Alessia smiled. The importance of the moment didn't go unnoticed by her. She started laughing. Until her gaze fell on the blood bag. The laughter died, and the smile faded. "I've gotta get out of these scrubs," she blurted out as she hurried from the room.

Gabriel looked down at the bag, his laughter now a distant memory. He moved to the kitchen, popped the bag into the microwave, and set it for thirty seconds. As the blood warmed, the microwave's vent blew the coppery odor into his nostrils. He felt his body react, reminding him of when he was a child smelling brownies baking in the oven. The microwave chimed its completion, sounding to Gabriel like a cowbell calling cowboys from the range and to the wagon for dinner. He didn't remember opening the microwave and removing the steaming bag. He didn't remember sinking his fangs through the plastic. He only knew the sublime exaltation as the warm fluid rushed over his tongue and down his throat.

As the blood coursed through his body, images of faces and familiar places flashed through Gabriel's mind. It was nothing he could put together, but he knew that these weren't his imagination; they were memories.

39

Roman Dvanaesti's Estate, Italy

Jacquelyn guided the ibis-white Audi R8 Spyder around the fountain in front of Roman's villa and to a stop in front of the left staircase, loving the sound of the crunch of gravel under the tires. She could have accepted her father's offer to have his car and driver meet her at the airport, but she hadn't. She could've taken an Uber, but she didn't. Instead, she'd rented the convertible sports car and driven herself. After all, it was a beautiful day. And this was Italy.

She gave the pedal four quick presses, knowing her father would hear the engine's roar no matter where he was on the grounds. A smile had split her face wide open when she'd first listened to the engine's purring in the rental parking lot and had not left her face since. Not even now, as she cut the engine and sat in the silence that enveloped her as sweetly as the Italian sun and countryside, the car would cost her a little over a thousand euros a day.

Worth every centesimo.

The ninety-minute drive from the airport to Roman's villa had done wonders for her psyche, taking her out of the tedium of her father's plans and into the present. She wasn't thinking about anything. Her mind was clear. Her spirit was high. No present. No future. Carpe Diem was the Latin term everyone liked to quote. Seize the day. But she preferred the Italian saying, vivi per il momento. Live for the moment. Another phrase drifted into her brain like the breeze—Vivi per adesso.

Live for now.

Jacquelyn knew that, like the breeze causing her hair to dance on her forehead, that last thought was not her own. It was his. That was the other thing she loved about that drive. No one was in her head, either. Not her. Not him.

Concentrating, she blocked her thoughts. Once she felt her mind was in a tightly sealed box, she exited the Audi. As she grabbed her bags, her eyes fell on the fountain. Though she'd seen it many times, it always unnerved her. Jesus Christ. Standing over nine feet tall. Water flowed from his hands, feet, and a hole in his side. The water never stopped. Roman had seen to that. Twenty-four Seven, Three Sixty-Five. For centuries.

She'd never understood Roman's obsession. He never spoke of it, but Isabella had shared what it meant to him. And why. Still, Jacquelyn couldn't help but wonder if Roman ever crossed His mind.

Control your thoughts.

Jacquelyn climbed the steps and opened the front door.

"Welcome, Mistress Jacquelyn," Mia, one of the servants, called out in genuine warmth.

"Ciao, Mia," Jacquelyn replied in kind, setting her bags down.

After exchanging light kisses on each other's cheeks, Mia said, "Master Roman is attending to Mistress Isabella in the east wing. Should I announce your arrival?"

Jacquelyn shook her head as she looked in that direction. "No. That won't be necessary. He already knows I'm here."

Mia smiled as she picked up Jacquelyn's luggage. "Of course, Mistress. I'll take your bags to your room."

"Grazie Mia," Jacquelyn said as she headed down the corridor towards the east wing.

"Greetings, daughter," Roman said without even turning to look at Jacquelyn as she entered the room. "Come and see your mother."

"How is she? Really?" Jacquelyn questioned.

"She is healing quite well. It won't be long before she is fully recovered," Roman responded. "How are things going with your new position?"

Jacquelyn rolled her eyes before turning to face him with a forced smile.

Control your thoughts.

"Everything's going according to plan," Jacquelyn replied. "I exploited a recent tragedy in Mr. Darby's life that should prove useful in expediting things." She struggled to muddle her thoughts. Like the one she had now. He wouldn't ask a question he didn't already know the answer to. She knew that most conversations with Roman were rhetorical.

She knew that he had eyes and ears everywhere and that little took place that he wasn't aware of. However, she prided herself on the fact that over the years, from time to time, she could still surprise him.

"You get that from your mother," Roman said.

"Get what?" She stomped her foot and shrieked in frustration as if she were three years old. "Would you stay out of my head and just have a normal conversation with me for once?"

"Normal," Roman repeated, rolling the word over his tongue with amusement. "This is *normal* for us, daughter. Would you have us pretend that we are nothing more than livestock?" Roman asked.

"I suppose not, Father," Jacquelyn replied. Then she laid eyes on Isabella. "Mamma." And no other thoughts entered her mind except her mother's well-being.

40

Venice, Italy

Gabriel lay on the couch, eyes open, hands folded over the waistband of his jeans. Anyone looking at him would think he'd been laid out in the perfect coffin pose. They might even believe he was dead if they noticed his chest was still.

But Gabriel wasn't dead. And he wasn't sleeping, though that was as good an explanation for Gabriel. Sleep was the only thing he could compare with what was happening. Had been happening. Even when he wasn't in his right mind, not much more than a mindless beast, he understood that the sun was not a good thing. Not like he would burn if he were caught in its light. But he felt drained. Weak. Bleary, like he'd been drinking. Not drunk, but tipsy. It wasn't a pleasant feeling.

At night, he was aware. Alert. His hearing and eyesight were straight out of a James Bond flick, only he didn't have to wear a gadget and flip a switch. His eyes worked better than any night vision goggles the public or military could purchase. He saw every detail, whether at a distance or up close, focusing automatically without even thinking about it. It just was. He'd learned what entered his eyes wasn't exactly colors, but only the color green. His eyes, though, could see more wavelengths of green than he thought existed. His brain added the colors. He'd learned he could adjust the colors just from concentration. In complete darkness, he could still see. His brain translated his hearing and echolocation into an image.

In daylight...it was like when you've been in a dark room for a couple of hours and someone flips on the light switch. Only, it wasn't some lamp or bulb in a light fixture. It was stadium lighting five feet in front of your face. His eyes never adjusted. No ballcap or expensive dark glasses provided any relief. He also knew his body required rest. It wasn't sleep, exactly. He didn't close his eyes, but he didn't see anything, either.

Well, that wasn't true. He saw color moving through the blackness like mist dancing on a gentle breeze. The first few nights, the color was crimson. Watching the color dance eased the sting in his thirst, numbed his frenetic mind, and soothed the growl in his gut. Once he began feeding on rats, the color slowly changed to aqua. Now that he fed regularly on human blood, the color had changed again to a soft amber hue.

Gabriel was also piecing together his past from the flashes he would receive every time he fed. He couldn't remember the names of the faces or the locations he was seeing, but he knew his memory was slowly coming back to him.

Just moments before the sun would rise, he'd feel a tugging in his core to prepare for this state of rest. He didn't need to lie down. He could enter it sitting or standing. But since sleep was what he was accustomed to, he would generally lie down. He didn't close his eyes, but the blackness would come, enveloping his sight. And then the color. His body would feel heavy, like when the technician lays a lead blanket over your body when taking an X-ray. His other senses still worked, watching over him. His brain processed what he heard, smelled, and felt, and only alerted him to leave this state if it decided that sound, odor or feeling to be dangerous. Real danger. Rats crawling across his face in the sewer didn't qualify. In this state, he was just another piece of concrete or metal. Nothing that smelled or tasted like a food source for them. When he wasn't, the rats fled. They understood they were prey.

He would stay in this state, his body keenly aware of the sun's progress through the heavens. As the sun set, Gabriel could feel the lead blanket slowly lifting from his body. The color would continue to dance, but it would slowly evaporate like mist on still water in the early morning. Then the blackness would fade into white noise, and finally his vision would return.

At that moment, the blanket was lifting, but he could still feel it. The color still danced. The blackness still enveloped him.

Click.

The blanket was ripped away, and the color and blackness evaporated like a light switch. Gabriel sprang to his feet in a blur, glancing at the clock on the wall.

8:13.

Alessia wasn't due home for hours. Closing his eyes, Gabriel relied on his senses to identify the danger. He heard two distinct heartbeats thundering on the other side of the front door. He expelled every last atom of air from his lungs and inhaled a slow, deliberate breath through his nostrils, smelling their blood. Neither was Alessia.

Gabriel turned and ran for the window that led to the fire escape. Except there was no fire escape. "What the—?" Gabriel gazed out the window and saw only the building across the alley. He'd just assumed that by the age of the structure, it'd have an exterior staircase like an old building in America. He realized he'd never checked to see if that assumption was accurate.

He heard the handle on the door turning behind him as he opened the window. Looking back, he saw two men entering the flat in black tactical gear, their faces hidden by balaclavas. They carried sidearms, not assault rifles, and moved with speed, precision, and efficiency. Cain didn't know who they were or who they were with, but he did know one thing.

These are not my friends.

One man moved to the right as he scanned the perimeter. The other moved to the left. Gabriel didn't move as his eyes tracked the men's movements. The men stopped as they both caught sight of

Gabriel at the window. The one on the left tossed what looked to Gabriel like a small hockey puck across the floor towards him. It hissed, and gas billowed from it as it rolled.

Gabriel didn't wait but turned and jumped through the window, dropping three stories to the concrete alleyway. As a teenager, he'd jumped off the roof of his house on a dare. The house he'd grown up in was a one-story ranch, and he'd landed in grass softened by a day-long rainstorm. Still, his feet and ankles had stung, and his knees had buckled. He'd just jumped over thirty feet, landed onto concrete, and had only felt a soft thud as if he'd hopped off a kitchen counter. Glancing up to the window he'd just leaped from, he stared in disbelief.

There's got to be a vampire user manual I can get.

One of the men's heads popped out of the window.

In a blur, Gabriel turned towards the alley entrance and stopped. Standing in the middle of the alley, hands tucked into the pockets of his black suit, stood a man Gabriel thought he'd never see again.

The man nodded. "Good evening, Gabriel."

Gabriel frowned. "Marcus."

All the images Gabriel had seen while feeding flooded his mind as if he were watching a film, but at high speed. Some things remained a mystery, but he knew this man's face.

Marcus. Caiaphas. The Illuminati.

41

Venice, Italy

Marco placed a hand on Antonio's shoulder, stopping him from knocking on their boss's office door. "You sure you want to do this?"

After leaving the Grasso residence, Antonio made some inquiries. Wondering if other Italian cities or provinces might also be experiencing an influx of dead rats or an unknown suspect seen drinking from rats, he reached out to various stations. He started with the stations closest to Venice and worked his way out. No other city, province, or region had any reports like what Antonio was describing to them. A couple of detectives had asked if he'd been drinking his lunch. Antonio hadn't been surprised. After all, if other stations were investigating something so bizarre, wouldn't they have done exactly what he'd done, reached out? He thought of the detective who'd cursed him out for wasting his time before hanging up on him and reasoned maybe not.

But without reaching out, how would they know of the elderly couple? Why make the trip to Venice? Why not call the Venice station and request either the interview notes or an interview to be conducted on their behalf? However, Antonio returned to the fact that no one outside of Venice was experiencing these occurrences. No other stations were investigating. No one had contacted the Venice station, and until that day, Antonio hadn't reached out to any other station. So, where had these detectives come from? How had they learned of the witnesses? Why hadn't they met with Marco and Antonio while in Venice to compare notes? What if they weren't detectives at all? If not, then who were they?

Antonio had brooded over a Margherita pizza and Peroni. Piles of dead rats had begun to appear behind restaurants and grocery stores. The rats looked like they'd been drained of their blood. A man had been seen in at least one of the scenes. An assault victim reported a man matching that description killing her attackers and drinking their blood. The scene shows evidence of an assault, or assaults, with blood from multiple persons present, but no bodies. That same man was spotted again, but this time covered in blood. Two men claiming to be detectives interviewed his witnesses.

Taken separately, there was nothing of interest here. No one would mourn the loss of the rats, especially since the carcasses were immediately cleaned up, tested, and found to be disease-free. So, rats were dying, but people weren't. The attempted rape of the Mantalto woman angered him. Antonio hated the fact that sexual assault occurred in his beloved Venice, and it was rough when he arrested a suspect. She probably hadn't been these two suspects' first victim, and she wouldn't have been their last. If what she claimed had happened to her attackers was true, Antonio could rest easy; there were two fewer monsters on the street. It was annoying that detectives from another jurisdiction hadn't exhibited professional courtesy, but that was hardly cause for alarm.

Together, however...

What was that phrase his mother used to say when he was growing up? *Once is a chance. Twice is a coincidence. Thrice is a pattern.*

Collections of dead rats had been recovered throughout Venice. But their concentration, the sighting of the man drinking from them, the Mantalto assault, the elderly couple's sighting of presumably that same man, and the visit of the two "detectives" all occurred in the same general locale. What were the odds that it was all just chance or coincidence? He had a better chance of being eaten by a shark while eating his pizza. No, Antonio thought as he finished his Peroni, this was a pattern.

He'd shared all of this the following morning with Marco, who was his usual unimpressed self. He'd only shrugged and, after swallowing a bite of his fette biscottate, said, "I guess it depends on what toppings are on your pizza."

Antonio had said nothing. He'd stood up and walked towards the chief's office. That's where they were standing now, Marco's hand still on his shoulder.

"I'm just doing my job," Antonio responded. "Telling Donatello what we've discovered."

"What *you've* discovered."

Antonio shrugged off Marco's hand but said nothing. Turning, he knocked on the door, opened it, and entered without waiting for permission. "You got a second, chief?"

Marco rolled his eyes but followed Antonio.

Both inspectors could see the look of disappointment on the chief's face as he looked up. The chief gave them a curt nod as he gestured to the two chairs in front of his desk.

"The couple who reported seeing the homeless man covered in blood," Antonio started as he sat down.

"What about them?" Donatello snapped as Marco plopped down in the other chair hard enough to make a teenager proud.

Antonio continued, "I went to interview them, but they said they'd already spoken to the police. It wasn't us, and we're the only ones working this case."

Several uncomfortable seconds passed as both detectives watched Donatello, who leaned back in his chair, frowning. "The mayor," he finally said.

"Excuse me?" Antonio felt he'd been slapped in the face.

"The mayor interviewed the geezers?" Marco exclaimed, leaning forward.

Donatello rolled his eyes. "You're an idiot, Scalia." He turned his attention to Antonio. "Next year is an election year. Even though the mayor can't run again, he doesn't want a city full of dead rats and a blood-covered homeless man to be his parting legacy. You two haven't been able to solve it yet, so he's requested the Carabinieri's assistance."

Marco pumped a fist in victory.

Antonio bit his bottom lip. "The mayor has asked for the military police to take over the case?" He didn't try to hide his disbelief. He hoped Donatello heard it loud and clear.

Donatello ignored the attempt. "Have your report on my desk by the end of the day. I'll make sure it gets into the right hands."

"Will do, Chief," Marco chimed, standing to leave.

Antonio remained seated. "Mr. Grasso said the two men who interviewed them were in suits, not Carabinieri uniforms. Maybe we should call the mayor's off—"

"Don't push it, Antonio," Donatello cut across him. "You're lucky the mayor didn't demand I put the two of you on foot patrol." His frown turned into an oily smile. "But that could be arranged."

"That won't be necessary, Chief," Marco said as he grabbed Antonio by the arm and pulled him from his seat. "We'll have that report on your desk ASAP." Marco ushered them out of the office.

"Close the door on your way out," Donatello barked, picking up his phone.

Marco nodded as he shoved Antonio through the door and closed it behind him.

Throwing off Marco's hold, Antonio fumed back to his desk and dropped into his chair.

Marco plopped down in his chair and popped a Cannoli into his mouth. "We dodged a bullet on that one," he said as he chewed. "What?" Marco asked, seeing Antonio's glare.

"You don't think that was strange?" Antonio questioned.

"I don't get you. You're handed a get-out-of-jail-free card, and you want to set it on fire?

Antonio held up his index finger. "The mayor calls in the military police to investigate some dead rats and a homeless guy because it's an election year *next* year, and we're not doing our job." He held up his middle finger. "Donatello doesn't take our heads off because the mayor's called in the Carabinieri. When's the last time you saw him not lose his mind because a crime wasn't being solved fast enough?" He stuck out his thumb to illustrate his third point. "Not only does he *not* come down on us, he doesn't even mention it to us, till *we* bring it up." The glare dropped from Antonio's face as he leaned back in his chair, shaking his head. "Something's not adding up."

"What's not adding up?" Marco asked. "Neither of us wanted this case to begin with. Donatello only gave the case to us because people were complaining, and he was mad at me." He fished another Cannoli out of the box. "So the mayor freaks out about his legacy and calls in the big guns. So what? All that's above our pay grade." He stuffed the Cannoli into his mouth and chewed. "Who cares if it adds up?" Marco said after swallowing, "I'm out of the doghouse with him." He held up the box of treats to Antonio. "So do us both a favor and let it go?"

Antonio wasn't convinced, but he withdrew a pastry from the box.

Marco nodded. Setting the box down, he said, "Tell you what. You start typing up the report, and I'll grab us both an espresso." Marco stood from his chair and walked away.

"You're just trying to bribe me so you don't have to type," Antonio called out.

Marco only raised a hand and toodled his fingers.

Antonio couldn't help but chuckle. Maybe Marco was right, he thought. He did feel a little lighter. Taking the case folder from his drawer and comparing it with the notes in his notepad, Antonio was just about to start typing when he looked toward Donatello's office.

The man stood at the glass wall, watching Antonio as he spoke to someone on the phone. Seeing Antonio watching him, Donatello nodded as if to say, *Get back to it.* Then he turned away.

Antonio couldn't help but think that the subject of the Chief's conversation was him. He popped a Nicorette lozenge into his mouth. Rubbing the Chantix patch on his arm, he thought, something's not adding up.

"Four sugars, no cream. Just the way you…" Marco stopped mid-sentence as he stared at Antonio's empty chair. The case folder and notepad were gone.

42

Venice, Italy

"Turn around," Gabriel shouted at the back of Marcus's head. Watched as Marcus turned in the gondola to look. "We have to go back."

The gondolier hadn't flinched, just kept moving the gondola smoothly through the water, eyes straight ahead. The man was dressed in the traditional uniform of black slacks, black shoes, a black and white striped shirt, and a black hat with a red ribbon. He looked like any gondolier on the water, but Gabriel smelled something more. Confidence. Bearing. Alertness. The man knew everything going on around him, and Gabriel was sure he would be just as deadly with a weapon as he was capable with the boat.

"I'm afraid that's out of the question, Mr. Hawthorne," Marcus finally responded.

"We have to go back for her. If you found me, then that means they will too," Gabriel pleaded. He felt a thrill of horror as his mind's eye flickered the images of Alessia returning home, calling his name as she removed fresh blood bags from her backpack. Screaming as someone who looked like the vampire in the cowboy boots, jeans, and denim jacket he'd come across the first time he met the Illuminati, emerged from the shadows, smiling, fangs protruding.

"They?"

"You know who turned me," he made a gesture taking in all of himself, "into what I am."

"Miss Montalto is of no consequence to the Illuminati or the vampires. In fact, removing you from her apartment might have saved her life if she'd been there when they found you." Marcus was

189

silent, letting that last nugget of truth sink into Gabriel's brain. "My instructions are to bring you in, and that's what I intend to do," Marcus replied.

He sat for a moment, thinking. Marcus was probably right. Alessia was in danger because of his presence. If, and it was a big if, the vampires were looking for him, then his presence in her apartment put her at risk. They wouldn't want to leave any eyewitnesses behind. And Caiaphas didn't care about her, so the Illuminati didn't care about her. The fact that she was gone when he left with Marcus, and the vampires would soon know he was now in the hands of the Illuminati, if they even cared, there'd be no reason for them to bother with her. Again, the vampires would have to know and care that he was now a vampire and keep an eye on him or recruit him to their ranks. Either way, Alessia was safe. And yet...

"No."

"No, what?" Marcus turned an exasperated look at him.

"No. I'm not going with you."

Gabriel listened as the oar cut through the water and propelled the boat forward. He could hear Marcus's heartbeat in front of him and the gondolier behind him. Smelled the pungent tang of salt and algae in the Venetian canal water. He found that he relished it. It cleared his mind. Alessia may be inconsequential to the Illuminati and the vampires, but she was very significant to him. Gabriel inhaled a calming breath before speaking. "Look. I know Caiaphas doesn't want to see me, just so we can catch up. He wants something, and may even need something. Whatever it is, he wants and needs me to do it."

"And your point?" Marcus's eyes and tone betrayed nothing of what he might be thinking.

"My point is, if we don't go back for her, I won't do whatever Caiaphas wants or needs me to do."

Marcus stared at Gabriel for a long moment before looking at the gondolier. He watched as Marcus's thoughts played out on his face. If he ignored Gabriel's demand and took him to meet Caiaphas, exactly how pleased would he be with an uncooperative vampire so close to him? How much manpower would be wasted guarding an uncooperative vampire until they could decide what to do with him? Or would they just kill him outright? Either way, they would've wasted a lot of time, money, and resources just to kill him once he brought him to Caiaphas. On the other hand, Caiaphas had only ordered Marcus to bring back Gabriel. How would he feel if Marcus showed up with an unillumined civilian? Not to mention the cost of time, money, and resources spent to get her there. Would they kill her if they decided to kill him?

Gabriel was about to say, *Never mind*, when he saw Marcus glance at the gondolier.

"Turn around."

43

Venice, Italy

Chief Inspector Alberto Donatello sat at one of the outside tables of the L'Obmra del Leone. It was a café-bar he visited often, mainly for the view. It was truly magnificent, across the Grand Canal toward the Basilica of La Salute. He also loved that it was a very public place. Alberto shot a nervous glance at his watch as the sun started to set.

"Caffè?" The waiter asked, gesturing towards the empty cup on the table.

Donatello looked up to see the waiter gesturing towards his empty cup. He'd been so preoccupied with why he was here tonight that he hadn't noticed the waiter arrive. Slipping, he thought. You're slipping, and you're getting too old for this.

"Sì, grazie." Donatello forced a grin.

As the waiter refilled his cup, Donatello scanned the entrance to the alfresco dining area on the Terrazza. He saw the man he was waiting for. The man wasn't alone. He didn't recognize the second man, increasing Donatello's agitation.

Man? Donatello would've laughed if his mouth had been able to make any saliva. The sight of the first one had dried his throat. Now a second? One vampire was bad enough, but two?

The waiter finished pouring the coffee and left after receiving a perfunctory nod from Donatello.

He stood and offered an anxious grin and wave to announce his location.

The two vampires ignored Donatello. They'd only been waiting for the waiter to leave before joining him at the table.

Donatello didn't even know the first vampire's name. They'd been introduced when he was a teenager by his father, a major in the Italian paramilitary police, the Carabinieri. Donatello's father had also been introduced to this same vampire when he was a teenager by his father. His family had been working for the vampires since the time of his great-grandfather, a cabinet minister. The vampire stood over six feet two inches with a lean athletic frame and looked exactly as he did when he'd met him thirty-four years ago.

However, the vampire following looked like a silverback gorilla someone had dressed in a suit, which was so tight on his frame that Donatello thought it might explode if he sneezed or coughed. Do vampires cough or sneeze? Donatello wondered. He'd never seen it.

Slipping, Donatello. This is not the time to let your mind wander, old man.

The first vampire sat down and casually slipped his Halliburton briefcase under the table next to Donatello's identical case. It gave Alberto a sense of comfort to see it. They'd been using this method of passing payment and information for years.

"Good evening." Alberto hated the quaver he heard in his voice, and his smile was anxious as both men seated themselves.

Neither vampire responded in kind.

"You wanted to discuss a development." The first vampire's voice was as biting cold as the north wind coming off the Alps.

Donatello glanced at the second vampire and immediately regretted making eye contact. The icy cold that ran down his spine made him shiver. The man's eyes were lifeless. Black as pitch. It was like staring into a well in the darkness of night. He remembered a quote from Antonio Gramsci. *The old world is dying, and the new world struggles to be born; now is the time of monsters.* And he served these monsters. Served them, not as a mercenary but as a prostitute, like his father before him and his father before him. As such, wasn't he, and his father and grandfather, also monsters? If so, why did staring into the eyes of a monster just now turn his bowels to ice?

"I'm waiting." The first vampire's words weren't an observation but a command.

"Y-y-yes." Donatello cleared his throat, still staring into the second vampire's eyes. "I...I wanted to inform you that my investigators discovered that some of your people were also asking questions. About the rats." He gulped like a drowning man breaking the surface and filling his lungs with fresh air. "And the homeless man."

"Our people?"

The stone-coldness of the vampire's tone finally helped Donatello drag his eyes away from the second vampire. He found the first vampire staring back at him with eyes burning.

"D-Don't..." Donatello licked his lips. "Don't worry about it, though. I've closed the investigation. Our inspectors will be set to other duties."

"We've had no one asking questions." The first vampire's eyes narrowed, and the flames there burned brighter. "Why did *you* order an investigation?"

"My apologies," Donatello breathed. His bowels were quickly melting, turning to liquid. He tried to swallow, but his mouth was too dry.

"No loose ends," The first vampire said.

Donatello nodded as if he were a bobblehead.

"Your life depends upon it." The second vampire's voice was the rumble of distant thunder.

Donatello nodded understanding, sure his bladder would've released, it was full enough, if every muscle in his body hadn't just seized in terror.

The two vampires stood in unison. The first vampire now had Alberto's case in his hand as they turned and exited the Terrazza.

Donatello exhaled a breath and gasped for another. He'd been so scared that he'd forgotten to breathe as he watched them leave. It may have been a trick of his brain, but he swore he smelled death in every lungful of air. He tried to pick his cup up for a sip, but his hand trembled so much he spilled coffee across the table, the spreading stain reminding him horribly of blood.

The waiter was instantly at the table, muttering apologies and offering to fetch more coffee as he dabbed at the tablecloth.

Donatello waved him away with a curse. Alone again at the table, he closed his eyes so he wouldn't have to see the soiled tablecloth and tried to regain his composure. Once he felt he had control of himself, he threw a few euros on the table, grabbed the case, and walked towards the exit on legs made of rubber.

"What are you going to do?" He thought to himself, then frowned. He knew exactly what he was going to do. He was a fourth-generation servant of the vampires. He would not be the last.

44

Illuminati Compound,
Caja del Rio Plateau, New Mexico

Alessia Mantalto paced back and forth, arms wrapped across her chest, in an exam room that reminded her of the rooms at the hospital E.R., except the door was locked from the outside. She'd also checked all the drawers and cabinets. They were secured as well. She tried them all again for good measure before resuming her circuit.

Two days ago, she'd been grabbed by two men in the courtyard just outside the emergency room exit.

Or was it three? Three days? Three men?

Unlike her two would-be rapists, these men were professionals. She never had a chance to react. She'd been immediately gagged, bound, and had a hood pulled down over her head. They never made a sound, not even a shoe scuff, as she was moved from the courtyard to a boat. It hadn't been a gondola. This one had been under power, though they didn't blaze through any canals. The motor was kept at a low and steady growl. From the boat, she was placed in what must have been a van. Alessia had always been keen on sounds and was sure she'd heard the sound of the sliding passenger door.

Alessia tried counting the minutes and thought she'd counted ninety. The ride was smooth, with few stops and turns. None of the men ever spoke or played the radio. They didn't even smoke.

The ninety minutes gave her time to think. This wasn't another sexual assault or mugging. These guys had been professional. Aside from the initial attack, she'd been handled as if she were some priceless statue. Other than the bindings, gag, and hood, they'd seen to it she was comfortable. Though they never asked if they could make her more comfortable. And they'd never touched her inappropriately.

If this were an abduction, then this might be a case of mistaken identity. Her family wasn't rich. She made more money than they did. No one in her family was a politician or member of the government. Every member of her family worked hard, paid taxes, and abstained from anti-government rallies and rhetoric. But she couldn't think of anyone she worked with who met those criteria either.

From the van, she was transferred onto a plane. She could hear the engines thrumming a steady staccato as they sat idling on the tarmac or wherever they were. She could only assume it was a private flight from a private airport. They ushered her from the vehicle onto the plane, and then the aircraft was airborne in moments. Once they were at cruising altitude, the hood was removed.

"Apologies," One of the men told her as he removed her gag and bindings. "It was for your safety."

Alessia stretched her jaw and muscles to work out the kinks, letting the anger build inside her. She opened her mouth to protest when a voice stopped her.

"Alessia." Gabriel stood and started making his way towards her.

"Gabriel," Alessia exclaimed in anger and relief. "What's going on? Do you know these people? How did you get here? Did you know—?"

Gabriel placed a finger on her lips to silence her. The gesture was so intimate, the touch so foreign yet familiar, Alessia felt her heart race and her skin warm. She remembered a sermon the priest delivered about a burning coal being placed on the lips of the apostle John. It could not have felt this hot or this sweet.

"I know you have a lot of questions. And I promise they will all be answered. For now, please do as they ask," Gabriel said as he sat across from her.

For several hours, Gabriel recounted his life, filling in the blanks for Alessia now that he'd filled them in for himself. He now remembered exactly why he'd come to Italy. They were served food as he told her how he'd become a vampire and who'd been responsible. He told her about Cain, Claudia, and the Illuminati. Gabriel explained how the images he had been seeing since he started feeding had been flooding his mind, but it wasn't until he saw Marcus that all of it came together. She'd had questions, but they'd been advised to rest. She found she couldn't keep her eyes open. They'd been led to sleeping quarters on the plane, and she'd been dreaming before her head hit the pillow.

She'd been awakened and informed they would be landing soon. She was offered an apology, but told she'd need to be blindfolded again. She looked up and saw that Gabriel had already been blindfolded. She suspected the blindfold didn't matter for Gabriel because when she'd looked at him, he'd nodded. She accepted the blindfold again as the plane landed. She hadn't seen him since.

Alessia assumed they'd been placed into separate vehicles. No van this time. No radio. No smoking. No talking. She'd lost all track of time. She estimated she'd spent ninety minutes in the van. At least fourteen hours on the plane, followed by another drive that seemed to take several hours as well, but she couldn't be sure. She'd tried counting again but realized she'd been distracted by the feel of the sun on her face through the vehicle window. She didn't have any idea of how long she hadn't been counting. So all she could assume was that it was day wherever she was.

Once the vehicle stopped and the blindfold was removed, she found herself inside a building. They'd parked in a motor pool. There were vehicles parked in slots and maintenance bays. This was quite an operation, she realized. She was escorted to the exam room, where she now paced. She rubbed the band-aid where her blood was drawn. She still knew very little about the Illuminati based on her earlier conversation with Gabriel. The one thing she was certain of: they took security very seriously. Alessia jumped at a knock on the door.

"Miss Mantalto. My name is Caiaphas." Caiaphas said as he entered the room. "My apologies for how you were brought here, but we have certain protocols that must be followed to secure our safety as well as yours."

A hundred questions buzzed through Alessia's mind. Where was she? Why was she brought here in the first place? What was going on? But those weren't the questions that escaped her mouth. "Where is Gabriel? What have you done with him?"

"Mr. Hawthorne is fine, I assure you," Caiaphas answered. "The two of you will be reunited shortly." He leaned against the wall and smiled. "I have to admit we weren't expecting you originally. But Mr. Hawthorne was concerned for your safety and refused to come without you. I believe he is quite fond of you."

Alessia's heart leaped at this observation, but she ignored it. Maybe later, she could entertain it, even luxuriate in it, but right now, she needed to know Gabriel was safe. "What do you want with him?"

"We have another guest with us whom Gabriel has...a history with. I hope the two will help each other adapt to their new situations. Just as you need to adapt now that you have been illumined."

"Illumined?" Alessia asked, a puzzled look on her face.

"It's the term we use when someone becomes aware that vampires exist. And then, by extension, our organization exists. I know Gabriel has shared a little with you, and I'd be happy to answer any further questions you may have. But first, I'd like to give you a tour of our facility. I think that will help to answer some of the questions you may have, as well as possibly show you an opportunity in which you can help us." Caiaphas opened the door and gestured for her to follow.

Alessia was taken aback. "Help you?"

"Yes, Miss Mantalto."

"Please. Call me Alessia."

Caiaphas smiled. "In time." He gestured again to the door. "Shall we?"

Caiaphas showed her the rest of the medical wing. It was state-of-the-art. They had a fully functioning operating room, laboratory, and radiology department with X-ray, MRI, and CT machines. The recovery and exam rooms were fully stocked with modern medications and delivery systems. The one thing they seemed short of was staff. It was the same all over the world, Alessia thought, even in super-secret anti-vampire organizations; not enough doctors, nurses, and technicians.

Caiaphas could tell that she was impressed by what she had seen. He was glad for that, considering the reality she was about to face. Never one to hide the whole truth from someone once that individual had been illumined, he showed her the rest of the compound. He was not surprised by her repulsion at the weapons facilities. Those drawn to healing never liked instruments designed to destroy life, even monstrous life.

The weapons facilities did repulse Alessia. She didn't like guns. Like most doctors and nurses, she thought the human body was a wonderful machine and abhorred anything that could wreak such destruction upon it. Like most Italians, she didn't consider owning a gun reasonable for someone who didn't have a reason, like law enforcement or hunting. Even with the low percentage of gun owners and gun-related crimes in Italy, as an E.R. and trauma nurse, she'd seen firsthand what a gun could do to the body.

Once they returned to the medical wing, Alessia asked, "So why did you show me all this?"

"I was hoping you'd consider helping us here," Caiaphas answered. "We need someone with your skills."

"I'm sorry, but I have a job. Besides, I don't even know where *here* is."

Caiaphas paused, choosing his words carefully. "Miss Mantalto, your life has changed irrevocably. You have been illumined. That's not something that you can unlearn. Vampires possess a unique skill set that enables them to influence humans to forget or change their perceptions. But it would depend on the age of the vampire. An older vampire would use that skill set. A younger one would most likely kill you.

"Mr. Hawthorne was on law enforcement's radar, to use the colloquialism. As a result, you were on their radar. His actions, the number of desiccated rats he was leaving in public, and what he did to your would-be rapids put him on their radar, which put him on our radar, and by extension, you. I can only assume the vampires would soon take notice. Your life can never be the same. You can't simply go back and pick up where you left off. To attempt to do so would most likely mean death. Or worse. You would also put friends and family at risk." Caiaphas paused, allowing Alessia to process what he said. "Why don't we find Mr. Hawthorne? I believe he is waiting for us in the cafeteria."

Alessia nodded. The thought of seeing Gabriel again brought her comfort, but Caiaphas's words still echoed inside her head.

"Luca," Alessia squealed as she entered the cafeteria with Caiaphas.

Sitting at a table, Gabriel held her cat. "I forgot to tell you I had them grab him for you." Gabriel stood and handed the cat off to Alessia.

Alessia took Luca into her arms and snuggled him into her neck. "Thank you," Alessia said as the tears started falling from her eyes.

45

Illuminati Compound,
Caja del Rio Plateau, New Mexico

Gabriel had no idea how long he and Alessia had been sitting at the table. They'd told each other what had happened after they'd been separated, tried to coax Luca's experience out of the feline, and then fallen into silence.

It was strange, Gabriel thought, how good he felt with Alessia. Not just happy, but good about himself. Maybe that wasn't the right word, he wondered as he watched Alessia nuzzle Luca's ears, stealing an occasional glance. She thought she was being furtive, but Gabriel's vampire senses didn't miss anything. He heard her heartbeat accelerate, smelled her fear dissipate, replaced by a tang of something sweet, and saw the light in her eyes brighten. Perhaps she was feeling what he was feeling.

That thought brought him up short. What was he feeling? Could vampires feel? Could he feel? That was absurd. Of course, he could feel. Hadn't he just been thinking about how good he felt with her? Hadn't he been wondering if she felt like he felt? Wasn't he now thinking more like a thirteen-year-old in junior high than an adult? Perhaps he should pass her a note in study hall.

"What?" Alessia asked.

"Hmmm?" Gabriel looked up, shaken from his reverie.

Alessia smiled as their eyes met. "You just chuckled."

"Did I?" Gabriel smelled that sweet tang and felt giddy, his mind blanking.

Alessia nodded.

Gabriel shook his head. "I don't remember." Maybe complete was the right word, he thought.

"Mr. Hawthorne," Caiaphas said from behind Gabriel as he approached the table.

Alessia jumped, then dropped her gaze and head. A sheepish grin crossed her face as if she and Gabriel had just been caught by the teacher passing notes in study hall.

Gabriel didn't jump. He'd heard Caiaphas's footsteps and knew who was approaching. He even recognized the man's voice. Another benefit of being a vampire, Gabriel realized, was the ability to recall moments and memories in high definition and surround sound. He knew Caiaphas's gait and voice as if he were a close family member. So while Alessia might have felt adolescent surprise, Gabriel felt annoyed at the interruption. Without turning, he asked, "What can I do for you, *old man*?" mustering as much sarcasm into 'old man' as he could.

"If I could steal you away for a moment," Caiaphas said politely as if he'd missed the slight. Smiling at Alessia, he added, "I'll have someone escort you to your quarters."

"This can't wait?" Gabriel asked as he turned to face Caiaphas, immediately regretting calling him an old man. It was too accurate a description. The smile was still warm. The light was still in his eyes, but they were red-rimmed and set deep in their sockets. His sallow skin hung loosely on his gaunt frame. His clothes appeared to be two sizes too big.

"This is Gin," Caiaphas said, gesturing towards a young woman who approached the table. "She will help you get settled in, and I will get Mr. Hawthorne back to you as soon as possible."

Alessia hesitated, looking between Caiaphas and Gabriel. She had no reference for the older man, the compound, or this situation. She might not even have a reference for the part of the world she was now in, other than TV and movies, once she knew which part she was in. Gabriel was the only common denominator with the older man, the compound, this situation, and this part of the world. She wasn't ready to have that taken away from her, even for a little while.

"It'll be fine. I promise," Gabriel said, smiling at Alessia, who was still snuggling Luca.

Alessia nodded, then stood and pulled Luca tightly to her chest before following Gin out of the cafeteria.

"May I?" Caiaphas asked as he gestured towards the seat across from him.

Gabriel's nod was more distracted than polite. Now that it was just the two of them, he couldn't help noticing how much Caiaphas's body had changed. What could have ravaged Caiaphas's body so quickly?

Caiaphas could see the wheels turning behind Gabriel's eyes. "Cancer," Caiaphas said.

All the annoyance and frustration Gabriel may have felt towards Caiaphas evaporated like a drop of water on a hot skillet. He wanted to tell him that he was sorry. It's what you say when someone tells you they've experienced a loss or just received a fatal diagnosis. He'd lost count of the times he'd said it in his lifetime. It had always sounded perfunctory at best to his ears. Even lame. No different from when we ask someone how they're doing, even though we don't really want to know or care to know. And what are we sorry for? We didn't kill her grandfather. We didn't give him leukemia. Or do we say 'I'm Sorry' because we had a moment, however brief and maybe even subconscious, where we thanked God it was not us who'd just lost his grandfather or been diagnosed with leukemia, and feeling guilty for that moment, we offer an apology? So, like the person who's been asked how they're doing and knows the asker isn't really interested in the answer, he responds with 'good.' We understand that the proffered *I'm sorry* has nothing to do with the loss or the diagnosis, but the shame experienced in that brief moment, and respond with *Thank you*. The social contract of congeniality between the two parties has been completed.

Gabriel shook his head. *Becoming a vampire has turned me into a philosopher.*

"Is there anything they can do?" Gabriel asked with genuine concern in his voice.

Caiaphas shook his head in a slow negative, but his smile never slipped. "But it's simplified matters. I'm more focused now. More direct." A mischievous light brightened his eyes. "Less interested in scheming."

"Well. No one could ever accuse you of beating around the bush, could they?"

Caiaphas's next statement wiped the smirk from Gabriel's face as if it'd been a dry-erase board.

"Cain Dvanaesti survived. He's here."

The words crashed over Gabriel like an angry ocean wave, disorienting him, suffocating him. Cain Dvanaesti was alive. How could that be? That couldn't. No one could survive slamming into the sea at more than five hundred miles an hour. No *human* could, Gabriel reminded himself. And hadn't he seen just how inhuman Cain had become that night at his mansion? Gabriel was pretty sure that wasn't even a vampire. No, Cain was something else entirely.

But what if, Gabriel had the sudden thought, causing him to cartwheel emotionally, hit by another wave, what if the newspapers and media had gotten it wrong? What if the plane hadn't gone down like they said? Or what if it had gone down, but the pilots had at least landed the aircraft in such a way that there could've been survivors? What if Cain hadn't been the only survivor?

"Ms. Bennett did not survive," Caiaphas said, as if reading Gabriel's mind.

"What happened?" Gabriel asked, feeling rage growing inside him. He stared at his hands, watched the knuckles turn white as they clenched into fists, and relished the sting as his fingernails bit into the soft flesh of his palms.

"Roman had his plane shot out of the sky. The transformation that Cain experienced at the mansion was neither planned nor welcomed by the vampires. Cain had gone from a very useful and powerful pawn to something that could potentially change the way Roman played his games. So Roman removed him from the board."

"And Claudia was just...what?" Gabriel seethed. "Collateral damage?"

"Ms. Bennett wasn't even a consideration," Caiphas responded.

Silence hung heavy in the air. Caiaphas let it. He knew Gabriel needed to process. He knew that while Gabriel no longer felt romantically for Claudia, he still cared for her deeply. She'd been his primary motivation for going to Miami with Rotty and the others once he'd been illumined. But he wanted Gabriel to understand that Cain Dvanaesti was not the enemy. He was only a pawn, and then a victim, of Roman Dvanaesti, just as Claudia and Gabriel were.

Pawn, victim, or willing participant, Gabriel didn't care. He only knew that Claudia would be alive today if she hadn't been on that plane. And why was she on that plane? Because Cain had asked her to be. Cain had thought that with him was the safest place for her to be. Why couldn't he see that the safest place for the woman he supposedly loved was anywhere he wasn't? If he'd seen it, he would have told her to stay right where she was. Then she would've learned, like everyone else in the world, of the "tragic" crash of Cain Dvanaesti's plane. She'd be heartbroken, devastated, asking the press to respect her privacy as she grieved. She may even think she'll never survive without Cain. But she would. It would take some time, but she would emerge from the darkness and maybe even find love again. Even if she didn't, she'd still be alive. So for Gabriel, Cain as good as killed her by asking her to join him on that plane.

"What do you want from me, Caiphas?" Gabriel asked.

"I would like your assistance in convincing Mr. Dvanaesti to help us in the fight against the vampires," Caiaphas replied.

Gabriel scoffed. "So you want to use the 'big bad wolf' to keep the other wolves at bay?"

"You fail to grasp the reality we currently live in. The vampires are not wolves attacking a flock of sheep or breaking into a chicken coop. No, Mr. Hawthorne. We," Caiaphas gestured to include Gabriel, himself, and every human on the planet, "are cattle. The vampires are the ranchers. We may not be branded, fattened, and herded to the slaughterhouse, but each of us is a member of a herd belonging to an Ancient.

"Roman and the other Ancients have operatives placed at every level of every government. They manipulate and control every major decision globally. That manipulation and control are used to keep their herds healthy and ignorant of the fact that they are cattle. That is what we are facing, Mr. Hawthorne. And if we are going to stand a chance of stopping them, we need both of you."

"You plan to take the fight to Roman and these other Ancients?" Gabriel asked.

Caiaphas nodded.

Gabriel was silent, staring down at the floor. He thought of how Alessia's life had been turned upside down. He thought of his friend Miguel Gutierrez in Miami and the threat against his wife and child. He thought of Claudia and felt his nails bite deeper into his palms. He thought of Stefan. Taking the fight to the people who'd killed Stefan and Claudia and turned him into what he was now, and the whole human race into nothing more than cattle, sounded good to him. Good? Drawing blood from the people who'd drawn blood from the human race in general and him in particular sounded great.

He thought of Stefan and the picture of the young man as a teenager. No one knew who'd photographed the moment, but the Lost Boys of Sudan had just scored a victory against a larger and better-trained force. Stefan, fatigues now stained with blood and gore, had his rifle above his head. His smile was all teeth as he fired his weapon. Stefan was not proud of that picture. It brought him no pleasant memories. There was no warm nostalgia. But Stefan kept a copy of that photograph in his wallet and on the wall of every room in his apartment to remind him of the monster he'd been, so he'd never become that monster again.

Relaxing his hands, Gabriel turned them over and stared at his open palms. They had already healed. There were certain advantages to being a vampire. So, how much fight could a vampire and someone who was more than a vampire take to Roman and the Ancients? How much blood could they draw? Surely that was worth forgiving Cain. Wasn't it? After all, they'd both loved and cared for the same woman. Both want to avenge her murder. And that's what it was – Murder.

"I'm in," Gabriel said as he stood from the table. "I need to get back to Alessia. I need to explain what's going on."

Caiaphas had not stood. "You need to help her realize the life she knew is over.

The fight drained from Gabriel, driving him back into his seat. "It's my fault." He began to rub his temples.

"Gabriel." Caiaphas said the name as a father would when trying to comfort his child.

Gabriel stopped rubbing his temples. Caiaphas had never called him by his first name. He looked across at the old man and saw compassion in his eyes.

"You can blame yourself for her current situation if you want, but if it weren't for you, Ms. Montalto would either be dead or, worse, living with what her attackers would've done to her." He placed a hand on Gabriel's shoulder. "You didn't ask for any of this. Not what happened to her, nor what happened to you. All any of us can do now is try to make the best of the hand we have been dealt. You can help Miss Montalto by convincing her that there is a place for her here. She would be a valuable addition."

Gabriel nodded as he sighed.

"Let's go find and help her get settled in, shall we? Then I'll have you visit Cain." Caiaphas said, standing and gesturing for Gabriel to follow.

"Sure. I'll show up with a bottle of wine. I bet he'll love that." Gabriel said with a chuckle.

46

Venice, Italy

Chief Inspector Alberto Donatello stamped out another cigarette as he watched Detective Antonio Frederico's apartment. He'd been standing in this alcove since just after nine p.m. It provided additional darkness and the best visual of his quarry's arrival home. He would've preferred more time to plan, but after the warning from the vampires, Donatello decided to take care of this sooner rather than later. He checked his watch.

2:06 a.m.

Without thinking, Donatello stuck another cigarette between his lips. The flame from his lighter almost kissed the paper before he realized what he was doing. Cursing under his breath, he extinguished the flame. Another cigarette wasn't feeding a craving; it was stalling.

Antonio arrived home at a quarter past ten. Twenty minutes later, the apartment went dark. Donatello assumed he'd gone to bed but decided to wait in case Antonio had only visited his abode to change clothes or collect an item. It wouldn't do to meet him on the staircase. Donatello had no good reason to call on him at this time of night, especially without a phone call first. No, better to wait. Give it an hour.

But one hour had given way to two. Then three. Now four. During those hours, Donatello had chain-smoked as he thought about Antonio. He liked the young detective. Admired his Pitbull tenacity for justice and fairness. That's the reason why Donatello was here tonight. He'd been wrong to assign the case to Antonio and Marco. He realized that now. He hadn't thought it through, hadn't consulted the vampires. He'd reacted with pure emotion. Anger at Marco for taking advantage of his sister. Humiliation by the mayor with his scathing phone call, as if the dead rats showing up in droves before an election was Donatello's fault.

The mayor.

Turns out he's on the vampire payroll as well. Donatello chastised himself. He should've known. But then again, maybe he did. Probably, he had figured it out, and the vampires caused him to forget. Either way, he'd worn his heart on his sleeve, and now a good cop would have to die.

Donatello lit his hiding position with his phone and quickly swept up and pocketed the myriad butts of his cigarettes. Even a rookie cop would be suspicious of that much litter across the street from a burglary gone wrong. As he crossed the street towards the apartment, he stole furtive glances in every direction. Satisfied that no one had witnessed his approach, he entered the building.

Turning left and keeping his head down to avoid the camera by the elevator, Donatello climbed the stairs to the third floor. As he approached Antonio's door, he pulled a lock-pick kit from his jacket. His hands found the two implements he would need to unlock the door while he looked both ways down the hall. Kneeling to insert them into the lock, he noticed the door was pulled closed but not completely seated. In one motion, Donatello dropped the tools and kit into his jacket, stood, stepped back, and withdrew his sidearm. He thumbed the safety catch off, took a steadying breath, leaned forward, and pushed the door open.

Light from the hallway pooled in the small foyer. Donatello squinted but could only make out shadowy shapes throughout the space. Pulling a small penlight from his pocket, he entered the apartment and closed the door behind him, plunging the entryway into darkness. Once he heard the latch catch, he turned on his penlight.

Donatello scanned the main living space. Signs of a struggle were everywhere. Overturned furniture, a broken lamp, a picture on the wall hung askew, its glass shattered by what Donatello thought was either Antonio's or his assailant's head. He continued deeper into the apartment and found Detective Antonio Frederico lying face-up on the floor in a pool of blood. A knife protruded from his chest, and Donatello thought of Excalibur buried in the rock. He felt a sudden and wild urge to pull the blade from Antonio's chest and proclaim himself king. He took a half-step.

"I was wondering if you would ever come in." A voice sounding like distant thunder rumbled behind him.

Donatello spun, raising his firearm before registering the Armani-suited silverback gorilla. Somehow, the vampire looked even scarier than at the L'Obmra del Leone café. In the shadowy darkness of the apartment, the vampire's eyes reminded Donatello even more of the abyss, simultaneously seizing his heart with terror and the almost overpowering desire to fall into it. He suppressed the shudder but couldn't keep the gooseflesh from crawling up his back to his scalp. Dropping his hand, he forced a casual smile. "I could have shot you."

The vampire looked at Donatello's hand.

Donatello looked down at his hand and saw that it was empty. He looked back at the vampire to find him holding his weapon in a gloved hand. He hadn't seen the vampire move, let alone feel the gun being plucked from his grip. He opened his mouth to speak, but his tongue was stuck to the roof of his mouth. His question was expressed on his face. *Why?*

The vampire read it. "Your services are no longer needed."

Donatello tried swallowing but couldn't. Instead, he only heard a dry click in his throat. He worked up enough saliva to plead in a whisper, "The mayor..." before his voice faltered.

"The mayor was also in our employ. This problem with the rats could have been solved if either of you had made one phone call." He added with a malicious smile, "Now he will be remembered less for his legacy and more for his martyrdom in the years to come."

The blood drained from Donatello's head and chest and pooled in his feet. His legs shook, and his knees threatened to buckle. Cold sweat burst from every pore, saturating his clothing. "Martyrdom?"

Donatello wasn't sure if he'd spoken, but the vampire seemed to have heard or read his mind.

Nodding, the vampire said in mock shock and horror, which he failed at dismally, "So sad. He and his entire family. Brutally murdered by political opponents. Wife. Daughter. Sons. Even the maid. It is a cautionary tale, isn't it?" The vampire locked eyes with Donatello, pulling him into the abyss. "To be careful of whom you offend. It was, as your son would say, a blood bath."

Two words yanked Donatello from the abyss.

Your son

His son's sixteenth birthday was just six weeks away. Like his father and grandfather before, he planned to sit the boy down that evening, just the two of them in the study, and over Campari and sodas, introduce him to the family business. The boy was bright and ambitious. Donatello had dreams of him rising to prime minister. Now...

"Your son will not follow in your footsteps." The vampire held up his hand at the look of abject terror on Donatello's face. "He will live and never know the truth of his family or vampires. You, however, will die miserably. Even more miserably than your colleague."

Donatello glanced at Antonio's body.

"It's a shame the two of you couldn't resolve your differences without violence." The vampire sighed with mock grief. "But you just couldn't stand his romantic advances toward your sister."

Donatello's head snapped back to the vampire. "But that was Marco," He protested. Knowing his son would live had restored his voice.

"That's not how anyone, including Marco or your sister, will remember it. You came here tonight to tell him to leave her alone. When he refused, you became enraged. The two of you quarreled. And though you were able to stab him in the heart with your knife, he was still able to snap your neck."

Donatello looked back at Antonio's corpse and recognized the hilt. It was a gift from his sister when he joined the police. He'd carried it for years. Everyone knew it was one of his prized possessions. He was never without it. Until...when? He looked back at the silverback in a suit and found the vampire smiling with fangs bared.

Again, the vampire seemed to read his mind. "Why am I telling you this? Why am I doing this to you? Because, unlike my associate or employer, I enjoy playing with my prey before the kill."

Donatello didn't see the vampire move, but he felt the impact of what he thought must be a freight train striking his body. He went for his second sidearm but felt the fingers in his reaching hand crumple the wrong way like a wad of aluminum foil. The sting of a thousand wasps burned his throat and stomach. He opened his mouth to scream and found it filled with saliva. Only it wasn't saliva, he realized. It was blood. His.

47

Illuminati Compound,
Caja del Rio Plateau, New Mexico

Marcus knocked on the open door before entering Caiaphas's room.

Caiaphas sat in an overstuffed armchair in the corner of the room, a blanket draped over his shoulders, while Stacy, the nurse assigned to him for the next twenty-four hours, took the thermometer from his mouth.

"Ninety-seven. Good." She offered Caiaphas a smile as warm as her voice was soft. She recorded the number on the clipboard, removed the blood pressure cuff from his arm, and stood. "I'll be back in an hour with your meds. Is there anything I can do for you before then?"

Caiaphas locked eyes with her.

Stacy nodded as she smiled again. She knew what he wanted: time alone with Marcus and no interruptions. She would make sure he had that. Patting Caiaphas's shoulder, she offered Marcus a cordial but curt nod as she looked at him.

Marcus understood the message. *Upset him, and I'll tear you a new one.* He did not doubt that she would, too. Stacy stood a hair over five-foot-two in her sneakers, and when off duty, she liked reading romance novels and circuit training. But when she was on duty, she was ten feet tall, bulletproof, and had a bite. He was sure even Roman Dvanaesti would think twice before messing with a patient under her care. He nodded back. *Message received.*

Satisfied, Stacy left the room, closing the door behind her.

Marcus hoped the concern and sadness he was feeling in the pit of his stomach didn't show on his face as he took in the shell of the man before him. Caiaphas had had some good days and bad days. This was a bad one. The man he'd grown to love like the father he'd never had. He could hardly recognize Caiaphas. It was only a few months ago that Caiaphas had confided in Marcus that his cancer had returned. Caiaphas had beaten cancer twice already, but this time, it had come back with a vengeance. Marcus remembered the wave of nausea that had washed over him when Caiaphas told him that the cancer had metastasized. That same wave returned as he watched his mentor waste away in front of him.

"Help me to bed, old friend," Caiaphas said, reaching toward Marcus.

Marcus resisted the urge to flinch as he took hold of Caiaphas's cold, clammy hand. It was yet another slap to his face. The cancer had stolen this man's vigor, stooped his back, emaciated his body, and soured his pallor. If there was anything to be thankful for, Marcus told himself as he assisted Caiaphas to bed and pulled the blanket he'd been wearing over him, it was that Caiaphas still had his full faculties. Fluffing and positioning the pillows gently behind the old man's head, Marcus asked, "Do you need anything?"

Caiaphas shook his head, his eyes closing.

The movement was so thin that Marcus was sure he would've missed it if he hadn't been staring at him. "The reports can wait till morning." His hand trailed down Caiaphas's shoulder to his hand.

Nodding, Caiaphas wrapped his fingers around Marcus's. "Just sit with me."

Marcus sat on the edge of the bed and wrapped his fingers around Caiaphas's, resisting the urge to squeeze tight.

They sat, lost in their private thoughts for a long moment, neither speaking.

Finally, Caiaphas broke the silence. "Marcus. I need to share something with you."

Marcus looked at Caiaphas. He knew what his mentor was going to say before he even spoke. He'd heard the sage words of wisdom many times over the years. On this, Caiaphas was, as his mother would've said, a broken record. *As a leader, you must show patience and restraint.*

"I know this is happening sooner than we ever expected."

Marcus's heart panged as Caiaphas struggled to speak the words.

After a moment, Caiaphas spoke again. "I wish we had more time."

Marcus wrapped his other hand around Caiaphas's. The old man's hand felt frail in his two. "Your mentorship- your...friendship," his voice broke on that word. "Has meant more to me than words can express."

"I will not, as the idiom says, beat a dead horse, Marcus."

"That's only because you're too tired to wield the switch," Marcus interjected, feeling his heart leap as a smile blossomed on the old man's face.

Caiaphas swallowed, his eyes remaining closed. "I need to ask of you a promise."

"A promise?" Marcus questioned, confused.

"Promise me you will show patience and restraint as a leader," Caiaphas said, opening his eyes and looking straight into Marcus's. Though his face did not show it, Caiaphas could sense Marcus struggling not to roll his eyes at this statement. "I know this is hard for you, but I need you to understand. We have only lasted by embracing this truth. Our existence is not only because of the vampires but by them."

"By? Them?" Marcus's brow wrinkled.

Caiaphas nodded. "This truth is passed on only when it's time for a Marcus to ascend to the role of Caiaphas. If I had passed suddenly or unexpectedly, you would've been given a letter I drafted shortly after your elevation to Marcus."

Marcus searched Caiaphas's face for a hint of a smile, something to indicate he was making a joke. "We exist *because* of the vampires and *by* the vampires?" He sounded each word out slowly. "I don't understand."

Caiaphas only watched his protégé, allowing him to work through his confusion.

Marcus inhaled, allowing his thoughts to line up in his mind. "We, the Illuminati, exist because...because the vampires...created us?" He looked at Caiaphas, who nodded encouragement. "And...we continue...to exist...because...the vampires allow us to." The thoughts lined up like dominoes and then fell. "Oh my God. The vampires created the Illuminati for their purposes and continue to allow us to exist because we continue to serve those purposes."

Caiaphas deflated with Marcus's realization. He nodded. "And that realization among our people could cause a lack of faith and devotion."

"But that makes no sense," Marcus protested. "Why create an organization that could destroy you?" Marcus didn't miss the faint smile on Caiaphas's face.

How long have the Illuminati existed?"

"Centuries," Marcus answered, knowing that Caiaphas was not looking for an exact answer.

"And how long have we been able to destroy a vampire?"

"Months."

"And what about an Ancient?"

Marcus had no answer and knew Caiaphas didn't expect him to. "Then why create us?"

"What better to unite the troops than a common enemy?" Caiaphas answered, sounding like the father and mentor Marcus had first idolized, then tolerated, then loathed, then admired, and soon, he realized, he would miss. Just like a son's relationship with his father. He'd missed what Caiaphas had been saying but tuned back in as he said, "The culling."

"The culling?" Marcus questions again with a look of confusion on his face.

"Vampires have the same concerns as humans in one respect: resources to sustain their population. The more vampires, the more resources are required. In this case, the resources are humans. And while humans are a renewable resource, we are renewing at a decreasing rate.

"The newer vampires are not as hearty as the older ones. They are more flamboyant. Less willing to remain behind the scenes. They are more reactive. More exploitative and wasteful of their food source. They're more likely to kill than mesmerize a human who's discovered their existence.

"So the older ones developed a method of population control to protect their anonymity and food source. They even have a name for it. The Culling." Caiaphas smiled as Marcus frowned with disgust. "I see you disapprove of their methods. Are you feeling sorry for the younger of their kind?" Caiaphas needled.

Marcus shook his head violently. "But to kill their own kind simply to protect their anonymity and resources? Monsters."

"Is humanity any different, old friend?" Caiaphas replied. "How many wars have been fought to take another's resources? How many atrocities have been committed to protect people and resources? How many lives have humans taken simply because they could? So ask yourself, what is the definition of a monster? If you are honest with yourself, I don't think you will like the answer."

After a long pause, Marcus nodded in agreement. "How long have we known of this...Culling?"

Caiaphas sighed. "The Illuminati had existed for more than two centuries before we discovered this truth, though how it was discovered is...nebulous at best. Except that this discovery occurred at the same time as another one." Now, Caiaphas frowned. "The truth is...Most of the triumphs we have experienced are thanks to the older vampires. The Ancients. Our advancements in technology and weaponry were given to us by them."

Marcus stared at Caiaphas. "I don't understand. Phase Two and Three weapons were...*given* to us? *By* vampires?" He was horrified. The implications were...well, they were horrifying. The Illuminati were working for the vampires. They were what? Their mules? Their errand boys? How closely were they working with the vampires? Were some of the Illuminati working with the vampires? Planning? Strategizing? Experimenting? Researching and developing?

"If this is true, then what hope do we have against them? If they know our every move? Control every outcome?" Marcus asked, feeling completely lost.

"Hubris," Caiaphas answered.

Marcus looked back at Caiaphas, startled. He'd almost forgotten he was there.

The expression on the old man's face was one of triumph. "Their hubris will be their undoing. Once we discovered the truth of our origins, we started making changes, small, insignificant changes over a long, significant time. We learned how to identify which of our members were manipulated by vampires. We learned how to plant incorrect information in their minds so that the vampires gleaning their minds would believe that information as fact."

"We?"

"Caiaphas," Caiaphas responded. "Each Caiaphas has taken up the mantle to guide the Illuminati to a point sometime in the future when we are equal to the vampires. We've understood that if this organization has any chance of ridding the world of vampires, we must play a very long game. Each Caiphas has understood that this cleansing will not happen in his or her lifetime." A savage smile spread across the old man's face. "Until now."

"So," Marcus said, returning the grin. "We're ready?"

"No. Not yet." Caiaphas rebutted, the smile fading. "It may be in your lifetime." His eyes narrowed. "Or the Caiaphas after you. That's why I know this promise will be hard for you. You need to understand that we may still be laying the foundation for an outcome that will not happen for another hundred years. This idea has to guide your decisions when you are Caiaphas. When selecting your Marcus. From this moment on, every thought, word, and action must be governed by this understanding. We have been willing to lose battles so that we may win the war. Totally. We've come a long way over the last two years, but there's still much we have to learn about our enemy before that victory is total. You may have to continue losing. Your Marcus may have to continue losing. His or her Marcus may have to continue losing." Caiaphas looked hard into Marcus's eyes, praying that he was heeding his words.

Marcus was paying attention to Caiaphas's words. He didn't agree with them, but he knew Caiaphas wanted him to. So he offered the word Caiaphas needed to hear. "I understand," Marcus said, nodding to Caiaphas. "I will do as you ask."

Caiaphas smiled as he drew a labored breath.

"Rest, my friend. We will speak again in the morning." Marcus said as he stood from the bed and left the room. Walking briskly down the corridor of sleeping quarters, he walked past his personal apartment and exited the building. Making his way across the compound, he ignored the sentries who acknowledged him as he passed. He marched to the structure that served as the garage and mechanical service facility. "Wrench?" Marcus yelled. "Wrench? Where are you?"

"Hold your horses," A voice yelled from underneath one of the vehicles. "Don't get your panties in a—...Marcus. I'm sorry, I didn't know it was you." Wrench said as she slid out from underneath the vehicle. "What can I do for you, sir?" Wrench asked as she stood, wiping the grease from her hands with a rag she pulled from her pocket.

"It's time," Marcus said with the savage grin he'd learned from his mentor.

48

Albuquerque, New Mexico

Marcus rubbed his temples as the Mercedes-Benz G-Class pulled into the last available parking spot in front of the unmarked warehouse. Looking out the vehicle's window, he frowned. To his right was Cornelius's blacked-out Escalade. On the other side was Josephine's Porsche Cayenne GTS in silver. His metallic blue G-Class looked small between the Escalade and Bartholomew's white Navigator. The FBI, DEA, or any of the federal acronyms would have a field day right now if they were surveilling this location or the criminal element looking for targets of opportunity, he thought, as he made a mental note to start traveling by more discreet transportation.

He pressed his forehead with the palm of his hand. The migraine was self-induced, he knew, a byproduct of the anxiety he experienced whenever he directly went against his superior's wishes. He'd been this way his entire life. Parents, teachers, or any authority figure, for that matter. The more perceived authority, the stronger the migraine. And this was by far the most defiant he'd ever been. His father told him that God had given him the migraines as a sort of morality tuning fork to keep him on the narrow path. His shrink in the Marine Corps told him it was a psychosomatic response, nothing more than a physical response to a psychological stressor. Marcus understood his father and the shrink were saying the same thing, and he learned how to cope. Migraine nasal spray and pills were always on his person.

Removing the nasal spray from his jacket pocket, Marcus tilted his head back and depressed the plunger twice in each nostril. He should only use it once, but he should've already employed the nasal spray he chastised himself. He hoped the extra medication would help it work faster. When it came to migraines and vampires, Marcus had no patience.

He thought back to the conversation with Caiaphas. The old man wanted him to wait. Wanted him to promise to continue the long game. Marcus had felt the throb behind his eyes the moment he'd looked Caiaphas in the eye and lied to him, knowing he had no intention of playing the long game. The time for waiting was over.

The only long game Marcus had been playing was assembling an alliance within the Illuminati. For months, he'd been identifying and reaching out to like-minded leaders. Cornelius, Josephine, and Bartholomew had already shown a tendency to act quickly and outside the box. They were also leaders with connections and lines of communication unavailable to Marcus. They'd been more than eager when he'd approached them, ready to shake up the Illuminati and, as Cornelius liked to say, end the vampiric carbon footprint upon this big blue marble.

Marcus stepped from the SUV, making another mental note to encourage a more modest lifestyle among the leadership as he entered the warehouse. His eyes were still adjusting to the dimness of the space when a familiar voice boomed from an office doorway at the other end of the structure.

"Marcus, my boy. How ya been?" Cornelius asked.

His voice reverberated through Marcus like a hammer on an anvil.

"Honestly, I didn't think you had it in you," Cornelius needled.

"That makes two of us," Marcus replied, unable and unwilling to sheathe his sarcasm. "The ability to think," Marcus answered in response to the puzzled look on Cornelius's face.

Cornelius nodded. "Funny." The smile on his face didn't reach his eyes or hide the bite when he spoke next. "That's funny. You know, coming from someone whose nose is so brown you can taste what the old man's eating."

Marcus bit the inside of his cheek in annoyance. He didn't mind the ribbing, but he didn't like anyone, especially Cornelius, referring to Caiaphas as the old man. Whatever he said, Cornelius wasn't using the term with affection. It was used derisively within the organization, especially by those at this meeting. They ridiculed what they saw as Caiaphas's refusal to act quickly and decisively against the vampires, his steadfast commitment to continue as his predecessors had, and his quiet, thoughtful leadership. Yes. Marcus had felt and even expressed the same sentiment when he assembled this group. But that was before Caiaphas had revealed those truths about the Illuminati. Even if he hadn't, as Marcus closed his eyes and remembered the frail body lying under the sheets, diminished in its vitality, the term reminded him of Caiaphas's mortality. Caiaphas would soon pass away.

Pass away? That phrase had never seemed so perfunctory to Marcus. So anti-climactic. Caiaphas would be dead. No more conversations. No more remonstrations. No more instructions. No more congratulations. When his second parent died, Marcus felt like an orphan despite being an adult. When Caiaphas takes his last breath, Marcus knows he'll feel like an orphan again.

Marcus opened his mouth to retort, but Tarzan beat him to it.

"You're just one big shiny bag of fertilizer, you know that, Cornelius?" Tarzan approached the man, looking him over with the same expression a father would have while perusing the dings and scratches on the family car after the teenager borrowed it the night before. He'd been given the call sign Tarzan shortly after joining the Illuminati, due to his tall, muscular physique, long dark hair, and habit of walking around the barracks without a shirt on. What secured the name was his affinity with the field. He adapted to each new environment as if he'd been born and raised by the indigenous wildlife. Some of his team members had teased him, saying he should have been a model for romance novels and suggesting the moniker Fabio. Rotty, however, hadn't approved. So, Tarzan. He didn't mind.

"You were born to wear a suit. Probably came out of your mama's womb in one." He stopped just inside Cornelius's personal space. "You may look like the C.E.O. of some Fortune Five-Hundred company or a high-powered politician, but you lack the intestinal fortitude to be Marcus or Caiaphas. You could never lead the Illuminati like Caiaphas has, and you'd never show the initiative like Marcus to assemble this alliance or insurrection or whatever we're calling it."

Cornelius's mouth worked like he was trying to free a piece of steak from between his teeth as his eyes narrowed to slits.

Marcus put a hand on each man's shoulder. "We're the good guys." He squeezed their shoulders. "Let's remember who our real enemy is." Patting Cornelius's shoulder, he added, "I know you were just joshing me."

Cornelius's mouth stopped working, but his eyes remained slits. "Whatever." He shrugged Marcus's hand off his shoulder and walked away from them towards the table and chairs in the middle of the warehouse.

Marcus watched Cornelius, feeling this was not the auspicious beginning he'd hoped for.

"He'll get over it," Tarzan said, patting Marcus on the shoulder. "As soon as you tell him it's time to," he screwed up his face and performed a reasonably accurate impression of Cornelius, "start reducing that vampiric carbon footprint."

Marcus couldn't help but laugh.

"Rotty would've loved this," Tarzan said as the others emerged from the office space and meandered to the table and chairs in the middle of the warehouse.

"No, he wouldn't," Marcus replied. "He would've loved what happens *after* this meeting.

Now it was Tarzan's turn to laugh. "True," he agreed. "But he would've loved learning you hadn't really changed when you opted for dress suits instead of battle dress uniforms."

"I'll never forget the look on his face when I told him I'd accepted the position of Marcus."

"I can't say I blamed him. He recruited you. Trained you. Thought you would replace him one day. The only thing that surprised him more than Caiaphas selecting you was your acceptance. We all felt a little betrayed."

The two men were silent for a moment.

Tarzan shoulder-checked Marcus. "I bet you had quite the migraine that day."

Marcus's grin was weary. "As bad as today's."

"Well, I'm glad you're back." He crossed his arms in front of his chest. "So. Before we join Delta Bravo over there and hash all this out, you want to tell me what you're thinking?"

The weariness left Marcus's grin. Pulling a folder from his briefcase, he handed it over to Tarzan. "This came across my desk a couple of days ago. As soon as I saw it, I knew."

"What is it?"

Marcus nodded at the folder.

Tarzan opened it.

"The vampires have a top-secret compound."

Tarzan thumbed through the pages. "Any idea what's there?"

Marcus shrugged. "We only found it by accident three days ago."

"And I assume you didn't pass this information on to Caiaphas?"

Marcus's smile was mischievous. "What do you think? But as soon as I saw it, I knew we had our next target."

Tarzan understood Marcus meant this alliance, not the Illuminati. "You think this crew will go for it?"

"I do."

"You ready for this?"

"I am."

"When do you want to hit it?"

"As soon as you're ready."

"And where is it—?" Whistling, Tarzan looked from the map in the folder to Marcus. "North Africa?"

49

Roman Dvanaesti's Estate, Italy

Jacquelyn walked past the open doors of the library, averting her eyes as she made her way to the study. The library was too much of a distraction. It was too easy to lose herself. All these years, and she was still impressed by it. Roman's collection surpassed most others. Not only was it for its sheer volume, but every item was a first edition.

When she was younger, she would spend days in the library, reading and re-reading every ancient tome in the grand room. By the time she left for university, she'd read each work at least three times. Roman had strict rules about how the manuscripts could be consumed. Special gloves had to be worn. There was a special table with a special chair. Jacquelyn wore the gloves, but she always lay on the floor.

Entering the study, she walked to the bar and poured herself a drink before sitting in one of the armchairs. She knew Roman would be joining her shortly, having felt his presence inside her mind since he summoned her. Jacquelyn bit her lip as she swallowed. She always felt his presence. It was a dull roar in the back of her mind. Over the centuries, she'd learned to ignore it, make it part of the background noise, like cicadas on a summer night. But Roman could break through to the front of her mind at his leisure. It was one of the downsides to having his blood coursing through her veins.

"I need your help, daughter," Roman said, appearing across from her in the other chair.

Jacquelyn wasn't startled by his sudden appearance. There was no need for pretense between vampires, but there was always a desire to show power. "And you decided to converse with me, rather than just planting a to-do list inside my head?" Jacquelyn didn't try to hide her sarcasm.

"I need your help while your mother is recovering," Roman said, ignoring her tone. "There has been a development with the Illuminati that I would like to speak with you about."

"What do you think? That I'm nothing more than one of your pawns, you can move around as you will? The work I'm doing in D.C. is vital. I have responsibilities. Which you gave me." Jacquelyn spat the last sentence with as much venom as she could.

"You should consider yourself a bishop or a rook." Roman's face and tone were expressionless.

Well, Jacquelyn thought, at least he doesn't deny it anymore. "What's the difference?" She asked. "The pieces are all the same to you. Nothing more than tools for you to manipulate and move to serve your purpose."

"You misunderstand, daughter. I do not need to send you on an errand. I seek your counsel," Roman replied.

This response caught Jacquelyn off guard. For more than two centuries, she and Roman had butted heads like a father with his obstinate teenage daughter. And like a mother, Isabella ran interference, soothed ruffled feathers, and protected her from Roman's wrath. It was a side of Isabella no one else ever saw. Jacquelyn and Roman rarely saw eye to eye, and Jacquelyn never shied away from sharing her opinion, always unsolicited. For the first time in her existence as a vampire, Roman was seeking her advice.

"What do you mean? Council?" Jacquelyn asked.

"I often rely on your mother to help me process and resolve certain issues. Especially the ones that may have long-term ramifications," Roman replied. "Despite what you may think, your mother's opinion is very valuable to me. I can see from the puzzled look on your face that this surprises you." Roman continued.

"To be honest, yes. I've never thought anyone's opinion mattered other than your own." Jacquelyn replied, bemused.

Roman leaned back in his chair and sighed. "I suppose you forming that opinion of me is no one's fault but my own. The truth is that I rely on Isabella more than I would care to admit." A sly smile curved his lips. "Especially to her. Now I need to know if I can rely on you while she is healing. I know your work in Washington is important, which is why I gave it to you."

Jacquelyn felt the tension in her body fading; her defenses lowered as Roman spoke. Despite the arguments, her rebellion, and the endless tension between them, she wanted his approval and respect. She'd never admit it, though, not even to herself sometimes.

"It's regarding your brother," Roman continued.

Jaquelyn felt the tension return like a lightning strike. Every muscle in her body went taut. Her hands balled into fists. Her lips pursed. "That half-breed is not my brother." Jacquelyn stood to leave. "And you know how I feel about it."

"Sit," Roman said in a soft tone.

Jacquelyn felt her body respond to the command involuntarily. As she sat down, she felt the release of his control over her limbs subside.

"As you know, Cain's plane crashed. Though the remains of the flight crew and his fiancée were found, his body was never recovered."

"And you have him stashed away somewhere while he heals."

"And why would I do that? I ordered the plane shot down." Roman waited a beat for that to sink in before adding, "No survivors."

This last statement got Jacquelyn's full attention. So, she thought, Cain was just another pawn after all. Those unfamiliar feelings of sibling rivalry were unfounded, just as Isabella had been telling her for the last three decades. It had irked her even more than when Roman referred to the half-breed as her brother, that feeling she was competing with him for Roman and Isabella's approval. Roman hadn't shared his plans for Cain with her, but Isabella had. Even knowing, she still felt that childish pang. Not anymore.

Jacquelyn leaned back in the chair and crossed her legs. "So. How can I help you? Father?" Jacquelyn asked with a wicked grin.

Roman returned the expression.

50

Vampire Compound,
Bir Tawil, North Africa

Sierra One Alpha was tasked with clearing the lower levels of the compound while Sierra One Bravo cleared the compound's topside. This facility was unique among any of the compounds the Sierra One team had been deployed to. To begin with, Sierra One was here without its counterpart team, Sierra Two.

While other vampire compounds had at least some semblance of minimal security with a vampiric presence, this one didn't appear to be a compound at all. Its façade had been designed to blend in with the environment. The Illuminati stumbled on its existence completely by accident. Upon breaching the compound, it was obvious that while vampires didn't want anyone coming into their other spaces, this one was meant to keep someone or something from getting out. The security was massive and faced inwards, not outwards.

And finally, Sierra One Alpha came to a space they'd never encountered in a vampire compound: A cell block.

"Well, this is new," Tarzan said as he stared at the massive steel door. "Bravo, this is Alpha," he said over his mic. "We've reached a brig." He tried the door and found it locked tight. Using hand signals, he called for explosive entry.

Blaze hustled up to the door and slapped C4 charges around the door.

"We're going to breach. Over." Tarzan watched Blaze work and wondered why the vampires would need such an area.

"Bravo, this is Alpha. Standby. Over."

"There's no way they can hear us," Jacks said, rapping the wall with a gloved hand. "There's too much rock between us. We have to be over three hundred meters down." Jacks received his call sign because he always treated everything like a game, especially killing vampires. Shrugging, he added, "You thought those stairs sucked going down?" He whistled. "After we go back up, we'll have our steps in for the year."

"Fire in the hole," Blaze announced as he stepped back from the C4 charges he had placed on the door. Unlike Tarzan and Jacks, Blaze hadn't grown up in the Illuminati. He'd been recruited. He'd been an explosive ordnance disposal, E.O.D., technician in the service and was drummed out after losing a SEAL team overseas. Like the Navy, he thought it was due to a mistake he'd made. It had been his first and only mistake in his career, but it had exemplified the unofficial E.O.D. motto of "Initial Success or Total Failure." Treated as a pariah by the rest of the E.O.D. community and unable to cope with the deaths of the sixteen men, Blaze started drinking heavily. He got into fights in bars, usually instigating no-win situations involving himself and three or more opponents. The Naval psychiatrist said he was suffering from moral masochism and recommended therapy stateside. The Navy and Blaze disagreed.

So one night, Blaze found himself a newly minted civilian. He decided to celebrate by picking a fight with a guy who looked and sounded like a Rottweiler and his four buddies. The bartender told them all to take it out back, and he wouldn't call the cops. Blaze intended for the guy, his buddies called him Rotty, to put him in a pine box. Rotty, it turned out, had been there to illumine Blaze. The young man had not made a mistake, but was made a scapegoat by the vampires. The SEALs had gotten too close to one of their operations.

The fourth man on Sierra One Alpha, call sign Ghost, never said a word. Never made a sound. He seemed able to walk through walls.

And in a firefight or hand-to-hand combat, he was straight out of a scary movie.

Light poured from the hole where the door had been, revealing a tunnel with steps descending for approximately one hundred meters and filled with light of the same hue as the lighting they'd used initially during the assault on this compound. After Miami, every soldier in the Illuminati knew that light. Except here, it was brighter. Stronger.

"What the...?" Tarzan spat as he peered into a tunnel

"Why would vamps be using Phase Two lights?" Jacks asked.

Tarzan shook his head, stumped. "Stay sharp," Tarzan said, his eyes never leaving the tunnel. His hand signals indicated he had point, and the rest were to follow as he entered.

"How deep does this thing go?" Blaze asked.

"That's what she said," Jacks quipped.

"Focus," Tarzan ordered.

"Roger that," Jacks said as he turned and tapped Blaze on the shoulder as if he'd been the flippant one.

Blaze raised a middle finger.

Jacks chuckled, puckered his lips, and kissed the air before turning back.

Ghost only rolled his eyes from his position at the rear.

The tunnel widened and ended at another steel door. Two large tanks secured to the walls consumed most of the space. Pipes ran up from the tanks and disappeared into the rock wall. A small panel housing a dial and a red button was set into the rock.

"Check it," Tarzan ordered.

Blaze looked over the arrangement. "One metric ton of Acetylene and a whole lot of oh two." He ran gloved fingers over the panel. "Ignition source and controller. Looks like someone's planning a barbecue of whatever's inside."

"You're mixing your metaphors again, Blaze," Jacks japed. "Or at least your units of measurement." Sticking his ear to the door, he banged on it three times. "Little pig, little pig, let me in." Jacks said in a singsong voice. "Or I'll blow your house up."

Tarzan opened his mouth to order Jacks to stand down, but didn't. Instead, he turned his ear towards the door. "Did you hear that?"

"Hear what?" Blazed responded.

Tarzan stepped closer to the door. "There. A voice."

"I don't hear anything." Blaze stuck his ear to the door.

"Wow, an E.O.D. didn't hear something. Who'da figured?" Jacks stuck his ear to the door. "I hear it too. More than one voice. What's that? All the models from this year's Sports Illustrated swimsuit issue? Still clad in your bikinis? You'd love to show us your appreciation if we let you out? You want to—?"

"Stow it, Jacks," Tarzan ordered, leaning his ear to the door again. "Sounds like a male voice calling for help." He looked at Blaze. "Can you open it," he glanced at the tanks, "without blowing us to smithereens?"

Blaze nodded.

The rest of the squad stepped back up the stairs as Blaze placed the charges.

"Fire in the hole," Blaze said as he joined the others.

The squad walked through the smoke into darkness as they lowered and activated their NODs, Night Observation Devices. Taking up formation, two to the right and two to the left, they cleared space.

The space resembled a large empty warehouse carved out of the rock by heavy machinery. The floor, walls, and ceiling were rough and unfinished rock. Pipes and tanks, similar to the ones in the tunnel, snaked across the high ceiling. Steel beams spaced sixteen inches apart, like framing, ran from the floor and met steel joists running across the ceiling. Secured to these beams were flood lamps. Their spacing and number ensured that when turned on, not only would no crook or cranny in the room be missed, but there'd be overkill of that light. In the center of the space stood a large rock pillar.

"Please," a frail voice whispered from the pillar. "Help me." The words sounded dry and scratchy, like old paper that flakes when exposed to air. The voice sounded old and not accustomed to speaking.

Each man snapped his weapon toward the pillar.

"Hello," Tarzan called out, gesturing for his team to position themselves around the pillar.

Circling the pillar, Tarzan found the source of the voice. In the green light of his NOD, the form at the pillar's base looked like the desiccated remains of an old man who'd sat down to rest and died many years ago. He was reminded of the pictures he'd seen of the concentration camps during the holocaust. Tarzan squeezed the remote pressure switch on the tactical Phase Two light attached to his weapon.

The old man twitched and grimaced as if the light had shaken him awake like a hand. "Please help me." He held up a pleading hand as he squinted into the light.

"Clear," Tarzan announced, breathing a sigh of relief that the man was not harmed or showing any signs of discomfort from the Phase Two light.

Sierra One Alpha converged on the old man, switching from tactical clearance of a hostile space to hostage rescue.

Blaze poured water into the lid of his canteen and handed it to the old man. "Take this."

"Thank you," The old man breathed as he accepted the lid and drank.

"Whadda we do, boss?" Jacks questioned as he ran his hands over the old man, checking for broken bones or other injuries.

"Liberate him," Tarzan answered. He looked for Ghost, wanting his best man covering the door, and found him already doing just that.

"We need a torch," Blaze said, now examining the chains and manacles around the old man's neck, wrists, and ankles.

"We don't have time. Blow the chains, and we'll deal with the manacles later," Tarzan said.

Jacks examined the heavy chain after laying his tactical vest over the man's legs. "Seems like way more than overkill for an old geezer."

Blaze fell backward, grasping his chest.

Tarzan froze in horror as he looked at the gaping hole in Blaze's chest. He looked to where the old man had been lying, but he was no longer there. Dropping to one knee, Tarzan raised his weapon and scanned the room. He found the old man, no longer manacled, eyes closed, an expression of sublime joy on his face, holding Blaze's heart to his mouth. His finger moved to the trigger as he aimed at the old man's center mass. Then Jacks was there, one arm snaking around the old man's neck as his fighting knife arced towards the old man's side. The old man and Jacks vanished.

A thud sounded to Tarzan's left. He'd been in this business too long not to recognize the sound of a lifeless body falling to the ground. His stomach turned to ice as Jacks's dead body filled his scope. He scanned for Ghost and found him, resembling his call sign in the green light. His body crumpled to the floor like a sheet as the old man disappeared again.

In less than thirty seconds, three of his team members lay dead. Men whom he treasured as brothers were now corpses. Rage seized Tarzan. A desire for revenge coursed through his veins. He thumbed his selector to Burst and pulled the trigger. Standing and running for the door, Tarzan continued to pull the trigger as he swung his rifle right to left and up and down. He had no way of knowing if he'd hit the old man.

Old man?

A laugh tore from Tarzan's throat at that thought. That hadn't been an old man locked in this cell, chained to a pillar. An old man hadn't clawed through breastbone and ribcage and yanked a beating heart from a body. An old man hadn't disappeared and reappeared at will. And that wasn't an old man now ascending the emergency stairway to the surface. That was a vampire.

"Bravo, this is Alpha. Come in," Tarzan screamed into his mic as he followed the vampire up the stairs. "Bravo, this is Alpha. Tango headed your way." He could feel his heart beating out of his chest as his leg muscles burned. He continued to climb, weapon trained up and ahead. "Bravo-"

Screams and gunfire filled his ears. Tarzan stopped climbing and leaned against the wall to steady himself as his hands shook so violently that he couldn't believe he still held his weapon. His sight blurred from moisture even as he reasoned with himself that what he heard wasn't what was happening. Bravo had been surprised, that's all. They'd been surprised, but then they'd quickly recovered. Now, they were making mincemeat out of that vampire. When he busted through that ground-floor door, he'd find Bravo talking trash about Alpha over the body of a dead vampire. He kept climbing.

Nothing but static was coming over the mic now. Tarzan continued up the stairs, lungs on fire, breathing hard and fast, legs moving on pure muscle memory. Bursting through the door, he made his way back to the entry point of the compound. There was nothing recognizable left of Bravo. Blood and body parts were strewn about. Not only humans, but also the vampires guarding the compound. As Tarzan reached the light of day, he let the sun wash over him. Taking deep breaths and slowly exhaling, he dropped his weapon and bent over, planting his hands on his knees, forcing himself to calm down. Once his heart rate was no longer thudding in his ear, he ran to one of the Oshkosh armored vehicles and grabbed the radio.

"Sierra One Alpha to Overwatch. Sierra One Alpha to Overwatch. Call sign Tarzan. Made contact with an unknown tango. Team has been compromised. I repeat. Team has been compromised.

"Overwatch to Sierra One Alpha. Understood, Tarzan. Do you need support or evac?"

Tarzan looked for a moment at the radio in disbelief, then looked back over his shoulder at blood and body parts that once belonged to humans and vampires. Hysterical laughter burst from Tarzan's lips.

51

New Orleans, Louisiana

Georges took another handful of painkillers and washed them down with a swallow straight from the absinthe bottle. The constant dull throb in his head was forgotten only when what felt like an electrical current ran through the center of his eye every few minutes.

It was the eye Isabella had punctured with her fangs. She hadn't sucked the viscous material from the socket but pierced the optic nerve. Then she'd done something he hadn't known was possible. She'd injected a thought into his mind like a surgeon performing a fine needle aspiration. Now, his brain worked against him, preventing the nerve from mending. The eye would heal, she told him. Eventually. In a decade, maybe two. He needed a reminder of his failure to help teach him; he needed to learn and never do it again. He also had a visual reminder every time he looked in the mirror. His eye was always bloodshot, and it wept bloody water.

One of the young women sitting next to Georges on the circular sofa of the VIP section, in a black bustier, her hair, lips, and nails dyed black, skin bleached white, reached to wipe away the fluid.

Slapping her hand away, Georges pulled a silk scarf from his vest pocket and dabbed it, clearing his vision. He squinted as the bright lights invaded his retina like a cattle prod.

As a human, he'd suffered from photosensitivity. He'd learned to avert his eyes when police and ambulance lights flashed. He didn't watch films containing strobe effects and avoided dance clubs with pulsating light shows. Once he'd become a vampire, that sensitivity no longer afflicted him, until now. Now the lights sharpened the pain in his skull while nauseating his stomach.

But Isabella had been clear. There were consequences to his actions. His decision to kill LeBlanc had been rash. Regardless of how tawdry the young vampire and his club were, they made money for House Dvanaesti. That would not change. Georges would oversee the operations of 'V' in addition to his establishment.

Georges had always despised this place with its relentless pounding beat from the music and lights. The stink of sweat, vomit, cologne, perfume, cigarettes, and pheromones. The sad excuse for vampires and wannabe vamps that exhibited their flesh night after night.

To highlight his disdain for the goths at the club, the woman in the bustier stuck her tongue in his ear and her hand in his crotch. She didn't see Georges move, didn't feel her neck snap. He lay her lifeless body back on the sofa, considered draining the cooling blood from her body, and dismissed the idea. He'd rather imbibe a Bloodsucker: 'V's house cocktail. It was nothing more than a Bloody Mary warmed in a microwave and served in a faux-medieval goblet.

I hate my life.

Georges rubbed both temples, staring at the floor to hide his eyes from the pulsating lights. This didn't help since his view now was that of the lime-green shag throw rug on the floor, complemented by the leopard-print sofa he was sitting on. His head started to swim with a wave of nausea.

And I hate Isabella.

"Georges."

His head shot up. The voice had invaded his mind, not his ears. Georges knew the difference. Isabella was the only vampire he knew with that power, but this had been a man's voice. Focusing across the turbulent sea of smoke and writhing bodies, his vision blurring as his eye kept up its relentless weeping, he searched for the owner of that voice.

"Georges."

The voice drew Georges's attention to a man standing at the club's entrance. He was dressed in a black suit with a black silk shirt. His thick, velvety hair hung like a curtain past his shoulders, accentuating the copper tone of his skin. The man was the essence of masculinity and virility, yet not another patron noticed him. No one shot him long, hungry looks, or made a beeline for him to make his acquaintance. It was like he wasn't there; not like a wallflower, but as if the space he inhabited didn't exist. No one stepped into it or tried to avoid it. He was there, yet...wasn't. It was captivating.

But what enchanted Georges was the man's eyes. They sparkled like blue sapphires in the sun. Georges imagined falling into them. It would be like falling into a bottomless pit.

"You're beautiful."

Georges didn't know if he'd said the words out loud or thought them. Would it matter? There's no way the man could have heard Georges over the music and chatter. If the observation was only in his head, then there was nothing to hear anyway.

Yet the man smiled as if he'd heard the compliment.

This was no man, Georges realized. He was a vampire. And a powerful one at that. More powerful than Georges could ever imagine a vampire to be. Isabella paled next to him.

The vampire disappeared and reappeared in the middle of the dance floor. Again, none of the bodies moving to the music invaded his space. No one jostled the vampire. The dancers were as unhindered by his presence as he was by theirs. He disappeared and reappeared at the ropes separating the VIP section from the rest of the crowd. Before the two vampire bodyguards could react to his presence, they dropped to the floor, grasping the space where their throats had once been a second before.

Georges gasped as he found the vampire now sitting next to him. He pushed back into the sofa as if that offered some protection and distance.

The vampire smiled. "If I wanted to harm you, there is nothing you could do to prevent it."

Georges had expected the vampire to speak with an accent. Perhaps end his words in hard consonants. *Wantedeh. Couldeh.* But he didn't. No emphasis on the wrong syllable. His pronunciation was flawless. There was nothing about his speech that hinted at where in the world this vampire had come from.

The vampire looked around the club, frowning with disgust. "Do you think this is what we are meant for?"

"What do you mean?"

The vampire looked hard at Georges for a long time. "You really have no idea, do you? Who our father is. How we came to be. Our purpose and design. Our history."

Georges stared back, completely dumbfounded.

"We are *gods*. Meant to rule and to reign over mortals, not fetch them drinks and provide them entertainment. Or play silly little games of politics with them." The vampire looked around the space, hissing as he sniffed the air. "I smell the taint of the dilution of our blood." The vampire leaned in and sniffed Georges as if he were inhaling cologne and smiled. "You bear the scent of greatness. Of power. You are meant to be worshipped. Feared. You are a prince. Not a court jester." He locked eyes with Georges. "Not a pawn on someone else's chessboard."

Georges's heart burned in his chest at the vampire's words. All his life, he knew, hadn't he? He knew he was meant for more than the menial or mundane. All his life, he'd not only yearned for the finer things but surrounded himself with them. He was meant for them. He was meant to be served, not to serve. Isabella had promised him freedom from humanity's afflictions, yet inflicted her miseries upon him. He had immortality and the finer things in life, but he still suffered. Still slaved.

The vampire reached out and softly touched Georges's face just below his injured eye. "Do you want to know our truth? Your truth? Are you ready to take your rightful place?"

Georges nodded.

The vampire smiled. He picked up a shot glass and poured out the alcohol onto the area rug. Using his nail, the vampire opened his wrist and filled the shot glass with his blood.

Georges watched the wound close as the last drop fell.

The vampire offered the glass to Georges.

Eyeing the red liquid with unashamed lust, Georges accepted the glass. His head snapped back as he swallowed the blood like a shot of whiskey. A pleasant heat rushed down his throat and exploded in his stomach. The flavor reminded him of his mother's homemade beef bourguignon, but richer. Better than the first time he tasted blood as a new vampire. He could now feel the vampire's blood hit his bloodstream. It was more intense than any rush of adrenaline he'd ever felt. It wasn't electricity flowing through his veins but lightning. He could feel his cells, nerves, sinews, muscle tissues, even his bones, strengthening. His eye tingled as his once-blurry vision sharpened and grew keener. Now, his mind swam with euphoric bliss as the knowledge of the Ancients saturated his gray matter.

"Master," Georges breathed, bowing his head to the vampire.

The vampire lifted Georges's head. "I'm not your master. I have come to set you free. Not to enslave you. He smiled. "Join me."

52

Illuminati Compound,
Caja del Rio Plateau, New Mexico

Cain Dvanaesti found himself walking a circuit around his room yet again. He hadn't realized he'd begun moving. Just a minute ago (or an hour?), he'd been sitting at the table, staring at a chessboard, observing the pieces, thinking of their uses, how they moved on the board. Their strengths and weaknesses. Their purpose. It's something he'd taken to doing every day: Contemplating who in his sphere, before the attack on his Miami mansion, had been what piece on the board. Today, he'd realized it depended on his father's scheme, and most people in his sphere didn't even rate a place on the board in his father's eyes. Not even...

Claudia.

Despair, anger, and guilt flowed through his veins like adrenaline. He could feel them empowering and destroying him at the same time. She was the one thing in his life he'd chosen for himself. And he'd chosen well. She was kind, honest, smart, funny, and beautiful. She always saw the best in people. She made those around her glad to be around her. She wasn't perfect, but she was perfect for him. Because of him, Claudia had gone from an insignificant human to a pawn sacrificed for his father's gambit. He'd been so consumed with his ruminations that he didn't hear the footsteps approaching his door. He was collapsing into the chair before the board as the door unlocked and opened.

"Hawthorne." Cain jumped to his feet.

If it weren't for his vampiric ability, Gabriel wouldn't have seen the movement. To the guards watching the monitors, it appeared to be a system glitch. One moment, Cain Dvanaesti was sitting at the table. In the next moment, he was standing face to face with Gabriel Hawthorne at the open door.

The perfect storm of emotions raging inside Cain finally broke at the sight of Gabriel. In Cain's mind, Gabriel was just as guilty as his father for Claudia's death. He could understand Gabriel's desire to undermine him, even forgive it. What would he have done if he'd found he had a rival for Claudia's affections? But this man is partly responsible for what happened to Claudia. Maybe even mostly.

Gabriel held both hands up in surrender as he stared into Cain's eyes, watching them transform into pools of black tar. Gabriel braced himself, hoping that Cain would be willing to listen.

Cain's hands found their way around Gabriel's throat and squeezed. He wasn't seeing red. He wasn't seeing anything. The world was as pitch black as his eyes.

Gabriel grabbed Cain's wrists and wrenched his hands from his throat.

Cain stepped back in shock as he watched Gabriel massage his neck where he had grasped it. Cain wasn't at full strength until he transformed into the beast, but the fact that Gabriel had the strength to escape his grip could mean only one thing.

"You're a vampire," Cain hissed.

Gabriel nodded, continuing to knead his throat. "Your father." Gabriel's voice was hoarse but not as rough as Cain would've expected.

Then again, Cain hadn't expected Gabriel to be able to speak at all. He knew that Gabriel had spoken the truth. Though the scent was faint, he could smell his father's blood coursing through Gabriel's veins. He cursed himself for still referring to Roman, still thinking of Roman, as his father. He hated the fact that they even shared the same last name. Cain felt himself deflate.

"Why are you here?" Cain asked as he sat down at the table.

"I'm here for Claudia," Gabriel answered, sitting at the table across from Cain.

"Claudia is...Claudia's gone." Cain said, stanching the tears pooling in his eyes. He suddenly wanted to swipe the chessboard and pieces from the table, but he had no heart. So he wiped his eyes again while he let those words take on weight and fall heavy on his shoulders.

"I know," Gabriel whispered. He stared beyond the chessboard and the table, bearing that weight on his shoulders as well. "And I know you blame me."

"You were still in love with her. And you couldn't handle the fact that she no longer felt that way about you. You couldn't handle that she was in love with me. That's why you're here now, and that's why you were in Miami."

Leaning back in the chair, Gabriel selected the knight. It was an exquisite piece. Carved from stone, it was a medieval knight in chainmail, sword at his side, hands resting on his shield before him. The details were exceptional. Gabriel felt the knight wasn't just surveying the carnage of the battlefield, but him as well. And it was heavy, a good weight. Gabriel side-armed the piece into Cain's chest.

The impact would have knocked a human being from the chair, perhaps leaving the stone embedded in his breastbone. But Cain wasn't a human being. He wasn't even a vampire. Still, it got his attention. He stared from his chest to the knight and then at Gabriel, stunned.

"You arrogant, self-absorbed, son of a bloodsucker," Gabriel exclaimed. "You want to make this about you and me? Okay, yes. I was *in love* with Claudia, and she was *in love* with me. Once. A long time ago. By the time I met you at your mansion for that fundraiser, I'd grown comfortable with the fact that she'd been the best thing to happen to me and that I'd screwed it up. I still loved her, but I wasn't in love with her. I didn't want her back, but because I loved her, I wanted the best for her. I didn't think that was you."

Cain smirked.

Gabriel returned the smirk. "It's not personal. You were a politician. Why would I think you were any different? My career as a cop ended because of a politician. I'd spent ten years digging up the bodies politicians had buried. Ten *years*. I always found something on every politician I investigated. Why wouldn't I think I would find something on you?" He selected the king and leaned back in his chair. "I started digging. And what I found convinced me." Holding up the king for Cain to see, he said, "Your father."

"Don't call him that," Cain spat.

Silence passed between the two men for a full thirty seconds.

Cain now realized he would never again call Roman Dvanaesti his father. Never see the man- No. The monster that way again.

Gabriel realized Cain was ready to listen. Setting the king down in the center of the chessboard, he said, "It's time for the monster to pay for what he did to Claudia," and tipped the king over.

53

New Orleans, Louisiana

Georges touched the corner of his eye as he checked his reflection in the mirror. It no longer wept. Electricity no longer surged through his socket. His vision was no longer blurry. He smiled, tugging at the vest that covered his black silk shirt. It reminded him of the one the vampire had worn when Georges first saw him at 'V.' Though the vampire had never verbally revealed his identity, Georges knew who he was after he drank his blood. He knew everything after drinking his blood. He'd become enlightened. So, though he knew the vampire's identity and understood and respected his desire for anonymity, Georges christened him Ra.

"The cars are ready, sir," Jessie, head of Georges's bodyguard staff, said as he entered the room.

Georges followed Jessie to two Mercedes-Benz S-Class sedans parked behind his more subdued club, followed by an entourage of four vampires. Jessie and Georges climbed into the first car with its driver while the four other vampires crammed themselves into the second. The vehicles traveled through the French Quarter toward Crescent Park alongside the Mississippi River. They would often call meetings like this on or near bodies of water. It was sacred amongst the vampires. It reminded Georges of the way churches were treated in the Highlander movies.

Until Georges met Ra at *"V,"* he'd never known the origin of how or why vampires were forbidden to shed the blood of another vampire near water. He didn't know of the Ancients. Didn't know of the Culling. Didn't know of so many things. But now all had been revealed to him.

The cars pulled into a parking area where several vehicles were already gathered. Georges knew that the climate of this meeting would be volatile. How could it not? Considering those attending. Sure enough, as Georges exited the sedan, he saw several groups of vampires gathered around, leering at one another. Most of the gathered were leaders from unsanctioned covens, created by fledgling vampires without their maker's permission. They and their creators were always the first destroyed in the Culling. Provided they were allowed to survive that long.

As Georges observed the leering and posturing, he could hear the dull roar of more than a dozen motorcycles approaching. The bikes, traveling in two columns, pulled into the parking area and then split to the left and right of the gathered vampires. Circling the group, the bikers sneered and offered hand gestures before reforming their two columns. Halting their bikes, they formed a barricade. None of the gathered vampires were leaving without going through the bikers and their Harleys.

On Miguel's signal, each biker throttled up his engine to a scream. When the last biker had throttled his engine, Miguel signaled, and this time, all the bikers began revving. The already vibrating engines blurred. The roar crescendoed to that of a caterwauling freight train as the bikers throttled their engines to a mechanized frenzy. The leering vampires broke their posturing to grimace in pain as they covered their ears with their hands.

Well, Georges thought, it was enough to invite Miguel and his crew, if only for that moment. Miguel was the founder and president of *Los Viajeros Oscuros*. The Dark Travelers. Georges liked the name. And it was the perfect moniker for what Georges had planned for them.

Miguel pulled his thumb across his throat in a cutting gesture. The engines were all cut off as one. He swung off his bike and stood to his full height. The others followed.

Georges extended his hand to Miguel as the gathered vampires eyed Miguel and his bikers with contempt but said nothing. "Welcome to New Orleans."

Miguel had only met Georges once before. He hadn't been impressed. Georges had been nothing more than a prissy errand boy toy. His initial instinct was to ignore Georges's greeting and outstretched hand, but something changed his mind. Something was different about him. The aura radiating from Georges was of power, strength, and confidence.

Miguel had never experienced such power or strength in a vampire, not even the one who'd made him. Instead of dismissing Georges's hand, he found himself...fearful. From the uncomfortable body language of the other vampires gathered, he was not alone. Miguel wasn't sure why, but he was sure Georges hadn't offered a hand to the others. And they were glad. He looked over the gathered leaders again. They were all either competitors or enemies of each other, and all were competitors and enemies of *Los Viajeros Oscuros*. Miguel accepted Georges's hand.

Georges looked around the gathered leaders. "Follow me." He looked past them to their crews. "The rest of you stay here." He turned and added over his shoulder, "And behave."

"Who put you in charge, pretty boy?"

The disrespect elicited laughter from the other leaders, which stopped just as abruptly as blood spurted from the hole that had once been the questioner's throat.

"Any other questions?" Georges asked as he pulled a scarf from his vest pocket and began to clean the blood from his hand. He made eye contact with each vampire. No one responded. George nodded before turning and walking to a table his entourage had set up.

Miguel and the other leaders followed, noticing a briefcase now resting on the table. Feeling he was the de facto spokesperson for the group because of Georges's handshake but preferring his throat to stay where it was, Miguel raised his hand like a third-grader waiting patiently for the teacher to call on him.

Georges turned and raised an inquisitive eyebrow.

Miguel ran his bottom lip between his front teeth. "There's no love lost for...," he gestured with a nod towards the fallen vampire's body, "...and I would venture to say that without that demonstration, we might all be at each other's throats right now, including yours." He looked around the group and saw agreement on the others' faces. He continued. "When you requested our presence here, you mentioned an alliance that would benefit us all. I sense in you something greater and more terrible than the rest of us combined. Perhaps even more than the one who created us." He summoned his nerve and locked eyes with Georges. "Are you offering us the opportunity to work for you in exchange for our lives?"

Georges's face lit up as if Miguel had just paid him the ultimate compliment. "Not for me. But it does involve your lives. In a manner of speaking." He looked around the gathered vampires. "I will ask a question. Where does wealth and power come from?" He waited a beat before answering, "Knowledge. It's more than having all the answers. It's knowing what questions to ask." He turned back and laid his hands on the briefcase. "I am about to answer questions you didn't even know you wanted answers to." Georges unlatched the case and opened it. "We've been lied to. Used. Treated no better than humans. Worse." Georges reached into the briefcase and extracted a tiny glass vial. Holding it up to the light, he stared reverently at the dark liquid inside. "All of us have been lied to. They have lied to us. They want us divided. Not trusting each other, not questioning them. They want us divided and distracted. They want us to be ignorant. Ignorance is controllable."

"They?" Miguel asked. "They who?"

"The Ancients."

"Ancients? You mean the ones who created us?"

Georges laughed. "The ones who created us aren't even mere children. They're infants. They're just as ignorant and distracted as we are." He held up the vial. "The knowledge of what we are, where we began, what we can do is contained within this blood." He handed the vial to Miguel. He extracted more vials from the briefcase and handed them out.

Each vial was accepted, but no one dared to unstop their vial.

Georges could see the excitement and reluctance on their faces. He approached Miguel and traded vials with him. Unstopping the vial, he opened his mouth and drank. Waves of pleasure and bliss washed over him.

Miguel pulled the cork from the vial and held it to his nose. His head swam from the aroma. He put the vial to his lips and drank. He remembered the first time he used heroin as a human. The only feeling more intense had been the first time he'd tasted blood as a vampire, until now.

Georges knew what Miguel was experiencing as he watched the biker vampire's head drift back and his eyes close: The origin and history of vampires.

It had only taken a moment, but to Miguel it felt like a millennium. A lazy smile enveloped his face as his eyes finally opened. He felt a heady power flowing through his body like an electrical current. "Drink," he commanded.

The others did.

Miguel waited for the others to open their eyes before stepping to Georges and embracing him like a brother. "When do we get to meet him?" He asked after he pulled away. "When do we meet..." he smiled, "...Ra?"

54

Roman Dvanaesti's Estate, Italy

"What, child?" Roman asked without even turning to look at the young vampire standing in the doorway of Isabella's room. The Ancients knew where all those they had created were at all times, even when they might not know what they were doing. Roman spent long hours at Isabella's bedside, overseeing her healing, watching her sleep. Yet, even as he only had eyes for the woman in the bed, no one ever crept up on Roman unawares.

"Master," Cinzia cried, startled by his awareness of her. So startled that she didn't realize he hadn't said the words out loud, but in her head. "There's news from the security room, sir. I was instructed to summon you."

"Summon?"

Cinzia heard the dangerous tone in Roman's voice. "Request," she breathed. "Yes. I was instructed to tell you your presence is *requested* in the security room."

Roman stood from the chair seated next to Isabella's bed. He bent over and kissed her smooth and flawless forehead. Isabella had fully recovered from the fire. There wasn't any sign of scarring, not one blemish to be found anywhere. Her hair had grown back. She looked as young and beautiful as the first time he'd seen her. The only thing left was for her to wake from her deep slumber. Roman turned and walked past Cinzia without saying a word. "It's all right, child. Thank you." Roman whispered inside her head before the man disappeared in a blur.

"Master," Dante, head of Roman's security, snapped to his feet as Roman entered the room.

"What news could be so troubling that you would send a child to summon me rather than relay the message yourself, Dante?" Roman asked in a soft, puzzled tone. Of course, he'd already guessed what the news was. Nothing involving his children happened without his knowledge. He thought of Cain secretly overdosing on his blood under his and Isabella's noses, and checked the sour grimace ready to spread across his face.

Almost nothing.

"My apologies, master. I meant no disrespect. I..." Dante's voice trailed off as if he feared what he was about to say would rekindle Roman's wrath.

Roman was growing tired of his children's incessant fear of speaking to him. True, his temper had been shorter since he'd retrieved Isabella's body and brought her home to Italy. He'd not been so mild-mannered, so soft-spoken. He'd been more likely to explode in a fiery tempest of emotion when interrupted from his vigil over Isabella. But after the explosion, all was forgotten. He didn't hold grudges. He didn't 'shoot the messenger,' to use the modern idiom. Or run the messenger through with a sword, for that matter. This last thought almost made him chuckle.

Almost.

But Isabella was mended. Soon, she would wake up. Roman was beginning to feel like his old self again. Perhaps he could take a breath, let it out slowly, and offer his chief of security the proverbial olive branch. "You...what, Dante? You feared that I would be upset that the Illuminati discovered what was responsible for all the dead rats in Venice? Or should I say *who* was responsible for all the dead rats? That they discovered it was Gabriel Hawthorne? And that upon learning he was now one of us, they would collect him?" Roman waved a dismissive hand. "It was only a matter of time," Roman said as a prideful grin brightened his face. "There's not much that gets past Caiaphas. His attention to detail, while at the same time seeing the big picture, is why I chose him."

Dante did seem relieved at his master's revelation, his body visibly relaxing as if he'd just dropped a heavy rucksack off his back. However, he still swallowed audibly before offering, "Marcus was sent to collect Gabriel Hawthorne."

"Curious," Roman muttered. "So, Caiaphas did not want to collect him before he harmed any of the herd, but..." Now his voice trailed off as he thought. "If not to kill him, then what? Learn from him? Maybe even," Roman scoffed, "persuade him to become an ally?" Roman's musings were interrupted by Dante's rising fear. It permeated Roman's nostrils like the stench of an unserviced public toilet. There was something else. Something he was too terrified to tell him.

Dante gasped as he was lifted off the floor by his throat.

Roman stared into Dante's eyes as he invaded his servant's mind. The Illuminati had attacked another compound. Not just another compound, but the *other* compound. The one only the Ancients knew of, and certainly not the Illuminati. The vampires who comprised its security forces had no idea of its importance or what they were securing. They only knew that certain death awaited anyone who failed to perform his duty to his utmost.

And Dante had performed his duty to his utmost. He'd learned that the Illuminati had discovered its existence. Dante hadn't known what it was, but he'd been intrigued. So he let it play out, watching as the Illuminati sent in its two special operations teams. No. Just one. Dante watched eight soldiers enter the compound and one soldier exit the compound, along with one...

Blinding pain shot through Dante's body as it slammed against the wall Roman had tossed him into as though he were a rag doll. Slowly picking himself up off the floor, he could feel the broken bones in his body start to reset.

"You should have started with that," Roman's voice roared inside Dante's head like a thunderclap. He slapped his hands to his head to keep it from splitting in two.

Roman wanted to pick Dante back up off his feet and rip him to shreds like so much papier mâché. Perhaps later he would, but not now. Now, there were more pressing matters. He needed to move and move quickly. But he needed several of his children with him, and they could not move as fast as he could. He also needed time to think, to process, to plan. He ground his teeth as he looked at his security chief.

Dante blanched as he stepped backward into the wall.

Roman ignored Dante's defensive posture. "Have the car ready, and make sure the jet is fueled and waiting for us at the airport."

Dante opened his mouth, the word 'us' forming on his lips in an interrogative expression, but snapped it shut as his mind filled with the answer. He only nodded, his body sagging from the relief that he would not die today.

Roman turned and walked out of the room. If artificial intelligence could feel, it would be green with envy at the speed with which Roman's mind worked. A supercomputer could not process the ramifications of what had just happened as fast as Roman. He and his siblings had built that compound with their own hands. So well planned and well hidden that they didn't need to program the human satellites or drones not to see it. None but his brothers and sisters, not even Isabella, knew of the compound or its purpose.

The vampires who served at the compound hadn't known where it was or what they were guarding. Roman made sure of that. Those who did begin to question why they were at the compound and what they were guarding found themselves wishing they'd been another victim of a culling. Roman also made sure of that.

Yet the Illuminati had stumbled upon the compound. When? They'd infiltrated the compound. How? Members of his security forces tasked with monitoring the Illuminati had watched and said nothing to him. Why? And why hadn't he or his brothers and sisters sensed it? Why hadn't any of them noticed they were no longer conscious of him? Where in the world was he?

The only thing Roman knew as he punched the button connected to Delilah's monitor was that he was no longer in Bir Tawil.

55

"If you two gentlemen are done catching up, there's something of grave importance I'd like to discuss with you," Caiaphas's voice said over the intercom.

"Come with me," The guard outside the room said as he opened the door. Cain and Gabriel looked at one another and shrugged as they followed the guard. He led them to another part of the compound that neither had seen yet. The guard gestured to a set of doors at the end of the hall he had led them down, as he took position outside the doors with the other guard already standing there as they approached.

"Welcome, gentlemen," Caiaphas said, standing from his chair at the end of a long conference table. Marcus remained seated as if afraid to relinquish the chair that signaled his position as second-in-command. "Please sit." Caiaphas gestured to the chairs opposite Marcus.

Cain and Gabriel made their way to the seats.

Cain looked at Marcus. "No coffee and Danish before?"

"Perhaps cigars and bourbon after," Gabriel suggested.

"Ah," Cain said with a smile.

"I'm glad to see you two are getting along so well," Caiaphas said with a grin.

"I don't know if I would go that far," Gabriel scoffed.

"Let's just say we've come to an understanding," Cain added.

"Can we stop wasting time and get on with this?" Marcus burst out.

"Looks like we've offended tall, dark, and moody over there," Cain replied.

"He's just sensitive. He's a really nice guy once you get to know him." Gabriel said, trying to hold in a chuckle.

"Enough," Marcus said as he slammed his fist on the table.

"I couldn't agree more," Caiaphas said as he turned to Marcus. "Could you please excuse us, Marcus?" Caiaphas's tone was soft, polite, and final. It hadn't been a request.

"Sir. You shouldn't even be out of bed in your condition." Marcus replied.

"And whose fault is that?" Caiaphas answered.

Anger bloomed on Marcus's face like a red rose opening itself to the first spring sunshine. Taking long, slow, deliberate breaths, Marcus said, "Of course, sir," as he stood and walked towards the door, shutting it harder than he needed to behind him.

"Looks like somebody got in trouble," Gabriel whispered with a smirk to Cain.

"Mr. Hawthorne. Please. I need both of your help. This is very important."

"My bad," Gabriel said, holding up his hands in surrender.

"What's going on?" Cain asked, smelling Caiaphas's stress. It mixed with a pungent fruity scent and carried the rancid undertone of rot.

Gabriel smelled it as well. He exchanged a concerned look with Cain.

Opening the laptop on the table, Caiaphas said, "I need you both to help me solve a mystery." He turned the screen to face them. "I need to know what this is."

Cain and Gabriel looked at the frozen image of a man, his clothing in tatters, raging at the camera at first glance. But upon closer examination, they could see the fingers were elongated, ending in what looked more like filleting knives than claws. The jaw was unhinged, the mouth opening wider than any human, revealing gums filled with long fangs.

Gabriel thought that if they were in a movie, this would be the moment he or Cain would make some cheeky James Bond-esque quip about how those were a set of choppers to make a shark proud. But this wasn't a movie. He and Cain weren't James Bond. And the image frozen on the screen certainly wasn't any Hollywood nemesis. He glanced at Cain only to see him glancing at him with the same expression.

"I don't know if you're aware, but most recording equipment, including digital cameras, records at twenty-four frames per second. Our equipment records two hundred forty frames per second. This gives us a more detailed view of our operations. What I mean is more clarity. It's the difference between watching a film on VHS versus Four HD. When, as they say, we have boots on the ground. Not only does each soldier wear a body camera, but a camera is also set up to provide what a filmmaker would call a master shot. It provides us with an entire overview of the operation. What you're looking at is from a body camera. What you're about to see is from the master shot. It's been slowed down to show still shots. Each still will appear for ten seconds." Caiaphas pressed the Enter key on the laptop.

The camera view was from an elevated spot overlooking the sand. Lots and lots of sand. It looked like a desert somewhere in Northern Africa or the Middle East with several dozen people in desert Army Combat Uniforms, ACUs, milling about an opening in a hill. The opening appeared to be man-made. Neither Cain nor Gabriel could tell who made it, but it looked old enough not to have been made by these soldiers.

The figure appears at the opening, raging at the soldiers before him. Somehow, he seems more terrifying in this picture than in the first shot they saw of him. Gabriel thinks he knows why. It's all about context. In the first picture, it's just this creature with no frame of reference. He could be a still from Caiaphas's favorite horror flick. *The Hills Have Eyes Part Thirty-Eight.* Or the winner of the best costume at the annual Illuminati Halloween party. But Caiaphas's concern, his admission that he has no idea what this is, and the literal frame of reference now provided by the master shot and the impending doom it's about to reveal give Gabriel the desire to turn away from the screen.

The next still fills the screen, and the figure is gone. The soldier who'd been standing closest to the entrance, but still a good ten meters away, is exploding as if a bomb detonated in his stomach. The heads and limbs of the nearest soldiers are flying like so much gruesome confetti.

The next still shows more exploding soldiers. Multiple gut piles appear where soldiers stood in the previous frame. Some soldiers on the fringes of the frame have turned to run into the desert.

In the next still, gut piles appear where the fleeing soldiers had been in the previous still. No one made it out of the master shot. No, Cain realized, that isn't correct as he stared at the creature standing in the center of the carnage, covered in smears of blood, bits of human meat, and strings of sinew.

The figure had gone in the next still.

Caiaphas pushed the Enter key.

Silence filled the conference room.

Gabriel felt his stomach roiling. He was glad he no longer ate human food. He was sure he would have deposited his last meal in the nearest receptacle. He needed to speak, so he asked the first question that came to his mind. "How long did that last in real time?"

"Less than ten seconds."

Cain asked, "Where did this happen?"

"Bir Tawil."

"Bear Twill?" Gabriel asked.

Caiaphas pronounced it slowly, "Beer Tah-Wheel."

Gabriel adjusted his pronunciation, but only just. "Where is Beer Twill?"

Cain rolled his eyes while Caiaphas chose to ignore Gabriel's deliberate mispronunciation. "It's between Egypt and Sudan. A land mass a little larger than Vatican City that neither country claims."

"Why?" Cain asked.

"It would weaken that country's claim on the more important Hala'ib Triangle."

"Beer Twill and Halitosis," Gabriel repeated the mispronunciations, "and vamps. Oh my."

Again, he was ignored by the other two. "So what were Illuminati soldiers doing in Beer Tawil?

"Investigating a compound which appears to have been a prison," Caiaphas tapped at keys on the laptop keyboard, and the initial image of the creature appeared on the screen, "for whatever that is."

"So you found this monster and what? Set it free?" Gabriel was incredulous.

Caiaphas's lips pursed into a line so thin they all but disappeared. "Along with the body cams, our teams wear mics that record all communications during an operation. The team that went in to sweep and clear the compound came across what they believed to be an elderly man in distress. They were providing medical aid and assistance when, as best we can tell," Caiaphas pointed at the screen, "this creature attacked."

"Were there any survivors?" Cain asked.

"Only one. He's been unable to tell us anything new."

Gabriel could tell Caiaphas was holding something back. This wasn't his vampiric senses, but his experience as a former cop turned political operative. "Except?"

"He believes the creature might have been posing as the old man. If that's the case..."

"Then it would mean this creature is also intelligent," Cain finished.

Silence fell between the three men.

"The team that went in. The soldiers outside. They were all armed with our latest technology. But this creature was so fast that they didn't even have time to use them." He looked back at the screen. "This creature poses a greater threat than we have faced to date."

56

Dulles International Airport
Washington, D.C.

Washington Dulles International Airport handles roughly eight hundred commercial flights daily, domestic and international. Many of those international flights, including Rome, are non-stop. Rome to Dulles is approximately ten hours.

Jacquelyn could have booked a first-class non-stop flight, but she felt that was a little too ostentatious. She could have used the family's private jet, but that's what the half-breed would've done. It worked for him somehow. *I might live in a mansion, my ride might be a limousine, and I only fly in a private jet, a gift from my daddy, but I'm one of you. When I smile and shake your hand, well, shucks, it's like you're looking in the mirror.* It made her blood boil and her stomach roil. She wasn't going to do anything that abomination would do.

Would've done.

That thought warmed her heart and placed a smile of sublime serenity on her face. If the half-breed wasn't dead, at least he wasn't in the public eye anymore.

So she flew business class from Rome to Paris to Dulles. She couldn't be in Europe and not have French. She just loved the French.

The plane touched down on the tarmac fifteen minutes early. She collected her personal belongings, exited the plane, endured the long lines at Customs, collected her baggage, and made her way to passenger pick-up, where a silver Rolls-Royce Phantom Extended waited curbside. The luxury car went unnoticed by security and passersby. Jacquelyn made sure of that.

Her assistant had notified her that Mr. Darby was sending a car for her. She'd been willing to travel business class and go through Customs, but she wasn't willing to wait once her Dolce Vitas were back on American soil. So she'd reached out and set up a mental veil. It was a little trick she'd developed over the years. Simple, really, as long as she kept it simple. She could use it in court while addressing a jury, a boardroom, or a classroom, before entering. She'd cast the veil like a fishing net over the space with one thought: Innocent. Or Guilty. Hire him. Fire her. Fear me. Whatever she needed. It didn't work on Ancients, she'd tried. But it was effective on lesser vampires and humans. When it came to that, what was the difference? Both were inferior.

She'd learned to cast it over distance with accuracy. So from the plane, she cast the net on curbside arrivals. The Rolls was seen parked at the curb, but it registered in the brains of those passing through the mental veil as nothing more than a concrete post to be avoided.

So the fact that a vehicle was waiting for her wasn't a surprise, but she wasn't expecting to see Darby's personal ride...

And Darby? She could smell his aftershave, his deodorant, hear his heartbeat, and his lungs rattle as he inhaled and exhaled. She could hear his thumbs hit the screen of his smartphone as he drafted an email while he waited for her. She'd been sure they'd send the company limo used for expert witnesses and the partners.

His chauffeur stepped from the curb, opened the door as she approached, and took her bags from her without a word. As she slid into the cabin, felt the suppleness of the white leather, noticed the bespoke dashboard with an image of Lady Justice, Jacquelyn had to admit the old man had class.

"How was the flight?"

He saw Jaquelyn's body deflate into the seat with a long, weary exhale. "Long. And I had a three-hour layover in France." Jacquelyn rolled her eyes. "At least I could walk around. But it's still waiting."

Darby's head bobbed with a knowing nod before asking, "And how is your mother doing?"

"She is doing much better. Thank you so much for asking, Mr. Darby," Jacquelyn answered, smiling warmly. The other thing she had to admit about this man was his eagle eye, even at his age. Nothing happened at his firm without his knowledge. She thought about the recently deceased Howard Williams and smiled inwardly.

Almost nothing.

Darby placed a hand on her knee. Not like a man might do with his lover, but a grandfather with a beloved grandchild. "I told you before to call me Harold," he said with a scolding tone softened by the kind twinkle in his eyes.

Jacquelyn accepted the rebuke with equal kindness. "Harold. So, did you come all the way out to the airport just to inquire how my mother and I are doing?"

"Actually," the kind twinkle was replaced by a wicked glint. "I wanted to speak with you about something. And I didn't want to wait until tomorrow." Gazing around the cabin, he added, "And I wanted more privacy than even my office affords."

"I'm intrigued," Jacquelyn said, shifting to face Darby directly.

"You know Judge Conners." It wasn't a question.

Jacquelyn nodded. "Of course. He presided over my last case."

"He's a dear friend of mine. We met on my first case as a defense attorney. He was the prosecutor." Darby leaned forward with a mischievous smile and a devilish glint in his eye. "I swept the courtroom floor with him."

With that smile and glint, and knowing his legal mind, Jacquelyn could see Darby sweeping the courtroom floor with most attorneys. He would be a formidable opponent, and she realized that without her mental veil, he might even sweep the floor with her. She remained silent, encouraging him to continue.

"We were having dinner the other night, and he confided in me his plan to announce his retirement next year."

"So what exactly does that have to do with me?"

"Well. He'd like to take a prospective judge under his wing and begin mentoring them now."

Jacquelyn waited, nonplussed.

Darby continued. "He wants to find someone who should be on the bench, not in front of it. Someone with a keen legal mind. Someone who serves the law. Both its letter and intent. He was very impressed with you."

"But I haven't been practicing law long enough to be a judge," Jacquelyn exclaimed.

"When it comes to the law, you, my dear young lady, are an old soul. You'll be wasted in a prosecutor's office. And I'm afraid a firm like mine can only offer you the trappings of wealth." Darby's eyes stared past Jacquelyn. "Eventually, though, that wealth is a wanton mistress, proof that justice is more equal the deeper the pockets." His eyes cleared as he looked at Jacquelyn. "You not only love the law, you're in love with the law. Sitting on the bench is where you're meant to be."

"I don't know what to say. I never even considered myself becoming a judge." Jacquelyn replied, delivering the lie so convincingly that she almost believed it.

Harold continued. "With our connections and Bart's tutelage, we can get you on the bench." He leaned forward, that grandfatherly gleam back in his eye. "Where you belong."

"I don't know what to say," Jacquelyn replied.

Darby leaned back, satisfied he'd won Jacquelyn over. "Don't say anything. Go home. Unpack. Rest. Get a good night's sleep. We'll talk more later. Okay?"

"Okay," Jacquelyn answered, again almost believing her tone of bemusement.

"Are you hungry? I can have the driver pick you up something on the way," Harold offered.

"No, thank you." Jacquelyn laughed as she patted her stomach. "I gorged myself while I was in France."

Darby's eyes brightened with delight. "I just love French cuisine. What's your favorite?"

"All of it," Jacquelyn answered with a nefarious grin.

57

Roman Dvanaesti's Estate, Italy

Roman watched Isabella stroll through the vineyard. It was like being transported through time, seeing the curves of her silhouette as her body passed from shadow to light and back into shadow. The sunlight passed through her long white sundress like water through a sieve, revealing the flesh beneath those curves. The gift he had given her prevented her beauty from fading, even after eight hundred years.

But the healing process had done more than restore her body; it had softened her. He couldn't remember when she'd strolled through the vineyard, along a beach, or even a market. A century at least.

"Ciao amore mio," Isabella said without turning around, keeping the smile that his presence always inspired a secret from him.

Roman had made his way down from the main house and into the vineyard behind her in seconds. Even the tone of her greeting was softer. He said nothing as he embraced Isabella, turning her around into his arms. Roman pierced his lip, drawing blood as he drew her in for a long, passionate kiss.

The kiss might have lasted a minute, an hour, or a year. Neither knew nor cared. It was eight hundred years ago.

Roman pulled away from the kiss.

Isabella's head swam as she licked Roman's blood from her lips. It was sweet, like the red wines she'd enjoyed as a young woman, but there was also an undertone of...

Over the centuries, she'd learned to discern Roman's blood, like the varietal aromas of the grapes used in wine. Moods, thoughts, and emotions affect the blood, and she'd learned how to differentiate those aromas in his blood. He didn't have to say a thing. His blood always told her more than his words or his actions.

Wrapping her arms around Roman's neck, she asked, "What's troubling you, my love?"

A sheepish yet knowing smile crept across Roman's face. "I should never lead a meeting with my blood."

Isabella tilted her head, a dimple forming on her right cheek. That hadn't appeared in more than eight hundred years of life as a smile warmed her face like the sun, and her eyebrows rose with delight. "Not if you want to keep something from me."

Roman's nod was knowing. He inhaled and then admitted, "Cain's plane went down over the Atlantic Ocean."

"What took you so long?"

Isabella's question was so matter-of-fact that Roman's eyebrows rose with surprise.

She dismissed his shock with a roll of her eyes. "It's been long overdue. I've been waiting for you to, as the Americans say, fish or cut bait." She curled the hair curling at his neck around her finger. "Well, maybe not a plane crash, but I figured it was only a matter of time before you tired of his impertinence. I'm surprised he lasted as long as he did."

"Only Claudia and the flight crew's bodies were recovered," Roman responded.

"You fear he survived?"

Roman nodded his head. "I think the Illuminati may have him."

The laughter bursting from Isabella was as hard as a sledgehammer on an anvil. She ignored Roman's agitation. "So one of your pets finally bit you," she chortled. Then she heard Roman's teeth grind, and while the sound quelled her laughter, nothing could remove the malicious grin from her face. "I'm sorry, my love, but you had to know it was only a matter of time before something like this happened. The Illuminati aren't like your other pets. Of course, they were easy to control and manipulate when they were first created. But with each new Caiaphas, their knowledge grew. They learned from their mistakes."

Roman's face flattened. His body stilled. To most who knew him, his stoicism was just the Roman they were accustomed to *before*. Before the attack on the Miami mansion. Before he dug Isabella from the soil and brought her back to Italy.

But Isabella knew better. She'd been his friend, lover, and confidante for over eight hundred years. His blood coursed through her veins. She always read Roman. She never misunderstood. And she understood now that she needed to extend the proverbial olive branch. Perhaps I have grown softer, she thought as her hands moved from behind his neck to his face.

Tracing his brow with her fingertip while her thumb brushed his bottom lip, Isabella said, "Do you remember that young poet? That one, you dictated some of your plays to?" Her thumb ran along Roman's jawline. "He was such an odd fellow. So young but...so prolific. And so were you. No one could tell the difference between the two of you. I especially loved the one about the dream." She tilted her head slightly as she looked up through her eyelashes, the dimple appearing again on the right side of her face. "You never have told me which one of you wrote that one."

Roman was unfazed by her coyness.

Her hands snaked around his neck again, fingers interlacing. "I've always been impressed by your artistic abilities. It's one of the many things that made me fall in love with you. To play like Beethoven. Sculpt like Michelangelo. Paint like da Vinci. So, be honest with me." Her head tilted. The dimple returned. "Who influenced whom?"

The smudge of a gloating smile appeared on Roman's face.

His smile still warmed her like the sun warmed the beaches of Lampedusa. She continued, "Speaking of painting. I noticed the one of Claudia. That's the first piece you've done in centuries. Does she remind you of...her?"

Now, he gloated for a different reason. "Are you jealous?"

"A little," Isabella replied, pulling him in for another kiss.

58

Illuminati Compound
Caja del Rio Plateau, New Mexico

After coming to some form of a truce with Cain and then witnessing what was set loose in that compound at Bir Tawil, Gabriel needed to see the sun and feel the breeze, even if it was only a whisper. He wanted to see Alessia, especially after watching what that creature did to the Illuminati's soldiers. He wanted to protect her. Keep her safe. At the same time, after the video, he wished he'd never met Alessia. If they'd never crossed paths, she would never have been illumined. She'd be safe in her life in Venice. She'd be living her life, working at the hospital, perhaps getting ready for a date with a doctor, falling in love, and introducing the young man to her parents. Instead, she'd been ripped away from all that, the life she knew, surrounded by water, and thanks to him, set down in a life she didn't know, surrounded by desert.

Cain had gone to his room, most likely to engage in his newest pastime of staring at chess pieces, but Caiaphas had offered to go with Gabriel onto the grounds. He hadn't said a word to Gabriel after the offer but walked alongside the younger man, seemingly comfortable with the silence, content to let Gabriel stew in his ruminations.

"Have you thought about what you're going to say to Ms. Montalto?" Caiaphas finally asked as he led Gabriel away from the main building to a cactus-covered mesa. Though the main building and outbuildings were still within their sightline, the mesa provided a semblance of privacy.

Gabriel stopped as if he'd walked right into one of the cacti. Had he spoken out loud? Or worse, had he and Caiaphas been discussing Alessia and he'd been so lost in the last moment he'd forgotten? Or was he just that transparent to Caiaphas? Should he ignore Caiaphas's question? Ignore Caiaphas's presence? He knew he couldn't do that. Didn't want to do that. It was strange, but just before Caiaphas spoke, Gabriel had wished for something he hadn't desired for in a long time: a father figure to talk to, someone to listen and offer advice. Still, Gabriel couldn't find words. Didn't know where to begin. So he remained silent.

"She trusts you," Caiaphas prompted.

Gabriel dismissed Caiaphas's words with a snort.

Caiaphas tried again. "It's obvious that you care for Ms. Montalto."

"Of course, I care for her," Gabriel replied. "She helped me when I needed it most."

"And you, her."

Gabriel looked at Caiaphas, taken aback.

If it weren't for your intercession in the alley that night, she wouldn't be the subject of this conversation," Caiaphas answered. "And you demanded Marcus go back for her."

Gabriel looked away. There it was. He'd come to her rescue in the alley. What choice did he have? He'd sought her help when he realized he needed blood. What choice did he have? He'd demanded that Marcus go back for her. He couldn't just disappear from her life, leaving her at the mercy of the vampires. "What choice did I have?"

Caiaphas heard the agitation in Gabriel's voice. He could see the helplessness etched on his face like a tattoo. Still, he continued. "We always have a choice. Perhaps you should be asking yourself why your choices include Ms. Montalto.".

Gabriel felt that helplessness constrict around his throat like a necktie drawn too tightly. "If you're implying that I have romantic feelings for her, you're-...You know what I am. How could I-...How could I have romantic feelings for...what I now see as a food source? And how could I ever expect her or anyone to have feelings for me?"

"Gabriel," Alessia called.

Gabriel and Caiaphas turned to see Alessia waving as she walked toward them.

Caiaphas waved back. "It wasn't romance I was referring to." Caiaphas didn't take his gaze from the approaching woman. "But that's not what's important at the moment."

"And what is?" Gabriel asked, not taking his eyes away from Alessia.

"Helping Ms. Montalto understand her new reality. Assisting her acclimation as smoothly and quickly as possible."

Gabriel's snort was flavored with humor. "That's easier said than done."

Caiaphas couldn't hide a knowing smile. "Most things usually are."

Alessia ran the last couple of steps and threw her arms around Gabriel. "I was worried about you," Alessia said into his chest as she hugged him tightly. "You've been gone all afternoon."

"That was my fault, Ms. Montalto," Caiaphas said. "I apologize for detaining him so long."

Alessa released Gabriel and stepped back, trying to compose herself. She'd forgotten Caiaphas was there as soon as she was in Gabriel's embrace.

"If you two will excuse me..." The sound of vehicle horns interrupted Caiaphas. His smile faded as he recognized the S.O.S. pattern they were sounding.

Guards ran to the gates, pulling them open seconds before two G.M.C. Yukons would've rammed them. The second vehicle clipped the gate with its bumper, sounding like a hand grinder on steel as sparks flew. The Yukons stayed at speed until they reached the main building. Slamming on their brakes and kicking up enough dust, Gabriel had the wild thought that it was like a smoke screen from a James Bond flick.

As the dust cloud cleared, Alessia saw the occupants pulling two badly wounded people out of the back of the first SUV and laying them on the ground. "What happened?" Alessia shouted as she dropped to her knees in front of the wounded individuals.

A side door burst open as four men dressed in surgical scrubs and carrying stretchers ran towards the wounded.

"Carjacking," one of the occupants answered.

Alessia saw that his T-shirt was smeared with blood and quickly assessed that it was not his own but that of the wounded. She returned to triaging the two wounded. She saw multiple gunshot wounds, significant blood loss, and shallow breathing. Their skin was pale and cool to the touch. She felt for a pulse. "Thready."

"Carjacking?" Caiaphas repeated. "Where?"

Alessia helped lift the wounded onto stretchers. "Let's go."

None of the orderlies questioned Alessia as they lifted the stretchers and returned the way they came.

Gabriel watched Alessia disappear through the doors as she walked alongside one of the stretchers. "This might not be as hard as we thought."

"It would appear Ms. Montalto is more resilient than either of us gave her credit for," Caiaphas replied as he and Gabriel followed through the doors.

59

Queens, New York

Georges approached the Minute Suites in John F. Kennedy International Airport Terminal Four. The woman behind the desk smiled as she accepted his identification. "We've been expecting you." Typing on her keyboard, she said, "I hope you had a nice flight." She inflected her voice upwards, turning the statement into a question.

"Yes," Georges replied.

The woman handed him his identification. "If you'll follow me." Gesturing for him to move around the counter, she added, "I hope it's been an uneventful day so far."

This morning, he'd been at his club in New Orleans when a courier arrived with a manila envelope. Inside was a Real ID with his face but a new name and an address Georges knew didn't exist, a plane ticket departing from Louis Armstrong New Orleans International Airport for John F. Kennedy International Airport in two hours, and a note from Ra instructing him to proceed to this location upon arrival.

He'd looked up to find the courier waiting. "We need to go to the airport."

The courier nodded, turned, and headed outside to his idling vehicle.

It occurred to Georges that the courier knew he would deliver the envelope and then drive Georges somewhere—he just hadn't known where. Slipping the note, ticket, and license into his suit coat pocket, he let the manila folder fall to the ground as he followed the courier. He also realized the man had entered the bar and evaded his security detail when he saw the looks of surprise on their faces as the courier walked past them. He waved them off as he passed. It hadn't been in the note, but Georges had understood. He was to come alone.

The man said nothing as he drove, offering neither to turn on the radio nor adjust the interior climate. It was understood that Georges had free rein to attend to his comfort. Georges was content to contemplate what this day had in store for him. It wasn't lost on him that he'd willingly leave at a moment's notice with only the clothes on his back and a new name when his master called. His mother loved those stories in the Bible. She hoped it would happen for her son one day.

"Business as usual," Georges responded as he followed the woman to his master, smiling with insouciance as she opened the suite door, and his eyes caught sight of Ra. His master's gaze fell upon him, and his smile widened as if he were a Pee-Wee baseball player stepping up to the plate and noticing his father in the front row of the stands.

The woman closed the door as Georges stepped into the room.

Ra was smiling as well. "Please sit." He gestured to the sofa beside him.

"Yes, Master," Georges said, sitting.

Ra frowned. "Georges, I've told you before, I'm not your master." His tone was gentle but stern, like a father trying to take a son's moment of insolence and make it a teachable moment.

"My apologies, sir. I-" Georges stopped as Ra raised his hand.

"You have been treated as a slave for too long. It's now the only thing you know," Ra said, his hand dropping to George's shoulder. "But that's over now. You are no longer a slave." His grip tightened. "You are a son." He placed his forehead on Georges's forehead. "An heir."

Georges felt the tears well and let them fall.

Ra let them fall, moving his hand from Georges's shoulder to his back, rubbing like a father consoling his son. "You will no longer be called Georges. You will be called Amun. My firstborn. Of all my children."

Georges's tears turned to sobs.

"It's alright, Amun." He didn't remove his forehead from Georges's as he continued to rub the younger vampire's back. "In time, you will see your value."

Ra and Georges stayed like that for a long time, Ra letting Georges continue till he finally gave a final hiccupping sigh.

Georges pulled his head away. "Why did you summon me?" Georges looked into Ra's eyes before adding, "Father."

"You did such a magnificent job of bringing the rival covens together, I wanted to place a greater burden upon you," Ra answered.

Georges waited in silence, a bemused look replacing the distraught look on his face.

"I've been using this marvelous tool you introduced me to." Ra turned the open laptop towards Georges.

Dozens of windows were open, each filled with an active chat room where Ra was conversing. English. Spanish. French. Russian. Several had to be in different Middle Eastern dialects. Others were in languages he didn't recognize.

"What is this?" Bemusement had given way to pure amazement.

"It's time for your brothers and sisters to join us."

Georges looked from the computer to Ra.

Ra locked eyes with George as he pointed to the screen. "These are covens around the world. Every country. Every continent."

Now it was Georges's turn to feel like a parent protecting his child from danger. Children might be tech-savvy, but no more than lambs surrounded by wolves on the vast plains of the internet. "We need to be careful with this. We wouldn't want...others...to find out about this. Agencies monitor the internet for strange or...unusual activity," Georges added, after receiving a blank stare from Ra.

Ra rolled his eyes and waved a dismissive hand. "I'm on the dark web." The term brought a crooked smile to his face. "And I'm using encrypted servers bouncing through more than a dozen VPNs worldwide." He chuckled. "No...*Ancients*...have a clue."

A thrill of horror shot through Georges's bloodstream like a shot of Naloxone injected into his heart. "I just showed you the internet two days ago."

Ra shrugged. He was just about to offer Georges a verbal shrug. *I'm a fast learner.* Instead, he thought this might be a teachable moment, another opportunity to impress Georges just how great his god was. "When I was a mere god-king, I built monuments. Statues. Temples. I was the designer and master builder of cities. I was in my early twenties when I designed and constructed Pi-Ramesses." He gestured at the laptop. "My military exploits were legendary. My peace treaty with the Hittites is considered a diplomatic milestone. My intellectual prowess was the greatest in all the world in my mortal lifetime. There was nothing I could not, and did not, master. And now, I have been a god for more than *three thousand* years." He waited a beat to let that sink in. "What could be beyond my comprehension?" He waved at the computer. "This is nothing more than a tool." He smiled. "Like a ploughshare or a sword. A tool built on a series of zeroes and ones. A tool based on input, process, and output. Garbage in, garbage out. And it works almost as fast as my brain does." Satisfied with the stupefied awe on George's face, Ramses slapped the laptop shut. "Let's go shopping."

"Shopping?"

Ra nodded. "Amun has places to go and people to see." He looked Georges over as if he were perusing the items of the two-day-old sale bin at a grocery store. "And he can't represent his father in Paris and Budapest looking like a two-dollar American hooker." Standing, he said, "We'll pick you up some Hungarian language CDs to listen to on the flight as well." He wrapped his arm around Georges's shoulder.

"Paris and Budapest?" Georges asked, allowing Ra to lead him out of the suite.

Ra stopped, turning the young vampire to face him. Cupping Georges's face in his hands, Ra spoke, "I am Ra. *You* are my first tear. You fall from my eye to this earth. Giving it moisture. Giving it life." He placed his forehead on Georges's. "I am Ra. And you are Amun."

"I am Amun," Georges repeated, his eyes closed in rapturous ecstasy.

Ra smiled. And as he purchased clothing and luggage for Georges at the Brooks Brothers and Coach retail shops in Terminal Four of JFK International Airport, his mind dwelt on the Washington Post article he'd read on that magnificent little device Georges had introduced him to just two days ago, of a young hotshot attorney and her most recent legal victory.

Jacquelyn Dvanaesti.

60

Athens, Greece

Delilah lifted her hand, silencing the architect who'd just opened her mouth to protest another of Delilah's design changes. "I don't want excuses," Delilah growled as she turned to look out her office window. "Get out."

The architect and her team scrambled to gather their drawings, blueprints, briefcases, and easels before beating a hasty retreat from the office.

"They're trying their best," Eleni, Delilah's executive assistant, said as she closed the office door behind them. "You have to understand. They—"

"Do not patronize me, Eleni." Delilah interrupted as she turned to face her. "You haven't lived long enough yet."

"I'm sorry. I meant no disrespect," Eleni blurted, dropping her gaze to the floor. "I was only pointing out that the Riviera Tower is already under construction, so to make the changes you are requesting will take time." She added under her breath, "And add expense."

There was no mirth in the laughter that escaped Delilah's mouth. "You silly child. You of all people should know I don't make requests." She could point out that Eleni had been tasked with quietly purchasing shares until Delilah was the largest shareholder in the Riviera Tower venture. She did not suffer monetary concerns, let alone time constraints. She could also point out that Eleni had been with her long enough to know when she was in a foul mood.

And she was in an extremely foul mood. It started two days ago. Her mood was already dark. Abisare had called and texted nearly a dozen times that day, making her wish she could add his name to the list of those to be sacrificed at the next culling. Her sources had confirmed that Roman had lost control of the Illuminati and that they may have rescued Cain Dvanaesti from the crash, or captured him. They only had Roman's word that Cain was on that plane when he shot it down, and Roman was proving less than reliable. The most recent situation caused by Roman evoked an emotion she hadn't felt in centuries: Panic. She didn't need Abisare's theatrical announcement and demands. Ronin couldn't be bothered by anything. He was getting as secretive and devious as Roman. Her other siblings, well, they were having "daddy issues." The fact that none of them had felt their father's presence after so long was having a detrimental effect on their psyches. And, of course, Riviera Tower was falling farther behind schedule.

And then it happened. She'd been in a board meeting, regretting ever agreeing to chair this particular board as the company's CEO railed on how his perceived incompetence was really vision when the white noise that was the constant awareness of her siblings lessened. For a human, it would be like the classical music in her earbuds suddenly changing to heavy metal music. Delilah flinched. The CEO mistakenly thought he was winning over Delilah and made the further mistake of laying his hand on her shoulder as he made his pronouncement. Greek newspapers reported the next day on the brutal suicide of a CEO after he was fired.

Their father, Cain, had purposefully removed their awareness of his presence—at least, that's what she hoped. Unlike Abisare, Delilah could not and would not accept that Cain was dead. She could tolerate his rejection, his disgust. But not his death. Especially at his own hands. All the other times she and her siblings experienced that lessening in their awareness of each other was when one of the siblings died, which had happened.

She'd immediately reached out to her other siblings. They'd all felt it. All hoped it was true. Abisare had volunteered to send a team to confirm it. He was closest, he'd argued. But Delilah knew, and she could see by Ronin's smirk that he agreed. Abisare wouldn't send a team, just himself, and he would travel in that ridiculously ostentatious airplane of his. However, as Delilah was the de facto head of the family in their father's absence, it should be her. The others agreed, even Abisare, though somewhat reluctantly.

It would've been faster for one of the Ancients to go, but no one, save Abisare, wanted to. Delilah didn't know what was worse, his arrogance or his foolishness. She could have acquiesced to Abisare, but despite the proverbial pain in the backside that he was, they couldn't lose him. So she'd sent a team of fledgling vampires, ones who, if they were lost, would be of no loss. Being so young, they could only travel at night. The flight would take longer than usual because it would need to avoid radar. They would jump from the plane over Sudan, move as far as they could, then hole up for the day. They'd be in Bir Tawil the next night.

The waiting was insufferable. She needed a distraction. So she'd called the meeting with the architect and her team to discuss changes to the building's exterior and interior design. It hadn't been the diversion she'd hoped for. Instead, the bickering and patronizing had only darkened her mood.

And then the message came—not by phone, fax, or messenger. Delilah had been reaching out and delving into the team's minds. She watched through their eyes as they arrived at the compound, witnessing the devastation, the blood, and the bodies, both vampire and human. They moved quickly through the compound, confirming its total loss of life. And then they arrived at the cell. The remains there were nothing more than putrefying soup. She knew. He was not among the carnage.

This had all happened in the time between when she had barked that she didn't want excuses and then growled for them to get out. It was the only way to save their lives. Now there was only one way to save Eleni's life.

"Leave."

Eleni stepped backward until her backside connected with the door. She exited, closing the door behind her.

Delilah sat down behind her desk. Opening one of the drawers, she took out a remote with a biometric scanner. She placed her ring finger on the remote, and it lit up. Delilah punched in a four-digit code on the remote and turned her attention to the wall to the right of her desk. The wall was made of stone with an image of the Temple of Dagon carved into it, disguising a seam. The wall separated, revealing a large flat-screen monitor, currently dark.

Delilah readied herself as she lay back in her chair, knowing the information she would share would not be received well. One by one, the screen filled with the images of her seven remaining siblings.

Only seven, she thought to herself, and she felt the heaviness of that thought on her chest like a lead blanket.

Her seven siblings stared at her silently, expectation carved deep into their faces. They sat so still and unblinking that Delilah had the wild thought her siblings were showing off the statues they'd had made of themselves. Then, the reality of why they were here chased the fantasy away.

"Ramses is free."

THE END